The Quest of Tyron

Book Two

MIKE SIROTA

Atoris Press edition 2013

ISBN: 978-0-9855794-8-7

Cover design by Karen Phillips

Library of Congress Control Number: 2013903349

For Logan Jeffrey Opp.
Welcome to the family, little guy.

CHAPTER ONE:
A CITY OF DEATH

One might have thought that autumn, still nearly two months away, had come early to the land. The slight chill that permeated the air was not indicative of mid-summer, though it hardly compared to the icy, bone-numbing gusts that surged out of the north during the months that the vast canyon was blanketed in white. Dark, turbulent clouds blotted the sun's rays for all but a few seconds at a time as they raced through the sky in an endless procession. Each ominous puff carried with it the hint of an overwhelming deluge, yet throughout the long afternoon this ever-present threat never once came to pass. Threat? Perhaps such a downpour might have been a gift from the gods themselves, for only then might the unimaginable stench from the more than fifty thousand putrefying corpses have been washed away from this canyon of death.

It was the first day of the seventh month in the seven hundred and eighteenth Tahreskian year, this according to the Berboran calendar. But few of the remaining citizens would have been able to advise one who might have inquired of this fact, had they chosen to respond at all. Five days past, the first Berboran had succumbed to the devastation that would come to be known as the Great Plague. Such was the length of time it had taken to level an empire that for over seven hundred years had stood firm, unconquered. Five days! Now their city was dead; the stormy Berbora many had known under the last of the malevolent aghors, and the peaceful, prosperous Berbora that they had so recently enjoyed during the all-too-brief reign of the beloved Vhalin, was no more. In its stead remained a ravaged shell of a city, a place of disease and decay, of hopes and dreams irreparably shattered for all time.

The bulk of Berbora's immeasurable toll had been exacted during the second and third full days. From dawn of the second day till sunset of the next, the malady had spread like flames grabbing hold of tinder, killing half of the city's seventy thousand inhabitants. This represented more than two thirds of the final death toll. None perished quickly or painlessly; on the contrary, the affliction toyed with its victims mercilessly for hours at a time before releasing them to the welcome folds of death. Those who went untouched by the disease bore witness to the unspeakable suffering of family and friends alike, until the few tenuous threads that bound them to their lifelong homes were severed. With the soldiers of Vhalin no longer able to contain them, they fled the once glorious city in all directions, their destinations unknown even to many of them. By the end of the fourth day nearly twenty thousand had departed, leaving in their wake little more than five hundred who, for one reason or another, chose to remain. Few of the latter could truly say why they did so.

Berbora's opulent Palace of Gold had been razed by late afternoon of the third day. The noble Vhalin and his loyal retainers fought valiantly against the unreasoning citizenry, who chose to vent their anger and frustration on the helpless aghor, and for a time he repelled them. But finally, Vhalin, tormented beyond reason by the loss of his beloved Jhennia; of Vhadron, his eldest son; and of Sahria, his only daughter, fell victim to the dreaded malady. Crazed by the fires of burning fever, the aghor exited the palace before any could stop him. His longsword waving menacingly, he ran screaming and howling into the courtyard, now occupied by a hateful mob. The strength of madness enabled him to dispatch nearly a score, but their numbers eventually overwhelmed him. Before the horrified eyes of those in the palace, Vhalin was torn to pieces, his remains left to molder alongside the Stone of Vorhashekkh.

With the death of the aghor, nearly all of his fiercely loyal men abandoned their hopeless task and fled into the city. Only a handful remained to protect young Vhalok, the sole remaining heir, who had been sequestered in an upper chamber at the outbreak of the rebellion. But Vhalin's death also served to incite the rabble, who stormed the Palace of Gold with renewed fervor. The few who sought to deter them were trampled beneath the onslaught, and the destruction of the palace commenced in earnest. Not until every stone was plucked from the walls, not until the once lofty golden towers sat atop a shifting heap of debris barely ten feet above the edifice's foundation, were the incensed Berborans satisfied. They returned to their homes, some to gather up what few belongings they could and depart the city, others to die.

The last victim of the plague within the city's walls succumbed shortly before dawn on the first day of the new month, an event witnessed by no more than three uncaring people. Another corpse fell atop the countless numbers that choked the city's broad avenues. Many others dotted the fields and plains surrounding Berbora, while a few bloated forms bobbed obscenely in the slow-moving current of the Shelkan. Thousands of flies swarmed over each body like a living blanket, while waves of wriggling vermin competed with them for a share of each grisly prize. Those Berborans who still lived were sorely pressed to keep the pestilence from their own flesh.

Toward the end of the morning, nearly half of the survivors gathered by the western gate. They had aged considerably on the surface during the terrible five days, and all were quite pale. But none displayed symptoms of the malady, and they felt reasonably certain that it was no longer a threat to any of them. A pennant was unfurled high atop a parapet to advise stragglers throughout the city of their location, and within hours the majority of those who still called themselves Berborans were reaffirming their loyalty to the principles first established by Tahresk, the revered founder of the empire, so many hundreds of years past.

Under the temporary guidance of a once well-to-do merchant, all embarked on a task they knew to be unavoidable.

While scores of them dug a huge pit in a fertile field just beyond the gate, the rest returned to the city's interior to begin the unpleasant task of gathering up the putrefying corpses. There were no horses, no elephants, no work beasts of any kind, all having fled in terror days earlier. Wooden carts were drawn by men and women, and these same quivering hands, sheathed in anything available, loaded the insect-ridden bodies of their brethren atop the back of the carts in heaps of from twenty to twenty-five. By the time the first of the transports arrived back at the west gate the hole had been completed, and within its confines a roaring blaze thrust crackling fingers of flame upward into the hazy sky. One by one the decaying masses of flesh were consigned to this inferno, the newly resultant stench at first overwhelming those who of necessity were forced to carry out the assignment. But soon they grew numb to even this unspeakable effluvium, as they had to everything else so far, for many days would pass before the thick smoke from this immense conflagration ceased to rise above the canyon of death.

###

Two men stood at the perimeter of the courtyard and gazed morosely at the remains of what had been the Palace of Gold. They were impervious to the survivors that passed on either side of them on their way to the western gate, not even affording them as much as a sidelong glance, for they did not care. Both had once been young, but the preceding days had also aged them. Their backs were bent beneath the weight of some immeasurable onus, this posture belying the graceful trimness of their athletic bodies.

One had been born within the walls of Berbora and had seldom ventured beyond them in his lifetime. His complexion was fair, his tousled shock of hair colored a light brown. Usually clean-shaven, the five days of stubble he bore made him appear unkempt, though this detracted little from his comely face. He wore a fine leather hauberk, as well as high-laced sandals of a similar quality, these marking him as a soldier in the Berboran guard. Countless superficial wounds and ugly bruises covered much of his exposed skin, the dried blood from these injuries, which he had not bothered to wipe away, forming a bizarre pattern.

His companion was of a similar height, just over six feet. He wore an identical hauberk, and his injuries were also many. But here the resemblance between the pair ended, for the latter's hair and fully grown beard were jet black, his complexion swarthy. He was not a native Berboran; in fact, he was not even of this time. His home lay a thousand years and an equivalent number of leagues away.

Dehril, the young soldier of Berbora, and Tyron, the Kalkh mountain man from another time and place, had shared a strong bond of friendship since the advent of the latter in the splendid city some months past. That they now stood silently together was strong testimony to this bond, for of those who occupied the death chamber of young Vhadron only days earlier and heard the shocking revelation of Mohrosk, the bantir of distant Fragha, only Dehril remained alive. Only Dehril knew that Tyron, who loved the royal family as though they were his own kin, who loved Khreelar, the physician, as one would love his own father, had unintentionally borne the Great Plague to Berbora, the malady that destroyed them all. Why had Dehril not driven a blade into the heart of the one responsible for all of this? How could he not feel malice toward the individual who had brought an end to the life he knew for all time? Dehril understood, as had Vhalin, that Tyron would have given his own life a hundred times over to see Berbora spared, to prevent the inevitable catastrophic occurrence that was already part of history and legend a thousand years hence. It was predestined, and therefore unavoidable. The Kalkh had been no more than an unwilling pawn, a toy of the many gods that men bent their knee to, both then and now. Vhalin had seen his eldest son taken from him, then his beloved Jhennia, and finally the innocent young Sahria. Was this motive enough for intense hatred? Undoubtedly. Yet at no time had the aghor blamed Tyron, not when the truth had been revealed, nor at any time thereafter. Despite his immense grief he realized that the Kalkh would bear this incomprehensible burden to his grave and beyond. No, Dehril would not have despised his tormented friend under any circumstances, and even had he chosen to do so, he would have been shamed by the example set by the noble Vhalin.

Only hours before Vhalin's death, Tyron had revealed everything to the aghor, with none other than Dehril in earshot. Now, as they continued to gaze silently at the ruins, the Berboran soldier reflected on the unbelievable events leading to this tragedy. Tyron's people were the Kalkhs, a nomadic tribe that wandered through the distant Yushan Mountains, a range known as the Yshins during the time of Berbora's glory. The restless young Kalkh heard the legends of Berbora from a traveler in the mountains, and the desire to set eyes upon even the ruins became an obsession with him. He journeyed across the hostile land of his own time, risking death often, until he finally reached the Krabharkian Forest. Here he saved the life of old Zathras, the sole remaining inhabitant of Berbora. Zathras, a descendant of magicians, was more than pleased to satisfy Tyron's thirst for knowledge regarding the once great empire, though initially he did not divulge the true reason for his elation over Tyron's interest. Not until half a day had been spent exploring the ruins of the city, an unforgettable experience for Tyron, did the old man reveal his motive. With the aid of the enigmatic Stone of Vorhashekkh, which still stood in the courtyard, he would see the Kalkh safely through the normally impenetrable barrier of time more than a thousand years to the days of Vhalin's reign. He would have one hundred days to convince the city of its pending fate and take all precautions to see that it did not occur. Zathras reasoned that if Tyron was successful, if the course of history could indeed be altered, then Tyron's eventual return to his own time would be amid a greater, more benevolent Berboran empire, where he would be welcomed as a hero. Once certain that the magician could make good his claim, the Kalkh accepted the challenge.

Dehril was well versed in Tyron's exploits since the latter's mysterious appearance in the courtyard, but he dwelled on them nonetheless, for they held much meaning to him. Tyron's inexplicable presence immediately marked him as a spy and a potential assassin, and Vhalin sentenced him to face the Three Challenges. The aghor loathed the challenges, but because he had only recently won the previously tainted throne he retained them, this by the insistence of the people. Tyron survived the first, a battle against four capable fighting men. Vhalin begged him to forgo the next two and accept a lesser sentence of labor in the mines, but Tyron refused. In the second challenge, a mismatch against five terrible serpents, the Kalkh lost one eye and was nearly killed. But he endured, and once again he returned to the floor of the arena to face the third challenge, one that had never been met throughout all of Berbora's long history. The suicidal challenge, against numerous deadly beasts, was more than the fair-minded Vhalin could bear. He entered the arena to assist Tyron, as did Dehril and some other guards, whose respect Tyron had won by this time. During the encounter Tyron rescued Vhadron, who had accidently fallen to the arena floor, from a vicious *tigher.* The other creatures were all destroyed, though Tyron remained on the brink of death for days thereafter.

After his recovery, Tyron learned that he had more than won the respect of Vhalin, but still he did not feel the time propitious to warn the aghor of the pending disaster. Instead, the Kalkh went underground to break up a conspiracy that would have overthrown Vhalin, an action that made him a hero to all. He was selected as the personal tutor and bodyguard to Vhadron, a position of honor. With the growing love and admiration between himself and the royal family, he felt that soon he would be able to warn them of the plague, still months away, and that they would believe him.

Ever restless, Tyron joined a party of guards assigned to bear the prisoners of the conspiracy to an isolated island as their punishment. The task was completed, though the vessel was damaged in a battle with an *orsogh,* a terrible sea creature. The ship limped into Zurgrava, a port city supposedly of the Berboran empire, although, unknown to them, it had recently sworn allegiance to certain hostile nations that would destroy Berbora. By deceit the Zurgravan governor poisoned most of the crew and guards, but with the Kalkh's help a few managed to escape to sea, where they sailed to Berbora to warn Vhalin of this dangerous alliance. Tyron, unable to flee, was captured and rendered unconscious.

The mountain man eventually awakened in the putrid hold of a Hoskon slave vessel, where strange beings of every kind sat in chains, many dying, some dead, all suffering terrible deprivation. Days later he escaped and, after floating ashore, he was nursed back to health by the inhabitants of Fragha, a village friendly to the Berborans. Here, for the first time, Tyron revealed his purpose, for time was of the essence and he required all the help that he could get if he was to return to the city in time. Mohrosk, the bantir, was at first incredulous, but with the assurance of a strange old *qassa* woman that Tyron's story was true, he relented. Once fully recovered, the Kalkh was given a swift steed with which to make the journey.

Tyron set off along the quickest route, which took him across the dreaded Plain of Horgrool. In this unspeakable place he was nearly destroyed, but he somehow survived, and he arrived in Berbora on the thirty-fourth day of the month, where he received a hero's welcome. Here he advised Vhalin of the pending disaster, and the stunned aghor chose to believe him. The city was immediately sealed off; no one could leave, nor could any caravans, individual travelers, or the like enter the gates. Those citizens with the most minor of illnesses were sent to a holding camp some distance away. With all precautions taken, the terrible wait commenced.

All went well initially, but soon a few were stricken by a strange and horrifying malady that consumed them within hours. As thousands died grotesque deaths it became evident that, in spite of his valiant efforts, Tyron had failed. The plague had struck Berbora. Vhadron was the first of the royal family to contract the illness, and shortly thereafter he died, to the overwhelming bereavement of all. Next stricken was Jhennia. Those who loved her waited helplessly for death to wrest the beautiful and gentle aghora from her torment.

In the midst of the unstoppable tragedy Mohrosk, the Fraghan bantir, unexpectedly appeared in the Palace of Gold. He was an aged, tortured soul, not the strong-willed chieftain that Tyron remembered. On the fifth day subsequent to Tyron's departure he had set off in the Kalkh's wake, for his own village had been leveled by disease, and he now understood. He passed through many dead or dying hamlets as he narrowed the distance between them, even daring the Plain of Horgrool. But there had been too many leagues to make up, and he was unable to accomplish his goal. That day, as Mohrosk neared the gleaming heart of the empire, he saw that he was too late. He knew that Tyron himself was the carrier of the dreaded plague, which he had contracted in the stifling hold of the Hoskon slave vessel!

Few noticed Mohrosk calmly take his own life, for all eyes turned to Tyron. The Kalkh, driven to the brink of insanity by this revelation, was heavily drugged. But he fought off the effects long enough to lay his body down on the Stone of Vorhashekkh near sunset, so that Zathras could draw him back to his own world. It was his one hundredth night in Berbora, the last night that such could be accomplished before he was forced to remain permanently. But at the final moment he relented, for he could not desert his friends, especially now. He sought out Vhalin, who gladly received him, and with swords raised they went forth to stand against the bitter mobs, which had turned their frustrations toward those within the Palace of Gold.

###

Amidst the city's crumbling ruins a thousand years hence, old Zathras waited to draw Tyron back. He remained for days beyond the allotted time before accepting the fact that the young Kalkh would not be returning. With head bent, shoulders stooped, the magician departed the remnants of the once great city to carry out Tyron's sole request: advising the mountain man's mother of what had come to pass. Zathras would never see Berbora again.

###

The rabble was initially kept at bay by Vhalin and his loyalists, who numbered little more than a score. Khreelar cared for the twins, Sahria and Vhalok, in an upper chamber, the physician calling forth all his skills in an attempt to concoct an effective immunizing agent for them. But his efforts failed, and young Sahria died quickly. It was believed that this tragedy, even above his own contracting of the illness, was the stimulus that drove Vhalin to his final action.

With the aghor dead, the loyalists who had not succumbed to the plague fled the palace, all save Tyron, Dehril, and two others, who vowed to protect Vhalok at all cost. But the enraged citizenry stormed them by the hundreds, and they were stoned mercilessly. The Kalkh was the first to fall beneath the stampede, though not before sending dozens of them to the depths of Sharn. Dehril dispatched only a few less before being overwhelmed. As the Great Hall grew black all around them, neither could conceive of ever again setting eyes upon the light of day. This did not trouble Tyron at all.

A dim spark of awareness returned to Tyron during the afternoon of the fourth full day of terror, the final day of the sixth month, though the mountain man could hardly know this. His breathing was shallow, the lungs and other orifices being clogged with dirt. Initial movement proved nearly impossible, for a considerable weight pinned him tightly. Only after his barely functioning brain began to unclog, only after he managed to part his eyelids a fraction, did he realize that he was buried under countless bits of rock, debris that had once been part of the Palace of Gold.

One arm was loosened, then the other, and with unbearable, agonizing effort the tortured Kalkh slowly drew himself upward from this premature tomb. Searing waves of pain coursed through his bruised body, and twice he blacked out. But with teeth bared he persevered, and after hours of torment he once again gazed upon the grey, cloud-filled sky. After a respite of no more than a few minutes, he rose upon shaky legs. The overwhelming stench troubled him little, nor did the sight of the countless decaying bodies, clearly visible from his vantage point, disturb him. His thoughts centered upon the vast cairn of rubble that surrounded him. He had endured, but what of Dehril, and Vhalok, and Khreelar? Was this heap of stones to be their gravesite for all time?

Dehril could recall the hand that firmly clasped his own, for was it not just yesterday? He had met the charging horde on the third broad step leading to the upper levels, and therefore was not buried as deeply as Tyron had been. The Kalkh, frantically hurling stones from the immense pile, came upon him within the first hour. Their reunion was brief, hardly pleasant under the circumstances. After a short rest, the Berboran joined his friend in a single-minded effort to locate the others. Only a few aimless wanderers ventured within yards of where they toiled, these lost souls hardly caring. Amid the vacuum-like stillness of the dying city, the pair hunted endlessly through the shattered debris.

At night the clouds dissipated, revealing a full, gleaming moon. By its rays they worked far into the late hours, denying their fatigue, their hunger and thirst. Finally, near dawn, they uncovered a bloodied hand, and for the first time they paused. Both immediately recognized the ornate ring on the small finger, the bauble that Khreelar cherished so dearly. They dug deeper, but they knew that their efforts were futile. The physician was dead.

With grief now added to their fatigue, they were at first unable to continue their efforts. But they knew that Vhalok had been in the care of the physician, that he was likely nearby. With renewed vigor they cast away tons of stones, hardly noticing the first trace of the morning sun as it topped the horizon. Soon it floated above the land, where it was blotted by the foreboding clouds that would fill the sky throughout the day. Not until they chanced to gaze upon each other in the daylight, where each saw a wild-eyed friend hovering on the brink of madness, did they grasp the reality of the situation. Vhalok was a small boy, a frail lad at that. He could not have survived the devastation, especially for this length of time. Their bodies shook as they crumpled upon the stones, each realizing the hopelessness of their labors. Blackness overtook them, their fatigue refusing to be denied any longer. Thus were they held for the remainder of the morning and the early part of the afternoon.

###

The fires that burned in their eyes had abated considerably, enough to allow them a more objective look at the scene of their recent monumental efforts. Dehril's grief over the loss of so many friends in the Great Plague could hardly be measured. But to the Berboran, who had been born and raised in the shadow of the splendid Palace of Gold, these shattered ruins represented a loss of another kind, for the edifice had meant so much to him. He wondered if anyone could understand such feelings.

Dehril glanced at Tyron, whose own steel-gray eyes were now turned toward a fly-infested corpse farther along the rim of the courtyard, about ten feet away. What must *his* torment be like? the young Berboran mused. Where had he found the will to live over the past few days? *If it had been me,* he thought, *I would surely have destroyed myself immediately.* To bear a burden such as this throughout one's life . . .

The saddened face of the Berboran suddenly altered to a look that bespoke grim determination. Tyron must not destroy himself! he thought. He *must not* live with this forever! Surely somewhere there can be a life for him, where he might at least try to forget the horror of these days. Until that time, I will protect him; *I must protect him!* Not from man or beast, for these are foes that he is more than capable of defending himself against. Tyron is his own greatest enemy, to be sure. He is my best friend, my *only* friend! He deserves to live a life free from the burden of the plague that he carries, a life free of bitter memories and haunting nightmares. I swear before Thur that I will devote my own life to seeing this achieved!

His future now determined, Dehril turned toward his friend and placed a hand on the bruised shoulder. Tyron's head snapped about, as though he had been disturbed in the midst of deep thought, and his gray eyes peered coldly at the Berboran. Awareness registered quickly, though the look softened only slightly, despite his companion's smile.

"Come, my friend," Dehril said. "It is time to go."

He strode purposefully across the courtyard, not once looking behind him. Tyron hesitated for a moment before following mechanically in his wake. Their time amid the rubble that had once been called the Palace of Gold was over.

CHAPTER TWO: ZARTHIK

The distance to the courtyard gate, most of which had been leveled by the raging mob days earlier, was about thirty yards. Dehril traversed the smoothly paved floor hastily, anxious to depart. But even as he neared to within an arm's length of the exit, he realized that this would not come to pass so readily, for Tyron, who had initially been close at his heels, now stood motionless in the center of the courtyard. The object of his rapt attention, as Dehril well knew before even turning around, was the enigmatic Stone of Vorhashekkh. Often in the past Dehril had observed his friend gazing wistfully at the translucent, emerald stone with its flecks of gold, though not until the truth had been revealed could the Berboran guess at what part it played in the Kalkh's presence. With a shrug he began to approach Tyron, but this time there was no haste. His steps were slow and deliberate, for in spite of the need to quit the heart of the recent tragedy, he was loath to intrude on the other's thoughts. Surely he could be allowed this moment with the sole remaining link to his own world.

As he neared the stone, Dehril noted that it had somehow gone untouched during the siege and subsequent leveling of the palace. Bits of debris, both large and small, dotted nearly every foot of the courtyard, but not even as much as a pebble sat atop the shimmering block, nor was there any on the floor within ten feet of its four sides. The rabble had given it a wide berth, to be sure, for all Berborans respected it, while most harbored some fear when in the circle of its inexplicable powers. Indeed, the Stone of Vorhashekkh merited such awe. Its height was three feet, its width the same, while its length was nearly nine feet. That the weighty block had been utilized in its dim past as some kind of sacrificial altar was a fact quite readily accepted, though words regarding this were seldom, if ever uttered. One need only gaze closely at the dark stains on its surface to realize the validity of this thought.

In what far off, dismal land of horror had the Stone of Vorhashekkh been spawned? For how long had it sat upon the face of this world? A thousand years? Five thousand? Longer? Even the magicians who had dwelled within its sphere could not hazard a guess regarding this. But its history in regard to Berbora could be more clearly defined. It came to the city from a dark place far to the north, this in the four hundred and sixty-ninth Tahreskian year, by a group of magicians opposed to the perverted, abhorrent practices of their dark brethren in a labyrinth far beneath Berbora. With its powers they drove the dark magicians out, and afterward they used the stone to practice a more benevolent form of their art. Only a fraction of its secrets became known to them, though each generation strove to learn more. Zathras, the last of them, had been able to master the traversing of time by reading scrawls within the dusty tomes of his ancestors. But he himself could not begin to grasp the full potential of the stone, this by his own admission, even with the compiled knowledge of numerous centuries at his fingertips. Perhaps the understanding of it would not be realized until the black and evil forces of Sharn itself walk the entire face of the land, an unwelcome but ever-present prophecy that few, if any, hoped would ever come to pass.

Dehril halted at Tyron's side, and the Kalkh immediately became aware of his presence, though this time he did not appear startled. His mouth was curled in a wry, humorless smile as he gazed at the Berboran for only a moment before again turning his attention to the stone.

"What are your thoughts, my friend?" Dehril asked in a hushed tone.

Tyron chose not to look at him as he replied, "The irony; the accursed irony of this whole incident never ceases to amaze me. It is almost amusing, in a perverse sort of way. I can still see old Zathras sitting amidst his beloved ruins, the dream of restoring an empire his very reason for living. He chooses me, *me,* to carry out his designs. A thousand years of time are crossed; a hundred days of cheating death on countless occasions are endured, and for what? Gaze around you and see the results! You used to laugh at the many times I returned from the dead, did you not, my friend? Why do you not laugh now? Here I stand, still among the living, while all around us a city continues to perish! Think of it: had death proven victorious but a single time, you might even now be racing your steed against the swift pony of young Vhadron alongside the Shelkan, while the rest of the city tended to the normal affairs of the day. Oh, you might have mourned my loss for a time, though the memory would eventually have faded. But what of *this?* Can you ever forget?"

"Tyron, please—!"

"Five nights past, while lying upon the stone and waiting for Zathras to draw me back, I thought of many things. At first I could not wait for the transfer to be done, so that I might tear myself from the stone and throttle the life from the old charlatan. Or worse, I would remain by his side until the affliction clutched at him and took his life slowly, painfully, as it had to those here. But, like myself, I realized that he could not have had the least inkling of what my journey to Berbora's past would portend, that his desires were no less sincere than my own. To destroy him would have been an act of futility. Better for him to meet his own death believing that he did all he could to try and prevent Berbora's destruction.

"I then thought of my affliction, something I must bear to my grave. In my mind I saw myself retracing the treacherous steps I had taken across the land of my own time. The Yushans appeared before me, their summits crowned in white. It was winter, and my people were camped in the lower elevations. I found them in the Fields of Kharg, and their boisterous welcomes echoed loudly off the rock facings. Jhalar, my mother, embraced me, while the long-haired beauties fought amongst themselves to touch me, to press eager red lips against mine. Old friends swore lustily as they pounded me on the back, their faces on the verge of cracking from the broad grins that they wore. All this I saw, Dehril, and I smiled inside, until the scene suddenly altered. The mountains now rang with the screams of the tormented Kalkhs as the flames of fever consumed them and drove them to madness. Pocked, bloated bodies writhed in the fields, each praying loudly for Zeth to be merciful and take them quickly. As I had destroyed Berbora, so would I have done to my own beloved people!

"I realized then that, whatever I chose to do, whether I remained here or returned to the age in which I had been born, I could never again approach within miles of any civilization, lest I kill them all. Never, *never* would I see my people again! Still, the ties to my own time were strong, and as the sun dropped toward the fissure I nearly let Zathras pull me through. But then I saw the face of Vhalin as he was advised of his son's illness, and I observed the lad's pale, twisted countenance as it appeared shortly after your Thur carried him beyond this lifetime. How could I bring this upon Vhalin, upon all of you, and then desert while it gnawed away at the foundations of your lives? This was the telling factor, and with few seconds left to spare, I tore myself away from the Stone of Vorhashekkh. Since then I have done what little I could for the aghor and my friends. Now the tasks are done, and with them my life."

"Wh-what are you saying?" Dehril stammered, fearful of the answer.

"Must you ask?" the Kalkh snapped. "Have your senses flown you? I carry the plague! Even if I choose to live with the knowledge of what I brought upon Berbora, which I assure you I do not, I must remain in isolation for all time! Never again can I know human companionship; never again can I bed a woman, knowing that within days her body might lay moldering in the dirt, infested with vermin! To me such a life would be worse than death itself! Can you not see this? I must be destroyed!"

"Tyron, no! You cannot—!"

"I will not ask you to carry this out, my friend. Though the taking of one's life is frowned upon in the eyes of Zeth, it goes without question that an exception will have to be made. Beyond this, it will be up to you to see to the proper disposal of my body. Burn it! Burn it until not even the bones remain; or hurl it into a chasm so deep as to penetrate into the depths of Sharn itself. Better still: carry it far out into the Khoric Sea. Cast it into the surging waves, heavily weighted. Should the orsoghs not find it, then at least it will rest forever far beneath the surface. Please, Dehril; I know that I rant like a madman, but I am sincere in what I say. As a carrier, mere death will not rid me of the curse that I bear. A reoccurrence such as this must not be afforded any chance. The corpse of Tyron must be erased from the face of the land forever!"

"Surely you cannot desire death," Dehril gasped. "Khreelar himself said that your will to live far surpassed any he had yet encountered in his long lifetime. You could not have lost this!"

"No, it is gone. Please, Dehril—"

"Tyron, no! You must hear what I say! Think of yesterday, and then admit to me truthfully that your desire to live is no more!"

The Kalkh appeared puzzled. "And what of yesterday?"

"When you regained consciousness, you found yourself buried alive beneath the ruins of the palace. You could barely move, lest the terrible pain further wrack your body and worsen the already numerous injuries. Yet your mind was still your own, and you were well aware of all that had so recently transpired. How simple it would have been for you, how convenient, to breathe one final sigh, close your eyes, and die. No more worry, no more pain. But did you do this? No! How agonizing it must have been for you to claw your way upward through the tons of crushing rock. Yet you persisted, until once again you saw the light of day. If not the will to live, then how would you explain your action? Can you answer me this, Tyron?"

The sinewy mountain man turned and stared at Dehril, his brow knitted in thought. His mouth opened, but a few moments passed before he spoke. "I—what transpired yesterday should not be misconstrued. My thoughts were only for the safety of the young aghorak, of Khreelar and you. Now this is over, and there is nothing left."

"That your concern for others gave you the strength to continue is commendable, and I concede that it played a small part in what you were able to accomplish. Do you hear what I say? *A small part!* It was your own desire to live, above anything else, that dictated your actions. You are young, and regardless of what has happened in Berbora, there is still much of life before you. Think of that, Tyron: you cannot wish to die!"

The tortured Kalkh could no longer remain standing upon his shaky legs, and accordingly he sank to his knees, his head shaking. After long moments he gazed upward at Dehril, his face twisted. His initial words were barely audible.

"I-I do not wish to die. You are right, my friend; I see that now. If the burden of the plague could be lifted from me, if the memory of this experience could be obliterated, I would truly desire to go on living. Even if only the former could be accomplished, I might somehow learn to live with the nightmare. But I fear that neither of these is within the realm of possibility. Do you understand, Dehril?" He turned toward the Stone of Vorhashekkh, and from his throat emanated a bone-chilling voice that seemed not to be a part of him. "There are no alternatives! *I . . . cannot . . . live . . . like . . . this!*"

Sobs wracked his injured body as he pounded his fists atop the Stone of Vorhashekkh. Dehril knelt at his side and attempted to soothe him, though for the first time since avowing his earlier commitment to Tyron he felt helpless, unsure, for he feared that his friend was right. He could offer no possible solution, nor did he even know where to begin seeking one out. Yet he could not allow Tyron to observe this doubt, for it would surely hasten the Kalkh's demise.

"Tyron, listen—" he began.

"Perhaps I might be of some help?"

The unexpected voice was soft but well-modulated, and it startled the pair. As one they whirled around and saw a bent figure standing no more than three yards from them. The old man wore a utilitarian robe and shoddy leather sandals, while under one arm he carried a hefty, leather-bound book that appeared considerably worn. The thin strands of white hair that grew from his nearly bald pate waved gently in the soft breeze, while his neatly trimmed beard, in contrast, was quite full. His eyes denoted wisdom and kindness, though he did not smile. Such an action could not have been expected of anyone still remaining within the confines of the charnel house that was Berbora.

Tyron was the first to rise as he gazed upon the fellow. His most recent actions were quickly forgotten, and his jaw hung low as he stared at the elder in unfeigned amazement.

"*Zathras!* In the name of Zeth, *it is Zathras!* How—why did you come here?"

"I beg your pardon?" the old man replied. "Surely you have me mistaken for another."

Indeed, peering through one clouded eye as he was, such an error on the part of the troubled Kalkh was understandable. Anyone of similar age and stature could momentarily have been perceived as the elderly magician that Tyron had known in another time. But even after staring at the old man for long moments, his conviction remained strong, for the resemblance of Zathras to this, doubtless his own ancestor, was uncanny.

"Why do you deny this?" the mountain man hissed. "Do you think me a fool? How would I not know—?"

"Tyron, please!" Dehril snapped as he grasped his friend's arm tightly. "You are indeed wrong. This fellow is Zarthik, the proprietor of a magic shop in the marketplace. I told you of him before, remember? It was Zarthik who helped Vhalin and me locate the tunnel entrances, this enabling us to flush Ghorus and his rebels from beneath the city."

The Kalkh rubbed the mist from his eye and stared disbelievingly at Zarthik, who chanced a meager, sad-eyed smile. Finally, with a resigned shrug and a nod, he accepted the word of his friend, though he knew that if Zathras were to stand at this old fellow's side, even Dehril would be sorely pressed to differentiate between them.

"It is not that difficult to understand the reason for your reaction, my young friend," Zarthik stated softly, knowingly, his previous puzzlement no longer in evidence.

Dehril's head suddenly snapped toward Zarthik, and he exclaimed, "What do you mean by those words, old man? How long have you been standing there?"

"Long enough," he replied.

"Then you have heard—?"

"I have heard enough to know that your friend here is in need of assistance. Beyond this, the retention or repetition of anything else I might have chanced to overhear is unnecessary."

"You—you know of the plague?" Tyron stammered.

"I do."

"Then you can free him from the onus of carrying it?" Dehril demanded, suddenly hopeful.

Zarthik shook his head sadly. "I fear that my limited powers are far from sufficient for such as this."

"But the Stone of Vorhashekkh—!" Dehril exclaimed.

"The Stone of Vorhashekkh can be utilized in learning whether there are any upon the land who might possess the means with which to assist your friend. Here, as an intermediary, might I be able to render aid."

"Is there anything you would have me do?" Tyron asked.

"I must know everything that you can tell me of this plague; not the symptoms and effects, for these, I assure you, have been observed from a short distance away. Where was the malady contracted?"

"In the cursed hold of a Hoskon slave vessel."

Zarthik nodded. "Tell me of those who shared this pestilent pit with you."

"Many were not unlike the strange folk one sees almost daily about our own docks. There were bearded giants, men with hair of blazing red. Small yellow folk with slanted eyes, their language an enigma to me, also occupied the hold. There were men and women of black skin, as well as those with flesh the whiteness of ivory. And—oh yes, the dwarves, hairless beings with fiery eyes and curled lips. I had never seen their like before. Then there were—"

"Wait!" Zarthik interrupted. "The dwarves you mentioned. Tell me more of them."

"The memories of those terrible days are so vague." Tyron shook his head. "I will do my best. There were five—no, six of them, some male, some female, though I cannot remember the exact number of each. The flesh was colored a sickly light tan, this background clearly displaying the bloated red tics that clung to them. They were chained closely together, hardly a considerable distance from where I was held captive. Any communication between them was at best crude, and was accomplished by a strange sibilant, sputtering sound. Amid these noises they coughed ceaselessly, this hacking at times coming in lengthy spasms."

"Is there anything else?"

"No, other than one of them had died by the time I made good my escape."

"What—what did the others do?" Zarthik asked, his altered demeanor indicating him to be almost fearful of the answer.

Tyron shuddered. "I could scarcely forget. They devoured him!"

"Thur!" the magician hissed through clenched teeth. "They were *Scambas!*"

The wide-eyed Dehril shook his head vigorously. "No! That is impossible!" he snapped. "From the time of my youth I was taught that Scambas existed only in legends brought to the docks of Berbora by seafarers of questionable reliability. Surely one as wise as you cannot believe that these tales have a basis in truth!"

"The Scambas do indeed exist," Zarthik stated with assurance. "That most have always thought of them as figments of one's imagination has likely been for the better. The reality of them is far worse than any fabricated tale."

"How can you be certain of this?" Dehril asked.

"That is unimportant. Suffice it to say that I now have the information I seek. There can be no doubt that your affliction was caused by contact with the Scambas."

"What is this all about?" Tyron demanded.

"Countless miles across the Khoric Sea there is a chain of islands," Zarthik began. "They are inhabited by a race of diminutive people called the Durvs, this an appellation in their own tongue for 'dwarf,' which they loathe. It is said that they occupied the mainland even before the time of Tahresk, that they were quite intelligent beings, as they still are. But their unique physical appearance made them the objects of derision, and they were eventually driven from the land. They settled on a few of these many islands, the ones surrounded by deadly reefs that were impassable to all save the Durvs' own tiny vessels. There, far from danger, they thrived for more than five hundred years.

"A deadly island malady eventually overwhelmed them, destroying nearly half of their population. While in the throes of this devastation, a cause was sought out, the solution not long in coming. A family unit of about twenty-five Durvs had recently arrived on Orma, the most heavily populated island, to partake in the trading of goods. These rural Durvs, inhabitants of an insignificant island in the chain, were generations removed from civilization, and the results were evident. They were surly, low in intelligence, and had little concept of sanitation. Bulging tics clung to the bodies of all, even the youngest children. The malignancy was in the system of everyone, and while harmless to themselves, the effect on the other Durvs was unspeakable.

"These Scambas, or Diseased Ones, were nearly torn to pieces by their incensed brethren. But the Durvs were a kindly people, and when their aghor petitioned for humanity, they acceded. The Scambas were deposited on the most remote island in the group, there sentenced to an eternity of isolation, for none possessed the skills with which they might have built a vessel, even a makeshift raft, from the trees that abounded there. This island was hatefully renamed Scambiost, and to this day it is still shunned by the Durvs.

"The natural resources of Scambiost were great, and the Scambas, despite the increasing degeneracy brought about with each passing generation, managed to multiply their numbers considerably. Within a few hundred years there were many thousands of them, crazed, infested little demons who wandered across the width and length of their confined land in search of food and physical pleasure, their only motivations for living. Predictably, the resources of the island petered out from their constant ravaging, leaving them with few alternatives to survival. They—they became cannibalistic, though at first they only devoured the flesh of those who died. But soon their appetite became insatiable, and they divided into quite a few small tribes, each seeking to destroy their enemies for food. Since then their numbers have dwindled, though still they continue to exist.

"Such are the Scambas, the Diseased Ones, offshoots of the noble and intelligent Durvs. The—the atrocities that I have heard spoken of as being carried out on Scambiost . . . *Thur!* I can speak of it no longer!"

Zarthik's body trembled uncontrollably as the shocking narrative was concluded, while Tyron and Dehril stared at him in thoughtful silence for long moments. The Kalkh finally pierced the quiet.

"What could the Hoskons have wanted with the likes of them?" he asked.

"Durvs are invaluable for labor in the mines," Zarthik replied. "Their size makes even the smallest of tunnels accessible. Until Vhalin ascended the throne, a few Durvs toiled as slaves even in our own mines. The aghor freed them and returned them to the home of their ancestors. As far as the Hoskons are concerned, such is the lack of intelligence in our western enemies. In their slaving foray they likely made the islands of the Durvs their final stop. Unable to penetrate the deadly reefs of the larger sanctuaries, they anchored off the hospitable shore of Scambiost, where they gathered up what inhabitants they could. Remember, not all believe what they have heard regarding the Scambas. Still, one glance at the filthy, tic-infested bodies should have sent them rowing in haste from the beach. But apparently their leaders required the small beings for their mines, and accordingly they cast the wretched creatures into the hold without thought of consequences."

"The slave ship that pursued Evath's brigantine as it sailed to warn Vhalin must also have contained Scambas," Dehril said. "Surely this is the reason why it gave up the chase in so odd a manner."

"But the journey from Scambiost must have consumed numerous days!" Tyron protested. "Why was no one stricken sooner?"

"There are many possible reasons for this," Zarthik answered, "though I could not select any one for certain. Perhaps a transfer from a tiny Scamba to a fully grown human consumes more time than from one of the dwarves to another. Exposure to the sea may have had something to do with it, or maybe the long years in which the disease has lain dormant in the systems of the Scambas and their descendants. Undoubtedly, you contracted the malady from your days of proximity in the hold, this exposure made considerably worse by the rending of the dead Scamba's body at the hands of its fellows. But know this, Tyron, it if be any consolation: the latter action of the Scambas most assuredly sealed the fate of the accursed Hoskons. Those of susceptibility aboard the slaver were likely dead before the day was out. If the vessel reached the port of Hoskon, then their city has resembled this for many days longer."

"As you said, old man, it is a small consolation," Tyron stated dryly.

"But why was Tyron not stricken with the plague?" Dehril asked.

"I had some of the symptoms!" Tyron said. "Do you not remember me telling you this? If not for the Fraghans, I . . .!"

The others shuffled uneasily as the Kalkh, now aware of his words, turned away from them and stared at the rubble that had been the Palace of Gold. Five, six times he pounded a heavy fist into an open palm, while Dehril, shaking off the brief lethargy, strode forth to calm him. But before he could reach his friend's side, Tyron whirled about, his action so rapid that he startled the young Berboran. The Kalkh's single eye was aflame, his teeth bared like some savage beast as he staggered toward Zarthik.

"Why me? *Why me*?" he shrieked, his words piercing the encompassing stillness. "Tell me the answer to that, you old charlatan! Why did I not die in Fragha? Why was I allowed to survive, to bring *this* upon Berbora? What makes me, above all others, a carrier of this accursed Scamban malady? Can you not answer me, *magician*?"

The unruffled Zarthik walked coolly past the raging, tormented man, not stopping until he stood only a few feet from the Stone of Vorhashekkh. With his eyes affixed straight ahead he replied, "To this I have no answer, my young friend. Knowledge such as this is for Thur and Zhon, as well as your own deity, to possess, and not to share with the likes of us. But as for carrying the malady to your grave, this your earlier concern, perhaps there is an answer. Now be silent, and leave me unquestioned to my designs!"

No reply was forthcoming from the pair. Zarthik glanced from side to side, noting that the flow of survivors to the western gate had abated. With slow, deliberate movements he placed the hefty tome atop the stone and knelt alongside it. Dusty pages in the volume were turned, until he found what he sought. His eyes were only inches from the parchment as he absorbed the contents, and once satisfied he pressed his palms against the side of the translucent block, while his forehead touched the top. Tyron, whose seething rage had been momentarily stilled, watched in silent fascination, as did Dehril.

For what seemed like an hour, but was in reality no more than a fraction of that, the magician remained so poised. His lips parted continuously, but the sounds that emerged were muffled, incoherent. Finally, deep within the green, shimmering Stone of Vorhashekkh, a faint glow appeared. For a time it grew in intensity, though at no time could it be considered bright. Zarthik, his eyes shut tightly, his teeth clenched, shuddered almost imperceptibly throughout the strange contact. Once, it appeared that he desired to tear himself away, as though wishing to deny some dark and terrible message that had been transmitted. But instead he held steadfast, likely by sheer force of will.

The glow abated, until it existed no longer. As the final vestiges faded, the old magician tore his trembling hands from the stone and lifted his head. He tried to rise upon shaky legs, but he failed, and had Tyron and Dehril not grabbed hold of his arms he might have toppled with a jarring impact upon the enigmatic talisman. They lowered him to the ground, and despite their anxiety they waited in silence while he regained his composure. At first he appeared pallid, but the respite sufficed, and he was soon able to face the pair.

"It-it is time to pass the knowledge on to my son," he gasped. "I grow t-too old for this strain."

"What did you learn?" Dehril asked.

"There . . . is a way," he replied, though hesitantly.

"May Zeth be thanked!" Tyron exclaimed.

"Please! Before anticipation overcomes you, I pray that you will listen carefully to all that I must say."

"Proceed, Zarthik," Dehril said.

"The dark magicians that were driven from Berbora so many years past were held together by some inexplicable bond, and accordingly they remained together in their flight. They ventured northward, far northward, beyond even the terrible land of Vorhashekkh itself. There they sojourned in a previously peaceful, pastoral land, and once their black secrets were loosed, the tranquility was no more. It became an unspeakable land, a place of horror, and those few of us who knew of its existence can scarcely utter its name without some trepidation. It is a bleak, uncivilized place called—*Lamnagha*!

"Who knows? By combining their forces, the dark magicians might again have arisen to challenge Berbora and the remainder of the civilized world. But petty jealousies displaced any such ambitions, and rifts were opened between them that could never be sealed. Many were destroyed, with only four surviving. The unquestioned giant among them was Zhusk, and individually, he could easily have crushed the others. But at the last moment this trio formed a tenuous alliance, and for the time being Zhusk was thwarted. He did manage, however, to drive the others from Lamnagha. They traveled south, not stopping until they reached the heart of Vorhashekkh. Before long, for the first time in hundreds of years the skies over Vorhashekkh again darkened as these new and unwelcome conquerors established their rule over the land and its semi-barbaric inhabitants—"

"The point, old man!" Tyron snapped. "Come to the point! You recite tales designed to frighten children. What—?"

"I waste no words, impatient one!" Zarthik replied testily. "Each is fraught with definite purpose. Please; I understand your feelings, but you must allow me to continue uninterrupted.

"The descendants of Zhusk and the others have waged this battle for so long that the original cause has been forgotten. But still it continues, with neither Lamnagha nor Vorhashekkh gaining the upper hand. The alliance between the three in Vorhashekkh immediately became strained, quite predictably, and their individual citadels were established at some distance from one another. But they maintained enough of a union to thwart the designs of their enemy, and the fathers of the current trio even once joined forces long enough to attempt destruction of the other. This was short-lived, I assure you.

"The magicians of Vorhashekkh are—remember the names well—Yathir, Shadil, and Dukkor. The ruler of Lamnagha, foremost of all dark magicians and every bit as powerful as Zhusk, his ancestor, is Cuhthic. Of all the names, never forget this one for a moment. Do you hear what I say, Tyron? Cuhthic is—may Thur forgive me for uttering the words—the only being on the face of this world capable of freeing you from the Scamban malady."

"A dark magician!" Dehril hissed. "By the gods—!"

"What does this matter?" Tyron exclaimed. "If Cuhthic be the only one who can rid me of this accursed plague, then so be it! I will seek him out!"

"As you said, old man, the gods will have to forgive us," Dehril added. "We *will* journey north!"

Zarthik glared at the two, his face a mask of rage. But before he could berate them, the anger passed and he shook his head sadly.

"The souls of the dark magicians are spawned in the depths of Sharn itself. Do you think that the likes of us would casually approach one such as Cuhthic and request a boon? Once, these demons co-existed with those not of their ilk during their sojourn in Berbora, but be assured that much tithe was exacted by them from the terrified citizenry to keep them in check."

"Tithes?" Tyron said. "You are saying that we must *buy* this favor from the dark one? Then it is done! What would he desire? Gold? Silver? I will find him all that he could need, and more!"

"Cuhthic could produce more precious metals by his own hand than you could ever hope to find, or even steal. No, much more will be expected for you to even approach him."

"Well, what then?" Dehril demanded. "Speak! Did the stone not provide you with some answer?"

"Y-yes."

"Quickly, old man!" Tyron roared. "I will entertain no more delays!"

"Cuhthic's tithe would be the heads of his enemies—the Three from Vorhashekkh!"

"Thur!" Dehril gasped.

"You would have me become a murderer?"

"It is not murder to rid the land of a dark one. This, I swear, is the truth. But—!"

"Then it will be done," Tyron stated grimly.

"Young fools! So long has it been since the dark magicians ruled the land that few, if any, have the least conception of what facing them might entail. You cannot begin to imagine—!"

"No, and I suspect that it is better if I did not try. What have I to lose, old man?"

"Nothing, I suppose," he conceded.

"How far might our journey be?" Dehril asked.

"Lamnagha lies six hundred leagues to the north, Vorhashekkh only slightly less. Dehril, have you ventured northward before?"

"Only once, as far as the mines."

"The empire's northern boundary terminates at the base of the Miskanthian Mountains, fifty leagues beyond the mines. From what I learned of you, Tyron, this lofty range should offer little challenge. But past this, more than a thousand miles of inhospitable, seldom explored land lies before the southern perimeter of Vorhashekkh. My own ancestor, Zavrhal, and forty others traversed this land many years ago in quest of the stone; only fifteen survived to reach Vorhashekkh. Had they not possessed the stone thereafter, I doubt that any would have seen Berbora again. Should you survive, you will come to Vorhashekkh. You will not have to ponder on your being there; you will know. Then—no, I will say nothing else. As you stated, Tyron, perhaps it is best not to be aware of your possible fate."

"So be it!" the Kalkh replied. "Then our task is well defined. But if we survive long enough to set foot upon the dark earth of Lamnagha with the grisly tithe, can we then be certain that Cuhthic will help me? What did the stone tell you of this?"

"The twisted minds of dark magicians are not within the realm of the stone," Zarthik said. "Even with the heads of his enemies laid at his feet, the unpredictable Cuhthic may refuse to assist you. He—he might even see you crushed."

"Then the journey will indeed have been for naught." Tyron turned and gazed questioningly at Dehril.

The young Berboran, who had observed a renewed sense of determination in his friend as the encounter with Zarthik progressed, now saw uncertainty, and he knew that he could not let this pass. With a smile and a firm nod, he assured Tyron that the venture was well worth undertaking, his resolve being the final impetus for the troubled Kalkh. Once again Tyron faced the magician.

"We will go," he stated calmly.

Zarthik nodded. "Then may all the gods go with you."

"Please, one final query," Dehril said. "Should this Cuhthic choose to help Tyron, could he also not expunge the bitter memories of this tragedy from his mind, so that he might find peace for the remainder of his life?"

Zarthik nodded. "The erasure of one's past is a simple matter. Even one of limited skills such as I can perform this."

"Then you must do it now!" the Berboran exclaimed.

"No!" Tyron snapped, his reaction at first confusing Dehril. "With no recollection of all that has transpired, what would my incentive be for such an arduous trek? Only at its end might this be accomplished."

Zarthik chanced a meager smile at this display of wisdom, and to Dehril he said, "Tyron is right, of course."

"He is, indeed."

For the first time, they noticed the two figures that stood just beyond the courtyard gate. One was a small, gray-haired woman whose soft eyes and kindly face bespoke gentleness. Alongside her was a boy of about fifteen, a scrawny lad of serious visage. Zarthik waved to them, and they returned the gesture.

"My family awaits me," the magician told the others. "I will leave you now."

He gathered up the weighty tome from the Stone of Vorhashekkh and began walking toward his wife and son. As he watched the stooped figure depart, Tyron shook his head in amazement, for the fellow's uncanny resemblance to old Zathras still left him with some doubts regarding his own sanity. But before the magician had left the courtyard entirely, he was able to shake loose from this feeling.

"Zarthik!" he called after him. The old man paused, and with an agile motion he spun around to face the Kalkh. "My thanks," the dark-haired mountain man said.

The magician acknowledged Tyron's words with a slight nod, and once again he continued on toward his family. When finally reunited, the trio set off around the palace ruins on their way to the western gate. Tyron and Dehril watched them until they were gone from sight.

CHAPTER THREE: TOWARD THE NORTH

With the removal of corpses not yet begun, many hundreds of them lined the street leading to the smaller northern gate. In places they were three and four deep, and nowhere could one proceed for more than a few feet before stumbling over a vermin-blanketed body. Though impossible to tell, the reality was that not all of the dead had fallen victim to the Great Plague. Many of them, women and children included, had been crushed beneath the sandals of the frantic, stampeding mob as they sought retreat from the doomed city through the narrow exit during the early part of the devastation. The same was true at the other three gates. How many more might have lived could only be speculated upon, though it went without saying that few who survived the disease really cared.

Untold numbers of insects sought the torn, throbbing flesh of Tyron and Dehril as they stepped gingerly amid the grim scene, forcing the disgusted pair to continual preoccupation with their removal. For an hour the merciless assault continued, this being the time that they had spent scouring the dead city for horses. Initially they could not have known that all of Berbora's beasts had fled in terror days earlier, that few remained within miles of the walls. But as their efforts continued to prove fruitless they came to realize this, and accordingly they wasted no more of their valuable time.

At the portal, they were forced to use their hands in casting aside the countless decaying, infested bodies through which they waded nearly waist deep. Once beyond the seething barrier they paused, for it became necessary to assist each other in removing the thick layer of insects that encased the exposed flesh of each, something they had been unable to accomplish during the few tense minutes that had just passed. Fortunately, the putrefying corpses outside the walls were widely scattered, and, once free of the parasitical covers, the men were sure that no repetition would be immediately forthcoming. But still they kept a wary eye on the small, buzzing clouds that hovered in the distance as they rubbed the soreness from the many bites they had received. Dehril, repulsed by the recent encounter, chose to vent his anger on a black beetle that crawled nearby, and with the heel of his sandal he squashed the thing into the dust.

They were finally able to cleanse their blood-caked bodies at a public well that sat alongside one of the roads leading into the city. Both appeared oblivious to the reeking death that surrounded them, as though it did not exist at all. Each drank deeply of the cool spring water from beneath the earth, this being the first time in days that they had refreshed themselves. Two spacious water skins were filled to capacity; longswords were taken from the rotting corpses of two soldiers that had fallen nearby. With few words passed between them, the pair began their northward trek.

Not until nearly two hours later, at the far perimeter of Berbora's adjacent farmland, did they encounter the last of those unfortunate enough to be within the city's sphere days past, when the Scamban malady first befell the populace. In spite of their numerous injuries, which included a slight ankle sprain incurred by Dehril during a fall at the palace, they had managed to place two leagues between themselves and the walls. Here, for the first time since their departure, and for perhaps the last time in their lives, they turned to gaze upon the dead city. From a slight incline they had a reasonably clear view, in spite of the gray haze that sat atop the canyon. Scattered corpses were tiny specks across the fertile fields, disconnected dots spreading outward from what had been a scintillating jewel in the heart of an otherwise drab land. Indeed, had the sun not been hidden that day, Berbora might yet have shone. Any onlooker might have been dazzled by the sun's rays as they reflected off the golden towers, or from the huge silver lions that stood silent guard over the main gate. But the gods would not permit this; the pall that enveloped Berbora was befitting of the devastation within its walls, the dense smoke from the recently ignited blaze only serving to enhance this effect. The sun would never smile upon this place again, Dehril thought, and as he gazed at Tyron he knew that the Kalkh's thoughts were no different. They shrugged simultaneously, and in silence they turned their backs on the city that both had loved so dearly.

For the next hour they trudged slowly across a dusty, lifeless plain. The northern hills, their goal for the day, had appeared deceivingly close all afternoon, but as dusk neared they realized that their ambitions had been far in excess of their capabilities. The fact that they had described a slight arc in bypassing the northern road, this for fear of any chance encounters with unwary travelers, might have accounted for the delay. But whatever the case, they could go no farther. Overwhelming fatigue had long since begun to tell, and their bodies could no longer respond to the demands made upon them. They crumpled to the hard earth, where neither stirred for long minutes.

After each had caught his breath, the brooding Kalkh watched curiously while Dehril fumbled about in the folds of his furs. Finally he produced a sack that had been woven of brown, hemp-like fibers. This pouch had been pulled tightly around a compact object some three to four inches in thickness. Dehril loosed the drawstring and displayed the contents, which appeared to Tyron as a tightly wadded mass of smooth, treated paper. Two of the uppermost layers were peeled away and returned to the pouch, while the third, a coppery red in color, was handed to Tyron. He turned it over more than a few times while gazing at it curiously.

"It is fruit, dried fruit," Dehril said in answer to the unspoken question. "The wax-coated parchment can preserve it almost indefinitely. Those setting forth on lengthy journeys to the empire's frontiers find it of great value. I came across this packet during our quest for horses, though it was the only one I could find. No matter, for even the smallest piece is quite nourishing. What we have here should suffice for many days."

"This method of sealing would also protect it from any possible—contamination," Tyron said with a thoughtful nod. He knew that Dehril would not have chosen to point this out. "You show much foresight, my friend. Were such details left to me, we would surely have starved to death before reaching Berbora's northern boundary. I had thought the drying out of fruit to be exclusive of old Zathras, but I see now that he had only been following a procedure handed down through many generations."

Dehril would have been pleased to see Tyron consume the entire piece, but the Kalkh instead divided it into two equivalent parts and handed one to his friend. The erstwhile mountain man was well versed in the lore of survival from his brief lifetime in the rugged Yushans, and despite the personal torment that dominated his mind, he was still capable of calling forth this knowledge when necessary. Dehril nodded his thanks as he took the proffered bit, knowing that such rationing would see them through for even longer than he had thought. For the first time since their emergence from the rubble, the young Berboran truly believed that Tyron was no longer a danger to himself, that his desire to carry out the questionable plan offered hesitantly by old Zarthik was indeed real. He smiled inwardly, knowing that he would sleep better.

They chewed absently on the sparse, leathery fare, which in truth proved to be as tasteless as it looked. But perhaps this was for the better, since the mass cremations had commenced in earnest near the city's western wall, and even the distance that separated them from the site was not sufficient enough to free them from the stench. Dehril knew that the next day they would pass beyond its sphere, though he doubted whether a hundred leagues, or even a thousand, could free them from the memory of the unspeakable odor. For the Berboran, this was by far one of the least inspiring revelations.

Shortly before darkness engulfed them entirely, the pair saw a dusty cloud sitting atop the horizon to the northeast. It continued to move steadily southward along the road leading to Berbora, while they observed it with something less than detached interest. But as the hard earth beneath them began to tremble slightly, the identity of the drifting puff became evident, and they leaped to their feet simultaneously in horror.

"Riders!" Dehril exclaimed. "By Thur—!"

"Hurry! We must stop them!" Tyron snapped. "We—"

The two stared at each other for a few tense seconds, though Dehril found it difficult to meet the bitter look reflected in the cold, steel-gray eye of his companion. But this hardened expression quickly altered to one of deep concern, and the Kalkh hastily indicated the dust cloud with a wavering finger.

"Quickly! Go quickly!" he shouted at his companion. "You have little time. I will await you here."

With no further hesitation the Berboran sped toward the road, while Tyron could do nothing more than stand helplessly by and watch him. It appeared that the respite had sufficed Dehril well, for the mile or so that separated the encampment from the well-beaten path fell away rapidly beneath his long, graceful strides. The topography was such that he alternately rose, and then vanished, amid a multitude of dry, rolling hillocks. From his own elevated vantage point, Tyron saw his friend top what appeared to be the last of these knolls, this simultaneously with the arrival of the unknown riders. Dehril immediately disappeared beyond the far side of the knoll, leaving the Kalkh in the dark as to what was happening. But within minutes, the answer was more than clear: the thunder of many pounding hooves, which had continually grown louder, now lessened. The dust cloud surged forth unhindered toward the grim city, where terrible death awaited many, if not all of the unfortunate riders. Dehril had failed.

The dejected Tyron chose not to watch his friend's sluggish return, which seemed to be made with invisible leaden weights on both ankles. Instead, he sat cross-legged on the hard earth and stared absently toward the west, where he watched the red sun drop beyond the curvature of the land after making one brief, less-than-spectacular appearance from behind the clouds that had shielded it through the day. Only upon hearing the scuffle of feet did he turn, where the grim countenance of his comrade further assured him of what he already knew.

"I-I was racing down the hill wh-when they passed," the breathless Berboran stammered. "There was no way they could not have seen me, and yet—they did not stop! Some even glanced in my direction, but it was as if they gazed right through me. I could not deter them!"

"Who were they?" Tyron asked. "And what of their numbers?"

"There were at least ten of them, though likely more, for their haste, as well as the upraised dust that engulfed them, made counting impossible. A few were soldiers, but most wore the drab garments that identified them as miners."

"Then the latter were prisoners. Perhaps this is why they did not stop."

Dehril shook his head. "Both prisoners and guards were of a single mind, I assure you. The expressions on the faces of those I could see bespoke great terror. And their steeds! Thur! All frothed heavily at the mouth, and none had to be urged to maintain their blinding speed, Never have I seen any Berboran soldier in such mindless flight. What could they be running from?"

"All that matters now is what they are running *to*," Tyron muttered. "They will find their destination far less hospitable than that which they fled from, regardless of what it might have been."

"Perhaps—they will fare better," Dehril said hesitantly. "With the Scamban malady gone from Berbora—"

"*I* am gone from Berbora, but not the plague! The city itself is also a carrier, though it has an advantage over me, for it can be freed from the burden. The remains of those who fell will have to be destroyed, an exercise that I suspect has already been undertaken this day. The buildings, the avenues, even the walls will have to be cleansed a thousand times over by the few souls who have chosen to stay within the city. All of this will likely be carried out in time. But as for the ones who passed you on the road, this time has not yet come. Some may live, but most will die."

Dehril did not dispute the Kalkh's words, which had been spoken with unquestioned assurance, for he did not doubt their validity. The rotted corpses were veritable breeding grounds for the disease, and indirect contact with them was unavoidable. Even now, the soldiers and their charges would be passing the first of them along the road. What would their reactions be as they grasped the magnitude of what appeared before them? he thought. What more could they be subjected to? Their pale white, twisted countenances flashed before him, and he tried to visualize the horror that had driven them to such a frenzy, but he could not. Had the preceding days not been enough for one to endure? No more, Thur! he pleaded silently. No more!

Darkness covered the land quickly, once the last vestiges of the sun had fallen from sight. The clouds of the day lingered, making the blackness nearly total and limiting visibility to little more than a few yards. The pair slept within the folds of the sleeping furs they had brought with them, thus negating any need for a fire, despite the coolness of the night air. Slumber found Tyron almost immediately, but Dehril's initial efforts met with little success. For half an hour he observed the troubled Kalkh, who writhed pathetically in the throes of the nightmares that assaulted him. When would he again know peace? the young Berboran mused. When would the torment end? With a shrug he turned away, and soon he too had penetrated the depths of sleep, though his own night visions proved only slightly less disturbing than those of the other.

CHAPTER FOUR: DARK LEGENDS

The trek resumed shortly after dawn, and within the first hour they had angled sharply enough toward the northwest to join the primary road. Here, Dehril assured Tyron, the hillocks were no longer in evidence, and they would be afforded a clear view for a considerable distance ahead of them. Tracks from the headlong stampede of the previous evening were evident, as they would be throughout the entire morning, but the dust had long since settled, and no more, save for the small puffs kicked up by their own footfalls, were raised during the early portion of the day's journey. The broad plain, save for an occasional rodent or a hovering scavenger bird, appeared lifeless.

Tyron had not been impressed by his initial view of the northern hills, nor was he any more affected two days later, when he and Dehril stood only yards from the entrance to the defile that split them. The loftiest of these jagged, dull-gray tors rose no more than five hundred feet above the level of the ground, this a far cry from the towering majesty of his beloved Yushans. Despite his own aversion to high places, Dehril looked forward to their arrival at the distant Miskanthian Mountains. There, in his own element, Tyron would experience a different kind of freedom, one that had proven elusive for so long, and the Berboran knew that his friend would revel in it.

The rock-walled path ran straight and level for the first two or three miles, where it gradually, almost imperceptibly, began to slope upward. Unlike the hard-packed dirt of the road on the plain, where all traces of travelers vanished with the next appreciable breeze, this path was rutted deeply in places by the wheels of carts that had borne heavy loads of ore to the city. Undoubtedly the gorge was subject to periodic flooding, a result of the torrential rains that often pelted the land, this accounting for the malleability of the earth. At present it was not even moist, for nearly a month had passed since the most recent storm. Both Tyron and Dehril hoped it would be at least that long before the next one.

Soon the incline became more pronounced, and the road, like some sinuous reptile, began twisting and turning amid the drab granite outcroppings. It was because of this that they did not see the solitary traveler until he stepped out from behind one of these stone sentinels little more than ten yards farther on. The fellow, like themselves, was on foot, and from his haggard appearance it was not hard to see that his recent days had been fraught with much hardship. The tattered garments that hung from his body were caked with dried blood, the product of at least a half dozen nasty wounds on his scalp and forearms. His round face was colored a ghostly white, while the numerous creases belied the fact that he had seen little more than twenty years. He froze in his tracks as he saw the unexpected pair, both of whom could easily read the terror in his eyes.

"Another tally," Tyron mumbled dryly. "But then, what is one more?"

Dehril, ignoring his friend's words, stated, "I have seen this fellow before, though his name escapes me."

He strode toward the other, his hand upraised in greeting, while Tyron followed resignedly. The frightened fellow at first took a few steps backward, and Dehril feared that he might run. But recognition somehow registered in his troubled brain, and the fires that burned within his eyes abated slightly. He held his own palm outward as he approached.

"Dehril! You are Dehril, of the palace guard," he rasped in a strange, chilling voice. "Likely you would not remember me, for more than a year has passed since we shared duties for a few days in the arena. I am called Sevaar."

"Sevaar, of course. But what has happened to you, my friend?"

"Water! First water, please!"

Dehril uncorked the skin and handed it to the parched Sevaar, who, without the other's guidance, might easily have drained half of it. The allotted portion went far in refreshing him, and when next he spoke, his voice was better modulated, though still tinged with fear.

"The two of you have come from . . . the city?" he asked hesitantly.

"Yes."

"Then you were among the fortunate ones, like me."

"You were in Berbora during the devastation?" Tyron roared, further frightening the pathetic shell of a man.

"Y-yes. I—"

"May Zeth be thanked!" the Kalkh hissed. "No additional blood to be cleansed from my hands!"

"What—what does he say?" Sevaar moaned. "Is he mad?"

Dehril placed a firm hand on his shoulder. "It is nothing, my friend, nothing, I assure you. Please, tell us of all that has transpired since you departed Berbora."

"I will tell you all, but let us first resume the trek out of this accursed gorge."

"Out? But we were journeying *toward* the mines."

Sevaar's eyes widened. "You venture—*there*?" He pointed northward.

"We do."

"Then you are both mad!" he snapped, as he tried to force his way past them. They wrestled him to the ground, though he displayed considerable strength, in spite of his obvious deprivation. For a few tense moments he thrashed wildly, but Dehril, with soothing words and a smile, eventually managed to calm him.

"We are not mad, Sevaar, this I swear. What we do is of necessity. Now please—"

"You need not ask again, Dehril," he replied as he sat up. "I departed Berbora some days past, exactly when I cannot say for certain, for memories of recent days are vague. Only after the last of my family had perished did I leave, though I did not flee in terror, like so many others. I journeyed to the mines, there to seek out my brother, Jeokh, one of the guards, and advise him of what had happened. His wisdom had always commanded respect, and accordingly I would have been content to follow through on whatever suggestions he had regarding our immediate future.

"Less than two leagues from the nearest of the mines, I was suddenly overwhelmed by a deafening roar, one that resounded off the rock facings. Only the fact that I could see ahead of me for about twenty yards saved my life, for over a dozen frenzied riders appeared around the base of a sheer cliff, and from the looks of their thundering, headlong rush I was certain that they would think little of running me down. I was able to locate a small crevice in the facing, into which I managed to squeeze, though just barely. My efforts proved justified, for the steeds raced by three and four abreast, their pounding hooves falling upon nearly every inch of the narrow road. I muttered my thanks to the gods for this fortuitous rift.

"Not until the pass was again engulfed by silence did I dare emerge, for the incident had left me shaken. I proceeded toward the mines with considerable caution, but I encountered no more riders. On the contrary, as I neared to within half a mile of them I saw none of the activity, heard none of the noise that had been so much a part of the place during previous journeys. No creaking ore wagons passed, nor did any prisoner transports. No sounds of guards barking orders, always audible even from such a distance, echoed from the cliffs. Had I not known better, I would have sworn that I still had many miles to go. But I knew that such was not the case, for the landmarks were quite familiar.

"Initially, I feared that the disease which leveled the city had been spread to even this remote place, but it did not take long to discover how wrong I was! After turning sharply around the corner of a large outcropping the road widened into a vast, circular canyon, this containing the bountiful mines of Berbora. I stood at the perimeter of the base camp, where I gazed mutely at a scene of unmatched horror before me. After the recent days I had thought myself numb to death and destruction, but not so. My stomach churned violently, and after falling to my knees I retched uncontrollably for long moments.

"Eventually I regained my feet, and once again I stared in disbelief across the floor of this natural bowl. That a force of incredible magnitude had passed through here could not be doubted, for the thatched hovels of the prisoners had been leveled, as well as the utilitarian wood cabins of the guards. The blood of countless mutilated corpses stained the earth, its glistening freshness indicative of how recently it had been spilled. And not all of the bloodied heaps were men, for I could distinguish the larger carcasses of both horses and elephants. Whatever it was that had committed these atrocities displayed little interest in the nature of the life form it tore apart.

"The fifty or so yards that separated this crude village from the closest of the mines were strangely devoid of bodies, though not so the ground that sat directly in front of the adits. From my position in the center of the devastated camp I at first found it difficult to believe what I saw, and because of this I staggered forward in order to verify the fact that I was not totally mad. At twenty yards away I halted, for I now knew that my eyes had not deceived me. Before two silver mines, these numbers six and seven, were piles of gleaming bones, the skeletal remains of both men and beasts alike! There were over twoscore of them, at least three-quarters of that number unquestionably human. From their whiteness, it would have seemed safe to assume that the flesh had decayed over the course of many months, perhaps longer. But upon closer scrutiny I saw the remains of garments stained with fresh blood lying nearby; I observed shreds of tissue and bits of muscle fiber clinging to the ribs of many. From this, I could surmise only one thing, no matter how inconceivable it appeared: *these bodies had been stripped of their flesh within the past few hours!*

"The subsequent time remains as little more than a dim shadow within the recesses of my mind. My legs were unquestionably inadequate to bear me, for these many bruises attest to the number of times that I stumbled. I drew no closer to the adits; or, if I did, then the memory has been erased. During this brief span of time, I was surely fair game for whatever demons roamed within the confines of the death-ridden canyon, my overwhelming torpor negating any possibility of pre-planned flight.

"A low, pathetic moan eventually snapped me from my lethargy, and as awareness returned I immediately noted the approaching dusk, this indicating the time that I had somehow lost. I sat cross-legged, just inside the camp's western boundary, this leaving me within an arm's length of two rent corpses. This foul sight was the final stimulus, and upon regaining my feet I quickly placed a few yards between myself and the bloodied heaps, which were infested with vermin.

"My attention turned to the sound that had initially penetrated my dulled brain, but a quick scan of the grim village did not reveal the source. In fact, for a few minutes the entire canyon was engulfed by silence, and I wondered if I had indeed heard anything, but as I staggered amidst the carcasses it was again repeated, and this time I was able to pinpoint the place from where it emanated. About ten yards to my left was one of the wooden dwellings that had served as quarters for the guards, before the inexplicable force had razed all but its foundation. From beneath a heap of shattered lumber there protruded a hand, a quivering, white-knuckled hand! And—this I swear, by the sword of Zhon—it was beckoning me to come!

"I covered the short distance in a few strides, though my initial excitement prevented me from realizing that I was once again in control of my movements. Despite the apparent need for haste, as well as my own anxiety, I removed each bit of wood slowly, carefully, a procedure that at times appeared endless. But eventually, I had cast enough of it aside to disclose the identity of the fellow, and I could scarce suppress a gasp as I gazed upon the shattered form of Jeokh, my brother!

"Only Thur could say why he still lived, for his stomach had been slashed open, leaving him to stare in muted bewilderment at his spilled entrails, which lay at his side. Waves of nausea coursed through me from the terrible sight, and I was overwhelmed by the unbearable stench that wafted upward from this living dead man. Why had he not been fortunate enough to find the merciful blackness of death, like those around him? Why had Jeokh, above all others, been selected to endure such unspeakable torment? But I did not concern myself with the answers, for, despite my puzzlement, despite my aversion, one fact dominated: *this tortured soul was my brother!* I could not turn away from him while he died!

"Jeokh's eyes, though opened wide, at first seemed devoid of life. I peered into them intently as I spoke to him. 'Jeokh. Jeokh, it is Sevaar, your brother. Can you hear my words?'

"No recognition registered in his eyes but, inexplicably, a trace of a smile appeared on his face. His lips parted, and a distant, tinny voice, one that I hardly recognized, replied to my query.

"'*Sevaar . . . why did . . . you come . . .?*'

"For a moment I thought of our family in Berbora, but I saw no reason for him to bear this knowledge beyond his life. Instead, I chanced a meager smile as I told him, 'I came to see you, my brother. Everything will be fine now. You need not—'

"The calm, faraway look on Jeokh's face suddenly altered to one of unreasoning terror, its unexpectedness startling me. With an effort that I could not believe possible, he raised a shaking arm and indicated the cairns before the sixth and seventh mines. Once again he spoke, but this time it was necessary for me to hold my ear within an inch of his face, lest I miss the words.

"'Earlier this day a . . . groundshake,' he gasped. 'Not uncommon here . . . Then . . . *they* came...! *They* . . . did this . . .! Sevaar . . . I beg you . . . go from here . . . now! It is . . . not over. They . . . come again . . .! Hurry . . .!'

"'Jeokh, please!' I cried. 'I do not understand! Who is responsible for this?'

"'*Corths* . . .! They were . . . *corths* . . . from the . . . mines!' He raised himself up on one elbow, this causing more entrails to spill forth. *'My brother. . . . please! You . . . must . . . leave . . . here . . . now!'*

"Jeokh's monumental effort was more than he could endure, and before another word could pass between us, he was dead. I might have remained to bury him, if only to keep the vermin from him for a time, had I not heard the sound that poured from the bowels of one of the mines. Only then did I fully understand the horror of the warning that he had attempted to relate, and I knew that, even on the brink of his own death, he had not lost his senses. A final look at the atrocities all around brought me to my feet, and with a silent farewell to Jeokh I set off toward the road leading from the canyon.

"I should not have been able to walk, much less run, for my fatigue was more than I could have dared imagine. Perhaps it was the horrible noise from the shaft, which grew louder as the seconds passed, that enabled me to tap resources of strength previously unknown. But whatever it might have been, I was far beyond the village within minutes. I paused briefly at the corner of the outcropping where the road curved sharply for, in spite of my terror, I still burned with curiosity. The shadows of dusk were upon the land, and from such a distance I could barely perceive the dark form as it emerged from one of the adits. Now freed from the confines of the mine, its cry resounded off the facings that ringed the canyon, though, aside from myself, there were none left to cringe in terror before it.

"After stifling a cry that had been welling up within me, I passed around the edge of the huge formation and sped southward, for the first time understanding what had driven the horsemen to such an action. Not until many hours had passed did I even pause to catch my breath, where I realized that I had long since freed myself from the sphere of the terrible echoes. Still, I knew that I could not stop. I traversed the road throughout the long night, as well as the morning, until our paths chanced to cross. That is all."

###

Tyron and Dehril had not spoken throughout Sevaar's chilling narrative, and they remained silent for long moments after, each absorbing its impact in his own way. It was the obviously puzzled Kalkh who first broke the reflective stillness.

"I do not understand. You mentioned—corths? What are they?"

Sevaar stared incredulously at Dehril. "He does not know of the corths?" the wild-eyed fellow shrieked. "How—?"

"He was a stranger in Berbora," Dehril interrupted. "Those of other lands could not know of our legends."

"Legends, *pah*!" Sevaar spat. "The atrocities I observed were not carried out by *legends*!"

"I'm sorry, my friend; I was not doubting you."

"Then you—you believe me?"

Dehril nodded. "We also observed the riders, and now we have seen you. I have no reason to question your story, Sevaar."

"My thanks," he replied, his tone calmer. "I apologize for my reaction. Until yesterday, the corths were naught but legends to *me*. Now—"

"Please!" Tyron snapped. "Will someone—"

Sevaar silenced the Kalkh with a brusque wave of the hand. "Of course, of course. I too am anxious to quit this spot, like you, though our reasons are undoubtedly leagues apart. Let us be done with it!

"Tales of the corths go back more than a thousand years before the time of Tahresk. It is said that these hills did not exist then, but rather a vast, searing desert, an inhospitable place within which existed a passageway that led into the very depths of Sharn itself. Even Thur and Zhon shunned the terrible land, though somehow, in a manner that could only be known to gods, they were aware of all that transpired there. They knew when the first of the corths emerged, and their anger was felt across the rest of the land. The skies darkened, and not until fifty days had passed, when their unimaginable task had been concluded, did the people again see the light of the sun.

"The corths represented but one type of the numerous lesser demons that were said to have been spawned in the black world below. They were vast in number, and by piling atop one another they were able to emerge onto the land, so the legends tell us. More than a hundred stood upon the burning surface, before the powerful arm of Zhon intervened. The war god cast bolt after sizzling bolt into their ranks, with few landing astray of a target. But for every one that he destroyed, two more crawled forth, until their minions stretched across nearly every square mile of the blistering sand. For the first time in eons, it appeared that the dregs of the underworld would overrun the land of man.

"Mighty Thur soon realized that his bellicose kin was failing, and he made his appearance known, this above the protests of the latter. Countless tons of stone rained down upon the searing desert, which was soon cooled by the foul lifeblood of the demons that were crushed in the devastation. The otherworldly passageway was tightly sealed with richly impregnated ores of gold and silver, minerals loathed by those of Sharn. Soon only a handful of corths roamed these newly formed hills, and their destruction was left to Zhon, who carried out the task methodically. On the fiftieth day the last of the corths was struck down, and the war god departed. No corth has since been seen, until . . .

"The mining of these precious metals began in earnest during Tahresk's reign, and the prisoners sentenced to work in the shafts immediately adopted the corth legends as their own. Some today even claim that the legends were perpetrated by these early laborers, though this, of course, cannot be. They believed that by removing too much of the gold and silver, the passageway to Sharn would again be open, for Thur had not meant it to be taken. Such was the tale that frightened many a newly arrived worker for the past seven hundred years, this one of the few diversions enjoyed by the unwilling miners. But did they themselves believe it? My brother had been exposed to the current group for more than six months, and he assured me that few entered the mines without some trepidation."

"And what do *you* believe, Sevaar?" Tyron asked.

The Berboran shrugged. "Jeokh stood face to face with the death dealers, and he thought them to be corths. For me, this is word enough. Some aspects of the legends, including a description of the corths, are vague, and therefore questionable. But consider this: what just happened in the mines followed close on the heels of Berbora's devastation, a tragedy that could only have been conceived in the depths of Sharn, for such was its magnitude. That the forces of the underworld are at work cannot be doubted. Therefore, the groundshake that reopened the passageway was a logical occurrence. The corths will finish what the inexplicable malady did not!"

Dehril immediately glanced toward Tyron, where he saw that the Kalkh's grim visage had not altered appreciably, despite the tormenting words of Sevaar. Indeed, the bearded mountain man appeared a bit puzzled as he gazed at his friend.

"What does all of it mean?" he asked.

"It means that this path is closed to us," Dehril replied.

"But why—"

"Dehril is right," Sevaar interjected. "These creatures, be they corths or otherwise, are savage flesh eaters. What they did to trained fighting men, to powerful horses and elephants, must surely be indicative of their individual strength. And, if I were to guess, I would say that their numbers are considerable; maybe not the thousands referred to in the legends, but easily scores of them. You will have little chance of survival."

"What are the alternatives?" Tyron asked.

"We must return to the plain," Dehril said, "and journey toward either the east or west to bypass the hills. Both are of similar distance, and would be equally as rugged, so the choice would not matter."

"And how much of a delay will this entail?"

Dehril looked toward the well-traveled Sevaar, who told them, "At least a month, perhaps more. There are many additional leagues to be traversed. And with no steeds—"

"A *month*?" the Kalkh roared. He gazed at Dehril, his troubled face pleading for guidance.

"The decision is yours alone to make, my friend." the Berboran told him. "I will say only this: whatever it may be, I will not desert you."

"There is but one choice to make," Tyron stated as he alternately glanced at the serious countenance of his friend and the twisted face of Sevaar. "We will continue along this road and, if the gods still smile upon us, we will journey past the northern mines!"

CHAPTER FIVE: THE CORTHS

Dehril would have provided Sevaar with food for the duration of his journey, but the latter refused, for he felt certain that he would reach the city quickly enough, and he did not wish to lessen the pair's limited stores. All that he requested was one final draught of water, which was given without question.

"Do not, under any circumstance, attempt passage through the mining village during the dark hours," Sevaar warned them, as the three exchanged parting handshakes. "The corths are as deadly by night as they are by day; more so, in fact, since one's own defenses would be hampered by the darkness."

"When near the mines, can they not be bypassed through the hills?" Tyron asked.

Sevaar shook his head. "The facings are sheer throughout nearly all the defile, and especially so in and about the adits. The hills themselves consist of row upon row of smooth, vertical outcroppings. There are no known paths through them. You might attempt such a passage, and you may be successful. But you would lose almost as much time this way as you would by skirting the range, and time, so I guess, is of value to you, or you would not wish to stroll so casually toward certain death."

After advising Sevaar of what he could expect to find awaiting him in the ravaged city, the pair departed. The former, despite his overwhelming desire to quit the gorge, stood silently and watched them for a few seconds, until the twisting path carried them from his sight. With a shrug he resumed his own interrupted journey, surely unaware of the effect that his final, sobering words were having on the already tormented minds of the purposeful duo.

By mid-afternoon the narrow, well-used road had leveled off, though it continued to snake endlessly between smooth, unscalable precipices. Tyron and Dehril walked alongside each other, the lengthy stretches of silence indicative of the deep thoughts that preoccupied them. But soon the Kalkh froze in his tracks, the unexpected action snapping Dehril from his own musings. He gazed at Tyron, noting grave concern etched deeply in the haggard, once youthful face.

"What is wrong, my friend?" the Berboran asked.

"We must turn back!"

"Turn back? But why?"

"Only after pondering the words of Sevaar have I realized my crass thoughtlessness. 'Certain death!' Those were his own words regarding that which we approach. And, after learning of his experiences, I believe him to be truthful. So withdrawn am I into myself that I have hardly considered you, Dehril. What right have I to lead you toward this suicidal encounter with the corths? You still have much of life to live, and I will not be the one to take this chance from you."

"Tyron—!"

"There are two options, and you must choose one now. If you still possess this insane desire to accompany me, then we will retrace our steps of the day and bypass the range. Otherwise, let us part here. I will seek my destiny northward, while—"

"Listen to me, you thick-headed Kalkh!" Dehril snapped, his voice echoing numerous times off the vertical facings. "My choice was made on the day that we crawled from the rubble of the palace, or perhaps even earlier, when I overheard the words of Mohrosk. No, you will not be rid of me so easily! As for altering the course of our journey, I would be no less loath than you to sacrifice the additional time required. Zarthik made it quite clear that the success of this venture was at best questionable. Beyond the Miskanthian range lies a thousand miles of deadly, unmapped land; past that, Vorhashekkh, and finally, Lamnagha! If our fate be predestined, then why prolong the inevitable by a month or more? Better to die now, with sword raised, in battle against the corths. But know this, my friend, lest you think me resigned to doom: we *will* endure, this I swear! The corths will not deter us, nor will anything else! Two months, four months, perhaps six months from now the peace you seek shall be yours, and I will be at your side to share it. This is all I have to say, and be assured that it is the final word on the matter!"

The steel-jawed Berboran resumed the trek, leaving the bemused Tyron to stare after his retreating form. Had Dehril chosen that moment to glance back, he would have witnessed the broad smile that temporarily lit the heretofore twisted countenance of his friend. But he did not, and seconds later, when the Kalkh again strode silently at his side, it was no longer there.

Dusk found the pair less than a league from the mines, this fact confirmed by the discovery of Sevaar's food pouch, which he recalled losing during his flight from the stampeding riders. They had traveled at a slow, steady pace throughout the long afternoon, for Dehril knew that they could not reach the mines before dark under any circumstance, and he saw no need to expend the additional effort. The contents of the pouch were meager, but there was enough to sustain them for one meal. After dividing the contents they dropped to the ground, their backs pressed firmly against a particularly smooth facing. Neither spoke for long minutes, nor was the repast immediately partaken of, for both were breathless.

"You're certain that we are far enough away?" Tyron finally asked, this after donning his heavy fur cloak to ward off a sudden chill.

"If the corths roam the land, then even two leagues would be insufficient to prevent them from scenting our flesh. But they emerged only yesterday, and there was still much meat at their disposal, according to Sevaar. I am certain that they have not yet left the mines."

But Dehril's words were hardly spoken with conviction, and his half-hearted attempt at assurance fell far short of calming even himself, much less the Kalkh. While picking at their food they cast numerous glances up the road where, even in the darkness, they were afforded a view of at least fifteen yards. Once, a small stone worked itself loose from high atop the facing, and as it clattered downward toward the road, the pair leaped to their feet simultaneously, their swords drawn. Only after gazing at each other sheepishly did they recognize their edginess.

"We act as children would, after hearing an especially frightening tale," the Kalkh stated as he sheathed the blade. "Go to sleep, my friend; I will see our camp safe from demons."

"Two hours, no more," Dehril insisted. "You must then awaken me."

Tyron nodded, and after wolfing down a few last bits of food, the young Berboran stretched out upon the hard ground in order to seek slumber. But it eluded him through most of the long night, as it did the Kalkh, for within minutes they heard the first of the sounds, and they knew that Sevaar had not exaggerated. It came from afar, of this they were certain, though the reverberations from the cliffs often made it appear that the source was within yards of them. Heavy, sporadic breathing was interspersed with a foul sputtering noise, as well as a lengthy, monosyllabic *ooooohhh*, the tone indicative of considerable pain. The steady, sequential repetition of the seemingly mismatched sounds was appalling, to say the least, and Dehril suddenly found it of necessity to don his own furs as clasping, gelid fingers pierced his flesh.

"By Thur's gray beard!" the Berboran groaned. "Have you ever heard the like of that before?"

Tyron shook his head. "Only in the depths of Sharn could such a sound even be conceived, much less uttered. There, undoubtedly, is one of Sevaar's corths!"

"Undoubtedly."

"And upon hearing this, do you still desire to risk facing them?"

Dehril shrugged. "Noises cannot destroy us."

A second corth, and then a third, added their unholy cries to that of the first, the ensuing cacophony such that it nearly drove the pair to their knees. Tyron stared at his wide-eyed friend, and for a moment he considered challenging the validity of the Berboran's most recent statement, but he thought better of it. Instead, he turned his attention toward the ghastly sounds. Was this how it had been for the miners and their guards, all but the handful that somehow managed to escape? Had these chilling unexpected cries momentarily frozen both men and beasts in their tracks, this enabling the savage creatures to carry out their atrocities at will? The truth in this seemed inescapable, for no Berboran would give in so easily to anyone, or *anything*.

Tyron again turned toward Dehril, and he immediately realized that his observation had been more than an assumption. The Berboran appeared under a spell as he stared northward, and not until Tyron grasped his shoulder gently did he free himself from the lethargy that held him. Then he listened thoughtfully to the Kalkh's words.

"Then we are indeed fortunate," Dehril stated, after Tyron had finished. "We at least have the opportunity of preparing for this. But can it truly avail us?"

"It is only a small edge," the Kalkh admitted. "But it will be more than the others had, to be sure. With the chance to defend ourselves, who can tell?"

More corths added their obscene cries to the nocturnal symphony of horror; dozens, perhaps, were now voiced simultaneously, though it was impossible to be precise. The din rose, until even from such a distance it grew to ear-splitting proportions, this amplification aided by the reverberations from the rock walls. But the strong-willed pair met the challenge with a new resolve, and by the time two hours had passed, they had grown as accustomed to it as they believed one could possibly be. The prospect of the morning's trek became just a bit less fearful, though one could have hardly accused them of overconfidence. They might have even sought sleep, had the sounds not altered so drastically in the middle of the night. First there was silence, an eerie, stifling silence that lasted for long, tense minutes. Then a series of new sounds arose, and they immediately knew that slumber would be impossible, though not because of fear, but rather revulsion. The sucking, slavering noises, along with deep grunts of apparent satisfaction, indicated but one thing: *the corths were feeding!*

###

Two bleary-eyed forms pulled themselves upright with considerable effort, for their joints were stiff, while their muscles throbbed painfully. The earliest traces of dawn had appeared, and they knew that, in spite of their fatigue, they could allow no more time to be wasted. It had been only two hours ago that the terrible echoes faded, this time for good, and, almost immediately they had been drawn into the deep bosom of slumber. Only the internal alarm of the mountain-bred Tyron had pulled them from the darkness, or they might not have arisen until midday.

After restoring some semblance of life to his pain-wracked body, Dehril brought forth a ration of food and divided it in half. The Kalkh stared disdainfully at the leathery morsel, and with a grunt he refused it.

"The performances of fighting men are known to be infinitely superior, once their bellies have been sufficiently filled," the Berboran scolded. "This is no joint of beef, and our water is hardly Kharkian wine; but it is food nonetheless. Besides, one never knows when a given meal might be his last one. Now, you *will* eat!"

"You are indeed encouraging this morning," Tyron growled as he snatched the fruit from Dehril's hand and began to gnaw savagely on it. "Where is the confidence of the previous day, that which would see us to Vorhashekkh, and beyond?"

"I . . . was merely generalizing, nothing more! Besides, what is one's disposition to be like after so little sleep on a bed of stone?"

"The prospects of the day are hardly inviting, are they, my friend? A brief rest on the cold ground, more miles, and finally, a less than pleasurable meeting with your demons of Sharn. How often in the past did you complain of your dull existence in the city? How many times did you confide in me regarding your desire for the kind of life known to so many of your ancestors, one of adventure, grave peril, considerable hardships and deprivation?"

"More times than I can recall."

"And now you would undoubtedly wish to take back these words?"

The Berboran drew his finely honed longsword and carefully fondled it. He pressed his thumb against the point once, twice, before gazing at Tyron. The somber expression that had dominated his face suddenly altered, leaving in its stead a broad grin.

"I would not!" he roared, the words resounding off the nearby facings.

Tyron, his head shaking, made a vain attempt to mirror his friend's beaming face, the result being something akin to a sneer. "Then you are indeed a madman and a fool, like me!" he replied. "Now, enough of this idle chatter! We have an appointment to keep!"

Dehril did not replace his longsword in its sheath during the ensuing miles but instead kept it poised for thrusting, as did Tyron with his own blade. Whether a necessary precaution, or an action of no more value than the bolstering of their courage, it was difficult to say. The fact that there were many sharp curves along the remaining distance lent credence to the former, since anything approaching from the other direction would not be discernible until little more than a few yards separated them. But whatever the case, they were able to proceed without the least hesitation, and the time passed uneventfully, much to their relief.

Though Dehril had been this way only once before, Tyron not at all, both immediately knew when they stood within a stone's cast of the devastated canyon. Had they not recognized the huge, knob-topped outcropping about fifteen yards ahead, the one that Sevaar had earlier described, they would still have found reason to pause. The unmistakable stench of death, now so familiar to them, assaulted their nostrils, and in the confinement of the defile it was no less overwhelming than that which they had known in Berbora. But it had little effect on them; or, if it did, one would have hardly known it from a casual observation. Had they desired to cough uncontrollably, or to vomit out their guts, they would not have done so, for such sounds were naught but a luxury. Stealth was a necessity; only by stealth, and the will of the gods, would they bypass the ravaged mines safely.

Tyron, his back pressed tightly against the facing, was the first to reach the corner of the outcropping. Slowly, hesitantly, he peered around the edge, his gaze remaining transfixed for long moments. Dehril, two yards behind him, waited impatiently for some sign to advance. But finally the seemingly interminable delay began to tell on the Berboran's taut nerves, and with great care he narrowed the distance between himself and Tyron. The pallid, death-like face of the Kalkh went unnoticed by Dehril as he stared past his friend's shoulder into the grim canyon. Had there been any doubts regarding Sevaar's narrative, they were quickly dispelled.

The nearest of the carcasses, that of a once beautiful stallion, lay less than twenty yards away from them, just outside the perimeter of the razed village. Its lifeblood had long since poured forth from a gaping chest wound, though as yet its flesh had not been stripped clean, this undoubtedly having something to do with its distance from the core of the camp. Beyond this, many other bodies lay scattered amid the wood and straw, all in varying degrees of decomposition. Hordes of tiny rodents gnawed methodically at the animal remains, of which there were few, while the human corpses, inexplicably, were so far untouched. As to the numbers, there appeared to be far less than Sevaar had reported, though a glance at the distant adits provided a simple, but grim, explanation. The twin cairns of bones were immense, in all likelihood nearly double the size of those observed two days earlier by the uncomprehending Berboran.

There could be no doubt that the terrible corths, since their untimely release from the underground, had indeed feasted well.

Save for the occasional scurrying sounds of rodents, or a scolding cry from a scavenger bird that floated high above the cliffs, this foreboding canyon was engulfed by the stifling silence that one could only associate with death. Because of this, every tentative footfall, each pebble accidently kicked, echoed from the facings with the force of an immense mallet falling upon an anvil of steel. Or so it seemed to Tyron and Dehril who, of necessity, had left the relative safety of the outcropping in order to traverse the center of the blood-stained bowl, a distance of nearly half a mile. They felt exposed, naked, for there was little concealment in the ruined village, and none whatever, other than two overturned ore wagons and a bulky elephant carcass, on the plain separating the camp from the northern pass. But what alternatives did they have? They could not skirt the rim of the canyon, despite the many boulders along this route, lest they pass within yards of the mine adits. Nor could they utilize the surrounding hills, as Sevaar told them, for the facings were sheer. Yet there were two facts that weighed heavily in their favor: first, Sevaar had spent the better portion of two hours in the canyon safely, this indicating that the corths, aside from their initial emergence, chose not to venture forth during the day. Second, the creatures had gorged themselves through the previous night and were even now far within the tunnels, all slumbering deeply. If so, it might be days before they again appeared, though the pair asked little more of their gods than half an hour to effect a successful passage.

The groundshake registered almost immediately, despite its gentle beginning, for their senses were heightened by the unceasing tension. Though not an especially forceful tremor, it caused the canyon walls to shake slightly. Tyron and Dehril, who stood directly atop its core, were brought to their knees after an unsuccessful attempt to maintain their balance. In only seconds it abated considerably, and by the time they regained their feet, it was past. A few stones had tumbled into the bowl, but no other appreciable damage was in evidence.

###

Rise up! Awaken! the dark and horrible sovereigns of Sharn seemed to be saying, as they shook their surface envoys free from the drug-like torpor that held them. *Hasten forth from the black pits, and see those who would tread upon the land that we have waited so long to regain. Stop them, children. Stop them!*

###

"Are you injured badly, my friend?" Dehril asked with much concern, as he observed the grimacing Kalkh rub his ankle vigorously.

Tyron, who had nearly stumbled with his first step as the pain registered, replied, "It is nothing. I bruised the bone on a rock during the tremor, though not until I placed my foot down was I aware of this. It is nothing to be concerned with. Now, we must—*Zeth! Look there*!"

Dehril whirled about as the mountain man indicated the canyon's east facing, more specifically the thirty-seventh mine. From the seemingly narrow adit there emerged a dark form, then a second, and a third. They had been silent during their journey from the tunnel's deepest recesses, for the groundshake had roused them from the far depths of slumber, and full awareness was not yet theirs. But now they saw the two intruders near the center of the naturally hollowed bowl, and an association between them and their own undesired awakening immediately formed in the wicked, miniscule brains. As one they loosed their incomprehensible cry, and even in the vastness of the circular canyon its intensity was nothing short of ear-splitting. The familiarity of the terrible cacophony left no doubts regarding the identity of the ones that voiced them: they were corths!

"Run, quickly!" Tyron snapped. "We may yet—*oohh*!"

The Kalkh fell headlong to the dust as the injured member refused to obey his will. Dehril quickly assisted him to his feet, and with one arm draped over his strong shoulder he attempted to bear his friend northward. But their progress was slow, while the trio of corths consumed the distance rapidly in long, leaping strides. No more than twenty yards soon separated them, and the two men knew that further flight would be futile. With blades held ready they faced the onrushing creatures, none of which paused until they had drawn within five yards of their quarry. Now, for the first time, they observed the true nature of these supposed legends, and they realized that even the most prolific teller of fables could not have visualized the mind-wrenching horror of these otherworldly nightmares.

Each corth had utilized its four appendages in racing across the floor of the canyon; but now, within range of striking, they rose tall upon their rear ones, much like the great bears that Tyron had often encountered in the distant Yushans. Yet this was the only resemblance between the majestic, glossy-furred cave bears and the horrors that stood before them. Despite appearances from afar, these corths displayed not the least bit of fur. Their smooth, taut flesh was the color of pitch, the only exception to this being their disc-like ears, which were reddish. From their clawed feet, to the uppermost part of their triangular heads, they stood nearly six feet, and had it not been for the permanent curvature of their spines they undoubtedly would have risen taller. The foremost appendages displayed vicious talons, even more so than the hind legs, with three gleaming, razor-sharp nails at the end of each sinuous member. What damage those rakes were capable of, what damage they had already wrought, was unimaginable. Two tiny, bloodshot eyes were deeply set in circular sockets, these located high atop what would otherwise have been considered the forehead. No proboscis was in evidence on any of the three, but rather a small, fleshy tumor, each displaying scores of tiny pinpricks that functioned as nostrils. In fact, the faces of the corths might have been thought of as nondescript had it not been for their mouths, the final atrocities of these black devils. Thin, curling lips showcased rows of savage, gleaming teeth, unquestionably designed for the rending of flesh. Two particular cuspids, inches longer than the rest, protruded downward as far as the upper portion of the broad, barrel-like chest. Thick, yellowish sputum poured forth at irregular intervals from the jaws, some of the vile discharge dropping in globules to the dust, the rest forming strangely patterned tributaries of slime as it trickled down the shining bodies.

It took but an instant for the sword-wielding pair to absorb this, yet even in this brief span of time at least a score of the horrors emerged from various adits, and they realized that they could delay the inevitable confrontation no longer. The throbbing pain in Tyron's ankle was all but forgotten as he and Dehril lunged toward the grotesque trio, this bold tactic hardly expected by the corths, who had only now begun their terrible cries anew. Fine Berboran steel whistled through the air, and so skilled, so powerful were the hands guiding the blades that their motion seemed continuous, which indeed it might have been. These dark ones, unused to resistance of any kind, now turned to the defensive, but their futile efforts were too late. The headless torso of one fell with a jarring impact upon the disemboweled carcass of another, their involuntary muscle actions causing the two dead hulks to thrash wildly for long moments. Their surviving fellow managed to crawl away, though barely, a thick, purplish gore spurting forth from the severed stumps of both foremost members, as well as one of the hind legs. Only the latter had caused any harm to the aggressors, this a deep gash in Dehril's shoulder from a raking talon. But the corth had more than paid for its affront, and now a toll was being exacted for past atrocities. The creature would die slowly, painfully, and not for a moment would it lose sight of its executioners.

Numerous corths now dotted the canyon floor, though for long moments they did not move, nor did they utter a sound, for the sight of their fellows' demise had left them uncertain as to their own subsequent actions. Dehril glanced at Tyron and was surprised to note that the Kalkh, spattered as he was by the corth blood, wore a grim smile.

"Your ancestors would have been proud, my friend," Tyron stated. "You handled yourself well."

"But what are we to do now?" the Berboran hissed. "Look at them! How many might we be able to kill, before . . .?"

"Let us begin backing away slowly. Never before have they encountered any who would dare fight back. They saw what we did to their kin, and they hesitate, for they are naught but cowards, like so many beasts of their ilk. Also, their bellies are still full. Perhaps all of these facts might ensure our safe passage from this accursed place."

Their dripping swords held before them, the pair stepped cautiously backward toward the northern defile. Tyron gnashed his teeth as he fought to deny the pain in his leg, while Dehril, despite his concern, kept his eyes glued upon the corths. The creatures continued to remain stationary as they stared in silence at the intruders, and for a time the Berboran thought that they might carry off their mad scheme, despite the agonizing slowness with which the yards fell away beneath them. But finally one of the corths, an apparent leader, shattered the stillness with its grotesque cry. The others immediately followed suit, and once their courage had been bolstered they raced forward to carry out a swift and terrible vengeance upon those who would dare destroy their own kind. Tyron and Dehril froze in their tracks.

"Back to back, my friend," the Kalkh said calmly. "Let us give these devils a bloodbath to remember!"

The swiftly moving corths quickly surrounded them, though none at first ventured any closer than ten yards, for memories of the recent slaughter were still freshly implanted in their tiny, wicked brains. But this did not encourage the men, for they knew that only a sign from one of the braver corths would be necessary to send countless fangs and talons at their throats. They described a full circle while observing the tightening ring, all the while denying the fact that the end might be little more than seconds away.

Some invisible, titanic stone might have been hurled to the earth from a hundred leagues on high by a vengeful god, for what else could have caused the land to be torn asunder in so many places? What else could have made the surrounding cliffs sway precariously, like trees caught in a none-too-gentle breeze? This groundshake commenced without prelude, unlike the earlier one, leaving both men and corths to thrash helplessly on the heaving canyon floor. The menacing cries of the latter immediately altered to shrieks of terror as rifts opened beneath them, sending the black devils, in threes and fours, to the unholy depths where they had been spawned. One of the gaping chasms was resealed tightly within an instant of its splitting, the foul gore that seeped upward from a tiny crack attesting to the fact that at least one of the corths had been afforded little progress on its downward plunge.

Dehril and Tyron, though only slightly less terrified than their would-be executioners, displayed the ingenuity of their species by regaining their feet with the aid of their longswords, the points of which were driven into the trembling earth. A cursory scan advised them of how fortunate they had so far been, for rifts were in evidence all around them, one barely a few yards away. By utilizing their blades as walking sticks they gingerly stepped over the narrowest of these cracks, though the direction was hardly of their choice. A screaming corth staggered toward them on all fours, the fear that gripped it making the dark creature an even more terrible engine of destruction. The slashing talons sought to tear them apart, but the pair reacted swiftly. Tyron raised his weapon high, and with a loud grunt he brought it down upon the charging creature. Its forward momentum carried the now headless beast to the brink of the chasm, which had widened considerably even in the few seconds that passed. The silent carcass toppled downward, while the triangular head, now permanently transfixed in a vicious snarl, followed in its wake after being kicked over the edge by Dehril, who was repulsed by the sight of it.

Three more corths were disposed of by the desperate pair, these being the last that stood in the way of their flight. Broad chasms were circumvented, smaller ones stepped over as they attempted to regain their northward path. The force of the groundshake did not abate in the least; on the contrary, the cliffs above the razed village began to crumble, sending tons of stone tumbling into the bowl. A hasty glance back revealed this, and they knew that in only minutes the facings nearest them would doubtless seal their own fate. This knowledge was the final stimulus, and with blades sheathed they staggered headlong across the shifting, turbulent canyon floor.

Less than a hundred yards from the northern defile, a violent surge beneath the ground sent the pair sprawling. By the time they regained their feet a new rift had opened before them, its length such as to make circumvention impossible. It measured nearly five feet across, and with each second that passed it continued to widen. Dehril, without pause for thought, raced toward the chasm, his graceful leap depositing him on the far side with some distance to spare. The Kalkh immediately followed suit, and under normal circumstances he might have topped his friend's effort by a yard. But the throbbing ankle hindered his approach, and his own jump was less than skillful. When his feet struck the far side, only inches from the rim, the pain that coursed through him was more than he could bear. With a loud moan he fell backward into the abyss, and had his fingertips not somehow found the barely yielding edge, he would have joined the foul corths on their homeward journey.

"Tyron!" the horrified Berboran cried as he saw his friend vanish over the rim. He raced to the crack, where only then he realized that the powerful Kalkh maintained a precarious hold on life. Yet extricating him proved a challenge, for the trembling of the ground was ceaseless, while the chasm continued to widen. Dehril himself was nearly hurled into the blackness on two occasions, but with grim determination he managed to secure a handhold around Tyron's wrist. It was here that the mountain man's numbed fingers could avail him no longer, and he reluctantly loosed his tenuous hold. Fortunately, Dehril had anticipated this, and he braced himself against the force that nearly tore his arm from its socket. With teeth gritted, he pulled the hefty Kalkh upward from the dark pit that sought to claim him for all time, his efforts being rewarded within moments. Sharn had been cheated again.

Their respite lasted little more than a few seconds, for the violent groundshake had by this time buried all but the northern perimeter of the bowl. Tyron brushed off his friend's assistance as he limped with surprising speed toward the defile, which they entered with only moments to spare. Clouds of dust wafted upward into the hazy sky as the pass was sealed behind them, though they did not pause to glance back, for neither believed that they were yet beyond danger. Other than escape, only one thought occupied their overtaxed minds: the gods had exacted their vengeance on the corths for the atrocities they committed. The passageway to Sharn, be it myth or reality, was again sealed, as were the famed mines of Berbora. Millennia may pass before their great riches would once more be withdrawn by the hand of man.

CHAPTER SIX: BRIGANDS

Two weary, blood-soaked warriors hurried along the narrow, walled pass for nearly a league before they finally paused, their overwhelming fatigue denying them any further movement. Tyron, despite his injury, had maintained a respectable pace, seldom falling more than a few yards behind the swift Dehril. But the events of the morning had now taken their toll on both, and their protesting bodies could no longer withstand the punishment heaped upon them. The Kalkh crumpled to the hard ground only moments after his friend fell, and much time passed before either of the panting duo raised their heads.

A great distance had been placed between themselves and the scene of devastation, though its proximity unnerved them throughout the flight. The echoes of their footfalls off the facings, as well as their own immeasurable fear, prevented them from knowing that the last vestiges of the groundshake had finally been stilled more than a mile back. But now, with their ears only inches from the ground and their own breathing barely detectable, they felt the deathly silence that pervaded the defile. This knowledge proved a worthy balm, for their ensuing minutes of rest were freed from the recent tension, and it served them well.

Dehril, upon catching his breath, examined his own body for signs of serious injuries. A few of the older wounds had been reopened, but these, along with more recent ones, were superficial. Only the deep gash in his shoulder, inflicted by the talons of the corth, bled appreciably, but he found no difficulty in stanching the flow. After cleansing this wound he bound it tightly with a strip of cloth torn from the thin waistcoat that he wore under his hauberk.

His self-ministrations consumed only a minute or two, for the young Berboran was concerned about the health of his friend, who had not yet stirred. Dehril traversed the few yards that separated them on his knees and, once by his side, he shook the Kalkh gently. Tyron emitted a low groan and slowly, painfully, rolled upon his back.

"We endured, my friend, as you said we would," he muttered. He tried to raise himself up on one elbow, but his grimace of pain indicated the magnitude of the effort, one that he abandoned. "Yet we paid a price, did we not? I feel that I will be unable to move from this spot for at least a month."

"A month?" Dehril replied in mock astonishment. "Then we indeed should have traveled one of the longer routes! To lose so much time, after what we have gone through—!"

"We will depart within the hour," Tyron announced, though in a tone something less than forceful.

"By Thur, here is the madman that I know!" the grinning Berboran roared. "Yes, you would subject yourself to more punishment so soon. We will leave in the morning, this dependent on your powers of healing. If not, the day after. Please! I will hear no arguments from you."

The sullen Kalkh stared at the top of the facings, and he all but ignored Dehril as the Berboran tended to his wounds. Most were minor, though a few required bandaging, lest too much blood be lost. The worst, unquestionably, was the large bone bruise that sat just atop the ankle, its color an ugly dark purple. It had already swollen to the size of one's fist by the additional demands made upon it. Dehril wished that he possessed one of Khreelar's foul-smelling salves, the like of which had wrought miracles in the past. But he did not, and of necessity he improvised as best he could. He drenched another bit of fabric in water and applied it to the discolored flesh, this initially relieving a bit of the throbbing. However, the liquid had not been appreciably cool to begin with, and its effectiveness was of short duration. The Berboran would have repeated the action, but Tyron, now well aware of what was transpiring, motioned for him to stop.

"Our water is far too valuable to be wasted for such as that!" he stated. "I will survive without it, I assure you."

Dehril knew that his friend was right, yet he hated to leave the injury go by untended. After seeing that his friend was comfortable he set off along the narrow path, the object of his search a mystery even to himself. But a few minutes later, the road curved sharply around the base of an eroded facing, and there, less than ten yards before him, was the answer that he sought. A slow but steady stream of water trickled out from a small rift in the granite wall, its numerous tiny tributaries snaking across the hard path before disappearing into some unseen subterranean shaft. The Berboran thrust his hand into the stream, noting that it was icy cold. After assuring himself of its purity, he emptied the contents of his own pouch and refilled it with the chilled fluid. Due to the sparseness of the flow the process seemed interminable. But the large skin eventually bulged to excess, and within minutes he once again knelt at his friend's side, where he applied a freezing compress. So rapid were his actions that, before the Kalkh could voice a protest, he managed to explain his good fortune regarding the discovery. Tyron first winced at the touch of the icy water, but soon the throbbing was overshadowed by its numbing effect, and the swelling decreased. By the middle of the afternoon the lump was no more, though the Kalkh himself was hardly aware of this, for he had long since found the welcome depths of slumber, much to Dehril's relief.

###

Because of the cloud-filled sky atop the narrow gorge, it was nearly impossible to accurately judge the passage of time. Tyron might have slept for an hour, or perhaps six, though he could not tell for certain. Only one thing was clear to him upon awakening:

the respite had revitalized the Kalkh. His wounds troubled him little, while the terrible lesion on his ankle, though still a bit sore, appeared all but healed. A chilled cloth was still draped atop it, one that he felt certain had been applied only recently. Indeed, Dehril had re-soaked the compress numerous times so that it would not lose its effectiveness. Tyron had been in capable hands throughout the day.

The young Berboran sat on a flat, elevated stone about five yards from where Tyron lay, his back against the west facing. He did not notice the Kalkh pull himself slowly to his knees for, despite his preoccupation with maintaining a vigil, his own exhaustion had begun to weigh heavily on his eyelids. They would gradually close, only to snap open as he jerked his head back. Tyron was well aware of how much he owed this loyal, unselfish fellow for all he had done since their emergence from the ruins of the palace, though being a man of few words he knew that he could hardly express his gratitude in such a manner. Yet something told him, even without the words being spoken, that Dehril understood.

Instincts long dormant once again became a natural part of the swarthy mountain man, and with a grim smile he closed the distance between himself and Dehril, his stealth reminiscent of a prowling Yushan lioness. The Berboran's eyes were momentarily shut, leaving him unaware of the form that knelt alongside the rock on which he sat. Tyron held his hand out and took a firm hold on the other's shoulder, a playful action that he nearly came to regret. The aroused Dehril tore himself free with a loud grunt, and in a deft motion he drew his well-honed blade while rolling sidelong off his erstwhile sanctuary. Once on the path he regained his feet, and with a savage yell he assumed the role of aggressor. His blade was thrust forward with the speed and skill one would expect of a Berboran soldier, and had Tyron not utilized his own agility to sidestep the sharpened steel, his quest would have been terminated prematurely in the defile that split the northern hills.

Before the uncomprehending Dehril could continue, Tyron extended his palms in a gesture of surrender. He could easily see the fires that burned in the Berboran's eyes as he shouted, "Dehril, no! It is I, Tyron!"

Awareness quickly returned to the rudely awakened warrior, and he was able to stay his hand only an instant before the next thrust. He lowered his blade slowly, and with an animated scowl he glared at Tyron.

"Has madness gripped you, that you would play such a prank?" he snapped. "I might have killed you!"

The Kalkh dropped his arms to his side, and with a shrug he replied, "You perform your duties less than capably. Had I been a corth, you would have been measuring the length of your entrails."

Dehril, who had straddled the line of exhaustion throughout the day, at first appeared enraged by these seemingly thoughtless words. But before he could respond, he noticed the slight smile amid his friend's bearded face, and he saw the once ever-present twinkle, so long vanished, in the mountain man's eye. This revelation more than offset his own anger, and he began to chuckle. Within seconds the many contributing factors had turned his laughter into hearty guffaws, these resounding off the facings and restoring life to the death-like gorge. Tyron, though as yet unable to fully participate in this much-needed release of pent up feelings, nonetheless felt much satisfaction over his companion's delight, and he observed the antics quietly.

"You—you are indeed a madman!" Dehril roared, after finally regaining some semblance of control. "Here I spend time concerning myself with your ability to walk, while you prowl around the camp like some predatory cat! I should have known better."

"Go to sleep, my friend," Tyron ordered. "You have been denied it for too long."

"You are certain—?"

"I am well rested, and considerably recovered. Now please—!"

"You need say no more."

The Berboran spread his furs on the hard earth alongside the flat stone, and within a minute he found slumber. Tyron walked around the camp for a short time to loosen stiff joints, as well as restore circulation. During this exercise he noticed the approach of dusk, this clearly indicating how long he had slept. Once resolved to allow Dehril an equal portion of rest, he sat down on the stone and commenced his task as sentry over the silent, lifeless defile.

Years of similar duty in the Yushans had left Tyron with the distinct ability of resting without lessening his awareness at all, and that night proved to be no exception. When Dehril awakened shortly after dawn, he would have sworn that the Kalkh slept soundly. But before he could even raise himself upon one elbow the black-maned head spun about, and the Berboran could see that his brain was not fogged by slumber. Dehril had been in capable hands.

They mechanically ate their morning meal, then set out immediately upon finishing. They paused at the small stream that flowed from the facing, where pouches were refilled and bodies cleansed. Dehril found the icy water almost intolerable, but a playful dousing at the hands of the mountain man, to whom such refreshment was a balm, quickly got him used to its frigidness. Subsequent to this they continued through the gorge, the makeup of which was identical to what they had passed through before reaching the mines. Not a word of the previous day's encounter was uttered, nor would it be spoken of for some time to come, if at all. What was past, was past; new challenges awaited them northward, challenges that would have to be met for them to realize their goal. Yet that morning, amid the quiet of the northern hills, even the immediate future was shielded from their thoughts, for they could not say for certain just when, if ever, such a peaceful interlude would again be known.

Save for a barely noticeable limp, Tyron's injury did not trouble him, and the pair was able to proceed at a rapid, steady pace. Late in the morning the pass widened, while the rocks on either side of them began to diminish in height. This trend continued into the afternoon, and when finally they chanced to pause, about two hours past midday, they were more than a mile beyond the last of the northern hills. Once again the road traversed a dry, dusty plain, much like the one to the north of Berbora. But the tundra did not stretch for miles ahead of them; instead, it terminated at the edge of a dense forest less than half a league farther along. They could see nothing beyond these trees, nor could they see past an equivalent distance to the east or west, for the elusive sun was still hidden by a low-hanging, gray haze. Both rued this fact, for they had hoped to catch a glimpse of the Miskanthian range's uppermost peaks, which Dehril knew were visible even from here. The breathtaking sight would have to wait, at least until nature chose to comply.

"What manner of folk are these of the northern frontier?" Tyron asked during the respite.

"Not unlike any you have yet encountered in Berbora's vast sphere," Dehril replied, "though perhaps a bit less self-sufficient than most. Their fields are hardly the most fertile, nor do they contain any minerals of worth. Still, they somehow make due, though it is at best a tenuous existence. Thievery is not uncommon here."

"Why were the people not relocated to more productive land?"

"These folk accepted Berbora's rule, but refused its aid. Past aghors have tried to re-establish them, but they failed. They are a proud and stubborn people, their roots steeped in barbarism. This is the land of their ancestors, and they would not leave it."

"And now they have little choice, even if they so desired, for the path to the city has been sealed, most likely for all time. In two generations, perhaps less, the last vestiges of civilization would have ceased its influence over them, and they will undoubtedly revert to what their forebears once were."

Dehril shuddered. "Hardly a pleasing prospect."

"No matter; whatever they are now, whatever their reception toward us might be, it is of no concern to us. We must avoid all contact, even if it diminishes our chances of acquiring steeds. Their villages must be bypassed. Do you know if there are many of them?"

"The first sits ten miles from here, within the forest, while the last is nestled at the base of the Miskanthian Mountains. In between, along the primary road, there are but four. Only two others exist, these in the wilderness to the east."

Tyron nodded thoughtfully. "Then our path is well defined. We will skirt the road to the west, and avoid all of them. What do you know of the terrain?"

"The maps indicate it to be rugged, though passable. It should not offer a significant challenge."

Their journey would have commenced within minutes, had it not been for the unexpected intrusion. So quietly, so skillfully had the four riders approached from the west, that not until they were within twenty yards of the pair was their presence even realized. They were young men, though they appeared quite hardened by their rugged element. Each sat atop a sturdy pony, three of which were identical sorrels, the fourth a pure, milky white. The latter steed bore the obvious leader, a brawny fellow with a thick shock of yellow hair. He had halted his mount in front of the others, a position he seemed natural in assuming. On his flushed face he wore a broad grin, one that exuded no mirth whatsoever.

Tyron, inwardly cursing himself for his lack of diligence, was the first upon his feet, with Dehril only an instant behind. Initially they did not even consider their own potential danger, but instead thought only of the likely death to which the riders had unwittingly exposed themselves. The Kalkh wished to run, to place as much distance as he could between himself and them, but he knew that such an action would be useless, for they were already close enough to contract the Scamban malady. He gazed helplessly at Dehril, and with a shrug of resignation he again faced the leader.

"What do you want of us?" he asked.

The grinning fellow remained silent for long moments, this further heightening the already building tension. Finally he replied, "Soldiers of the empire are always welcome to our land, though seldom have I ever witnessed any who arrived here on foot. This is a dangerous place under any circumstance, even more so without a swift steed to bear you through. You will need protection as you journey, and I, Wossekh, will be pleased to provide you with it."

Dehril eyed the brute carefully as he asked, "And just what do we need protection *from*?"

Wossekh glanced over his shoulder at the others, and the four shared a hearty, knowing laugh. He then returned his attention to the pair, his expression one of mock seriousness.

"Only in your wildest nightmares could you begin to visualize what lies before you," he stated, while the three continued to snicker. "Even two sturdy warriors such as yourselves will be hard pressed to reach your destination safely. But fear not! You are now in the hands of Wossekh and his friends. We will guide you safely to any village in the northern sector of our glorious empire. Of course . . ." He paused.

"Of course there is a toll to be exacted, is there not?" Dehril growled.

"A slight fee, nothing more, this for our time and the many risks we subject ourselves to!" the oily fellow replied. "Surely—"

"Enough of this foolishness!" Tyron roared, his tone startling the skittish beasts. "Begone from here, all of you, and let us go forth with our journey!"

"Well, if that be your desire . . ." Wossekh began. He again turned toward the others, and with the small finger of his left hand he sent an almost imperceptible signal. One of the riders urged his steed forward, at the same instant producing a lengthy, well-made pike that had been skillfully concealed behind his back. He raised the weapon high as he bore down upon them, the rippling muscles in his arm indicating that the force behind the cast would be considerable.

"Dehril, look out!" the Kalkh bellowed as he realized that his friend had been chosen as the initial target. Before the Berboran could react, Tyron shoved him forcefully from the path of the deadly missile, though not for an instant did he remove his eye from the attacker, now only yards away. The pike was hurled, but in a cat-like movement he leaped from its path. Then, in a blinding motion that defied most natural laws he grabbed the shaft of the weapon as it whizzed by. With teeth bared, the powerful mountain man snapped the pole in two over his knee and hurled the pieces away in disgust. So casually had this been done, so seemingly haphazard, that none could dare guess at the Kalkh's purpose, not until the sharpened end of the foremost half had lodged deeply in the throat of the erstwhile aggressor. The fellow's eyes bulged from their sockets, while torrents of blood gushed from his mouth, the unexpected spray terrifying his mount. He fell to the ground with a jarring impact after being flung from the pony, though he did not feel any further pain, for he was already dead.

"Roothuskh! By Zhon, they have killed Roothuskh!" the disbelieving Wossekh screamed. "They will pay for their act, this I swear! At them!"

The brigand leader, his eyes inflamed by hatred, raced toward Tyron, his lengthy pike poised for thrusting. His comrades, both stunned by the recent action, hesitated for a moment before deciding to assist him. But this brief uncertainty on their parts was all that the quick-thinking Dehril needed to gain the advantage. He scrambled on all fours toward the pair, and before fully regaining his feet he snatched up two handfuls of dirt, which he hurled at the heads of the sorrels. The blinded beasts reared in terror, each sending its uncomprehending rider toward the hard ground. Before fleeing the scene, the rock-hard hooves of one shattered the skull of its former master. The second fellow, though considerably shaken, managed to draw his sword and scramble to his feet, where the look of grim determination on the face of his approaching adversary all but assured him of the mismatch that would ensue.

Tyron deftly sidestepped Wossekh's initial thrust, and before the gleaming pony had sped too far past, he was able to leap atop its back. This additional weight was more than the animal could bear, and with a pathetic whinny it crumpled to the hard earth. Wossekh instinctively cast away his pike, lest he fall on it, an action indicative of much experience. With a roar of anger he hastily regained his feet, the speed of this movement worthy of Tyron himself, who only an instant before had scrambled up from the dirt. The two now faced each other.

"You will pay for this affront, *soldier*!" the burly Wossekh spat as he indicated the fallen Roothuskh.

The Kalkh chose not to reply, for he knew that men of this ilk were less than unreasonable. Instead, he ducked beneath a meaty fist that Wossekh swung at his head, at the same time landing a short, crisp blow to the brigand's midsection. Wossekh grunted loudly, but he did not fall. With a loud, animal-like bellow he raced headlong at Tyron, who showed surprise at the other's obvious lack of fighting skills. But the Kalkh did not dwell on this for long; he sidestepped the charge and grabbed Wossekh around the neck with one arm, wrapping the other around the burly fellow's head. Wossekh thrashed wildly as Tyron twisted, but his futile efforts were to no avail. His loud, piercing scream was silenced by a sharp crack, and he was deposited none-too-gently on the hard earth, where the scavenger birds and rodents would soon feast.

The outlaw leader would trouble no more helpless travelers.

Tyron immediately turned his attention to the surrounding scene, where he saw his friend casually wiping the dripping gore from his blade. Dehril had not even sustained a small cut, so quick and methodical had the dispatching of his foe been. He hailed the Kalkh, and after sheathing his blade, he strode forward to meet him. Together, in silence, they surveyed their grim work.

"Ironically, we most likely did them a favor," Tyron finally said. "In two days, perhaps less, they would have been praying for a quick and merciful death such as this."

The Berboran chose not to respond to his friend's statement, which, as he knew all too well, rang with truth. Instead, he pointed toward the west, where the four horses munched idly on some red-leafed shrubbery.

"If we can win their confidence, we will then have the steeds that we so long desired," he said. "Of course, once at the base of the Miskanthian Mountains they will avail us little. But there are still a hundred miles or so to be traversed, and for this distance they will prove more than useful."

They approached the animals slowly, both uttering words designed to soothe them. At first they bolted, but they did not run far, and the pair's next attempt met with success. Dehril took command of the white pony, and once this beast was under control, the rest followed docilely. The Kalkh selected the sturdiest sorrel of the three, with the remaining pair left to their own designs. Almost sadly, the latter two chose to stand alongside their fallen masters, and they all but ignored their fellows, who thundered northward with their new riders.

CHAPTER SEVEN: THE DEADLY HILLS

Despite their desire to make up some of the time that they had lost while traveling on foot, neither Tyron nor Dehril chose to push their newly acquired mounts beyond the limits of their endurance. Because of this, the sure-footed ponies responded well to their new masters, and within the first two hours their initial skittishness was tempered considerably. Their riders had guided them off the well-beaten road only minutes after departing the bloodstained scene of the recent encounter, but this troubled them little, for they were used to the rough terrain. The occupation of their past owners, quite understandably, had seldom seen them on the smooth path for any given length of time.

Late afternoon found them deep within the forest, their location, by Dehril's best estimate, about ten miles northwest of Fomm, the first village in this sector of the empire. They might have utilized the remaining couple of hours before sunset to gain more miles, but they knew that the horses were fatigued. Undoubtedly, they had been overworked by the brigands during the morning. Camp was established at the edge of a small brook, where the beasts were allowed to drink their fill. They were then tethered within easy reach of lush, dew-drenched shrubbery, which they munched on contentedly for the remainder of the day.

In addition to the pikes that each now possessed, Dehril had also gathered up the food pouches of the outlaws before leaving, and all that afternoon they had anticipated a more substantial repast. But now, as they emptied the contents of one pouch, they were immediately repulsed by the moldy, putrid fare. All the bags, in fact, contained the same vile stuff, indicating that Wossekh and his cohorts were something less than particular in the matter of food. Doubtless it was edible, but even had they closed their eyes, they could not have denied the terrible odor. With growls of disgust they deposited every last bit of it, woven pouches included, into the nearby brook, farther downstream. Dehril then dug into his own sack for the tasteless layers of dried fruit, now quite appetizing by comparison.

So negligible was the current in the small tributary that the undesirable stuff remained visible for a minute. Then, without warning, the still water began to churn all around it. The pair leaped to their feet, where they immediately realized what was happening. Scores of fish had risen from the bottom of the seemingly shallow brook to attack this unexpected feast, its large quantity driving them to a frenzied state. Between them, Tyron and Dehril skewered ten of the small, wriggling creatures with their pikes, surely more than enough for an ample meal.

With two small, flint-like stones and a pile of tinder, Tyron was able to ignite a blaze within minutes. Dehril tended to the broiling of the fish, while the Kalkh, moved from his apathy by the turn of events, scoured the nearby trees and bushes for additional food. A particular tree appeared nearly identical with one that grew along the base of the Yushans, a fact that was more than borne out by his discovery of soft-shelled, edible nuts that grew in clusters amid the upper boughs. By the time he returned to the camp with these, the first of the fish was done, and the two weary travelers shared a feast unlike any they had known for countless days.

###

They greeted the following morning with a new optimism, a rededication to the original purpose of this perilous journey that, of desperation, they had undertaken. Both men were well rested and equally well fed, as were their eager ponies. The fiery summer sun rose unimpeded above the eastern horizon for the first time since the devastation of Berbora, and the clear, azure sky above indicated that its welcome presence would be known throughout the day. And finally, if all this were not sufficient to heighten their spirits, they were afforded one additional revelation within an hour of breaking camp. After passing beyond the perimeter of the forest they were greeted by the sight of the towering Miskanthian Mountains, far to the north. They could see quite clearly that the range, even from such a distance, was no less majestic than they had thought it would be. Permanent white crowns sat atop the loftiest of the peaks, which rose upward for more than three miles. Fleecy clouds encircled these pinnacles, their auras indicative of, alternately, great beauty and mystery. To the city-bred Dehril, the sight was at the least awe-inspiring; but for Tyron, the range of emotions was broad. Though a thousand leagues and a thousand years from his beloved Yushans, the Miskanthian Mountains represented but one thing to the tormented Kalkh: *home*!

With each hour that passed during the sun-drenched day they drew closer to the immense range, which stretched endlessly to the west and east. Not for a moment, even when they descended into an occasional gully, did they lose sight of the great stone sentinels, which beckoned to them continually. But they did not hurry, for the plain was indeed rugged, with scattered debris and countless rodent burrows only a small portion of the obstacles. The least misstep would again see them afoot, as they well knew. Only three times did they view the ribbon of road that paralleled their path more than two miles to the east, this due to the topography of the land. They encountered no travelers, much to Tyron's relief, and just once did they catch a glimpse of one of the villages that sat along the road's edge from the summit of a lofty hillock. From such a distance it was difficult to distinguish any specific features, save for the fact that it was quite small, and doubtless far from prosperous.

Twenty leagues were traversed that day, this leaving the pair no more than a few hours away from the base of the mountains, which loomed large before them. Both were pleased with the progress that had been made, and they felt that, with an early start in the morning, their initial assault on the peaks would be equally as successful. From past explorations, of which there had been few, there were no known defiles through the Miskanthians, and Tyron had long since discarded any ideas of searching for one. Instead, he had selected one of the least imposing peaks from afar, this being the one that he planned on scaling. For himself, this range could not even be considered an obstacle; but he respected the fact that Dehril had never climbed any higher than the plateau that rimmed the Krabharkian Forest, which overlooked Berbora from a relatively short distance away. Accordingly, he would subject his friend to no more risk than was necessary.

They departed before dawn, and when the sun finally chose to top the horizon they were less than a mile from the base of the foremost sentinel. Here they paused, and both pondered wistfully for long moments on what they knew was inevitable. The sturdy ponies, to which they had grown attached even in so short a time, would soon have to be released. "If only there was some way that we could take them with us," Tyron mused. But they knew that they could not. The prospect of facing more than a thousand miles on foot . . .

"I have an idea," Dehril suddenly announced, the words snapping Tyron from his thoughts. "If we cannot take the steeds, then at least we can see that they are well cared for, along with assuring the safe continuance of our trek. The village of Shaaf sits a couple of miles from here. While you await me, I will journey to Shaaf with the steeds and exchange them for items of necessity: food, clothing, tools, and the like."

"Can you be certain of your welcome there?" Tyron asked.

"Like all those of the northern sector, the people of Shaaf can hardly be considered friendly. But they are still loyal to Berbora and will undoubtedly respect a soldier's garb, regardless of how shabby it may be." He indicated his tattered clothes.

"And, if nothing else, they are fond of a good steed. They'll be quite anxious to barter for the likes of these."

"Then go, by all means. I will await you over there." The Kalkh pointed to the base of a small knoll, about a hundred yards farther north. "But first, let me tell you a few things that would avail us greatly during the climb, items that would prove invaluable, should you be able to trade for them."

Dehril made a mental list of Tyron's priorities. After a parting handshake the Kalkh dismounted, and once the pike, as well as the other belongings, had been removed, the sorrel was led away. Tyron gazed after the retreating forms for long moments, until finally, with a shrug, he turned northward and began walking dejectedly toward the nearby hillock.

###

Shaaf proved to be even closer than Dehril had guessed, for not long after leaving his friend, he neared the boundary of the village's farmland. There were few in the fields at this early hour, for those of Shaaf were not the eager laborers of Heltha, of Sivla or Haskh, and the results of their disinterest were evident. The earth seldom yielded any more than was put into it, and often, to their frustration, it surrendered even less. How the Shaafians withdrew anything was a mystery to Dehril, for despite his own lack of experience he could judge a poorly plowed furrow, identify a patch of vegetables that had not been thinned, or note an overabundance of destructive insects, all of which were the rule here. But neither was it his concern, especially now.

Once upon the road, or what was left of it this far north, he urged the white pony to greater speed, and the beast willingly complied. But this was no more than a short burst for the fiery pony, for they quickly arrived at the perimeter of Shaaf. Here Dehril dismounted, and with the two steeds in tow he strode into the center of the ramshackle village, the population of which numbered little more than four hundred. Few saw him at first, but with each step he took, the hovels began disgorging their occupants in twos and threes. They were light-skinned, like most Berborans, and the women could hardly have been considered unattractive. But there was a hardness about them, this reflected in their lined, unsmiling faces, as well as their mean garments. For these descendants of barbarians, life in the shadow of the Miskanthians was not easy.

Dehril held his hand upraised in a gesture of peace as he continued toward Shaaf's hub, though he could see none who were of a mind to return it. They walked on all sides of him, none chancing any closer than five yards, their eyes darting between him and the two horses. Hands nervously gripped the hilts of swords and knives. Not a sound was uttered, this despite the number of small children and mongrels that darted in and out amid the crowd. The silence began to unnerve the Berboran, and he was determined to do something about it. He paused, his action bringing the villagers to a sudden, unexpected halt, and he glanced about before speaking.

"I would see your bantir," he announced with authority, his words piercing the stillness. But the Shaafians continued to stare blankly at him, and he repeated, "I would see your bantir!"

A crusty, middle-aged man broke through the crowd, and not until he stood less than two yards before Dehril did he pause. He appeared to be staring past Dehril as he squinted his rheumy eyes.

"Are you the bantir of Shaaf?" the impatient Berboran said.

"Yes," the fellow wheezed, though still his eyes did not meet Dehril's. "Where did you get them?"

"What do you mean?"

"The ponies! How did you come by these ponies?" he snapped.

"I—!"

"The white steed belonged to Wossekh, did it not?"

"It—yes, it was his," the flustered Dehril replied.

"And why is it now yours?" the bantir insisted.

The Berboran gazed at the faces around him for some sign, but they remained emotionless. "We—I was traveling alone near the southern edge of the forest," he told the bantir. If he had walked into a trap, then at least he might spare Tyron from being hunted down on foot. "Four men accosted me, and had I not defended myself, they would have left me to rot in the dust."

"Then—you killed them?"

"Yes; it was—"

"All of them?"

"Yes."

The bantir glanced at his people. *"This man has destroyed Wossekh!"* he shouted.

"He destroyed Wossekh!" the multitude, as one, repeated.

The ring of steel resounded off the nearest of the cliffs, as more than one hundred longswords and daggers were pulled from their sheaths.

###

An hour passed, and then half of another, while Tyron lounged in a sparse patch of grass at the base of the knoll and gazed upward at the higher elevations of the Miskanthians. Only once was his reverie disturbed, this by a low, distant murmur that seemed to come from the direction of Shaaf. But before he could concentrate fully upon it, the sound was gone, and his thoughts again turned to the mountains, In his mind he heard the hunting cry of the great mountain cat, saw the majestic aerie dwellers bearing huge rodents to feed their young, felt the coolness of a spring rain on his face as it brought life to the Malbash Valley. He wrestled with old friends, and made love to eager, long-haired beauties with crimson lips. Though the Miskanthians occupied his field of vision, it was the Yushans that dwelt within his thoughts, and his heart.

Concern over the tardiness of his friend soon displaced some of Tyron's yearnings, and after checking the position of the sun he rose to his feet and gazed toward the east, from where he expected to see the Berboran approaching. But Dehril was not as yet in sight; at least, not from within the immediate quarter of a mile, the distance afforded him from his less than advantageous position. He first considered setting off toward Shaaf, but then thought better of it. Instead, he began to ascend the knoll, hoping the elevation would provide him with a better vantage point.

Halfway up the slope, another sound pierced his thoughts, this one, though as yet unidentifiable, closer than the one he had heard earlier. He hastened his ascent where, less than five yards from the top, it was again repeated, this time much louder. Now there could be no doubt: the sound was that of a woman screaming.

The Kalkh topped the hillock, where he immediately absorbed the scene of horror unfolding on a boulder-strewn plain, this about thirty yards distant. Thoughts of his own safety were not a part of his mind as he raced headlong down the shorter northern slope, the reckless descent taking only seconds. He halted less than ten yards from the two figures he had observed from above, his pike poised for casting. But he could not hurl the weapon lest he injure the woman, who was being held tightly by her snarling, bestial assailant, the latter only now aware of the intruder.

In the few moments that he stood by helplessly, Tyron studied this incomprehensible paradox of life. The young woman, though shabbily attired and unadorned in any manner, was beautiful. She stood tall, barely half a head shorter than the Kalkh, with silken hair of yellow that cascaded far below her shoulders. The crudely woven garment that she wore failed to conceal her curves, nor could they withhold the full breasts that strained to break loose from their confinement in the midst of her struggles. Her trim, athletic legs tapered down to surprisingly thin ankles and proportionately small feet, these shod in plain working sandals. Her well-tanned skin appeared as smooth as the marble figurines of Berbora, without a flaw in evidence. A small, upturned nose sat atop a fiery slash of a mouth. The strong chin, the even rows of gleaming teeth visible between lips parted in terror, denoted a face so perfect as to seem illusory. Indeed, her own eyes might have been plucked from their sockets, to be replaced with a pair of well-matched flecks of jade. But her eyes were quite real; there was nothing false about this tormented beauty.

The grotesque bellow that emanated from the foul throat of her captor snapped Tyron from the momentary spell, and he gazed with loathing at the thing. It was ape-like, its height well over seven feet, its weight at least three times that of the Kalkh.

Coarse, grayish hair covered nearly every inch of its body, save for the fleshy face and the pink appendages that contained seven digits each. Two lidless, black eyes peered out from amid the folds of skin, these sitting almost directly atop a red, bulbous nose. Its jaws displayed numerous rows of sharp, seemingly filed teeth, while its thick lips were curled in perpetual rage. Any neck that might have existed was hidden by layers of hair, though the contours of the broad, ovoid head were clearly evident. Tyron did not doubt for a moment that it was possessed of incredible strength, and it was this fact that caused him to shudder, for he knew that the thing could easily destroy the woman if it so desired. No, it did not wish to injure her, or devour her, at least not yet. Its wicked, tiny brain held other thoughts regarding the golden-haired beauty.

The woman became aware of Tyron's presence only an instant after her captor, and apparently her agile mind conceived of a desperate plan. Doubtless figuring that the stranger would not cast his weapon for fear of killing her, she resolved to separate herself from the thing. While it concentrated on the Kalkh, she bent down and sank her teeth into its wrist. The beast roared in pain and instinctively raised the injured member. This momentary lapse enabled her to pull away, and before the creature could react, she had fallen to the ground and rolled more than five yards distant.

"The center of its chest! That's where its heart is!" she shouted while still in motion. "Hurl the weapon, quickly!"

Tyron, though momentarily startled by her unexpected action, nonetheless responded in an instant. He raced toward the enraged beast, now confused by the turn of events. Before it could effect a charge the Kalkh threw the well-balanced pike, his skill placing it precisely where the woman had indicated. Because of their proximity to each other, as well as the power of the muscles behind the cast, the shaft re-emerged from the creature's back, where it flew for another couple of yards before falling to the hard earth. The disbelieving thing clutched at the gaping wound, and for a few moments it watched its own life ebb. Then, silently, it crumpled to the ground.

"Are you injured?" Tyron asked as he raced to the girl's side and helped her up.

"It—it is nothing," she replied, though the grimace on her face belied this. "My ankle was twisted, but—*noooo*!"

Another terrible bellow shattered the short-lived calm as a duplicate of the first monstrosity appeared from behind a boulder some fifty yards distant. Its great bulk belied the speed at which it could travel, and before the pair could react it had narrowed the distance by half. The Kalkh would have retrieved his pike, but the girl held firmly to his arm.

"You could never reach it in time," she told him. "We must run!"

Tyron grabbed her hand, and they raced toward the nearby hillock. Under less adverse circumstances, the girl might easily have kept pace with the fleet Kalkh. But her ankle troubled her greatly, and before ten yards had been traversed she fell to the ground, her face a mask of pain.

"Hurry! Save yourself!" she cried. "I cannot—!"

"Listen to me!" Tyron snapped. "Try and make it to the top of this knoll, and beyond! Crawl if you must! I will attempt to delay its advance!"

"No! You must not—!"

But the Kalkh had already hastened forward to meet the shaggy horror, which had paused momentarily to eye its dead fellow. Now its wicked eyes fell upon the one responsible, and with a savage roar it bounded toward the object of its ire. Tyron drew his longsword and stood his ground firmly, the bold action bringing the creature to a halt less than two yards away. For long, tense moments they stared at each other, the beast finally choosing the offensive. It strode forward, the powerful arms outstretched, while the Kalkh arced the blade over his right shoulder, his strength such that he could easily have cloven the skull of the bestial assailant. But in a blinding motion that Tyron had thought it incapable of the thing lashed out with its left arm, the blow knocking the sword from his sturdy grip. The weapon clattered to the ground more than ten feet away.

Stunned by the loss of his blade, Tyron sought any means of defense within his reach, but there was none. The thing strode toward him relentlessly, its bellows resounding off the distant cliffs. The Kalkh dared not turn to flee, lest he lose sight of the creature for even an instant. He took three steps backward, then another, until his heel struck a stone that was solidly entrenched in the hard ground. Down, down he toppled, and with his reactions numbed by terror he was unable to brace the fall. The back of his head struck a jagged rock, and a dark, reddish mist clouded his vision. He was only vaguely aware of the snarling visage that gazed down upon him, even less cognizant of the pink, meaty paws as they were affixed upon either side of his head, where their vise-like strength would soon crush what they held between them.

CHAPTER EIGHT: LANIRA

The steel-tipped pike penetrated the thing's forehead less than two inches above the bulbous nose, its impact such that more than half a foot of shaft disappeared into the skull. With a loud, blood-freezing shriek the hairy creature lurched backward, as though it had been struck with a giant, invisible hand. For long moments it thrashed wildly on the ground, and in its death throes it might have unwittingly crushed the still immobile Tyron. But the weapon had been well placed, and with one last convulsive shudder the thing died, its huge form coming to rest less than two feet from the side of the Kalkh.

Awareness returned quickly as the copper mist faded, and Tyron was able to raise himself groggily to a sitting position. His vision was blurred at first, but soon it had cleared sufficiently for him to gaze toward the knoll, where he saw two figures hurrying toward him, the concern on their faces evident. One was the golden-haired beauty, the other—Dehril.

"Tyron! Are you hurt badly?" the Berboran asked as he knelt by his friend's side.

The Kalkh rubbed the small knot on the back of his head, and he chanced a meager smile as he replied, "Khreelar and you always accused me of being a bit hard-headed. Why should a blow such as this cause me any harm? But as for *that*—!" He indicated the nearby carcass. "I fear that even a skull such as mine would not have stood up against it. I wholeheartedly applaud your skills, my friend."

Shrugging off Tyron's gratitude, Dehril exclaimed, "But what, in the name of Thur, is that thing?"

"It is a *miskanth*," the girl, only now arriving at Dehril's side, informed them. "Those of its ilk dwell high in the mountains, which, as you now realize, were not haphazardly named. Only in the dark hours do they usually descend, and seldom as far down as this. The presence of these two, especially after sunrise, is a mystery." Her hypnotic eyes affixed themselves upon Tyron. "Had you not chanced by when you did . . ." She shuddered.

Tyron managed to free himself from their spell, and he turned toward the Berboran. "But what of you, Dehril? Your stay in Shaaf went longer than both our expectations. I thought that you might have encountered difficulty."

Dehril grinned, almost sheepishly, as he explained, "The people were quite morose when I first entered the village, and I feared that my plan had been poorly conceived. But then, after learning of what we had accomplished two days earlier before entering the forest, their attitudes changed drastically. They raised their steel on high in salute, and then they fought amongst themselves to lay tributes at my feet. Why, the bantir himself offered me his own honored title! I made certain that they knew of your role, thus making your name a part of their lore for all time. After politely refusing the bulk of their gifts, which would have required a score of steeds to carry away, I took what was necessary and departed. The entire citizenry accompanied me to the perimeter of their fields, where I begged them to turn back. Such was the nature of my delay."

"I do not understand," the girl stated as she eyed Dehril suspiciously. "I am from Shaaf, and I know my people well. The reception you were afforded there is most unlike them. What could you have done to warrant it?"

"Upon entering the northern sector, we were attacked by four brigands," the Berboran explained. "Of necessity we killed them, and we took two of their steeds. The Shaafians recognized the white pony that belonged to one of them—"

"The white pony?" she exclaimed. "The white pony of *Wossekh*?"

"Yes."

"You destroyed Wossekh?"

Dehril motioned toward the Kalkh. "With only his hands did Tyron dispatch the lout. Wossekh would have—"

The smooth-skinned beauty dropped to her knees, and before the startled Tyron could react she pressed her fiery, sensual lips against his in a kiss of passion quite unlike any he had yet known in his lifetime. He placed hesitant hands on her alabaster shoulders, but he did not push her away, for desires long dormant within him became aroused once more, and for a few moments he was the vital young man of his days prior to Berbora. But the euphoria quickly passed, for the girl freed herself from his embrace, though slowly, reluctantly.

"I-I do not understand," he stammered.

"If saving me from the miskanth were not enough, now I learn that I am rid of the accursed Wossekh forever! I owe you much; I owe both of you much!"

"What is your name?" Tyron asked.

"Lanira."

"Lanira," he repeated. "It is a beautiful name, in keeping with the one who possesses it."

The girl's exquisite face radiated an aura of joy as she gazed upon the handsome Kalkh, who could scarce meet her shimmering eyes. Dehril smiled inwardly as he observed the pair, until he suddenly realized the obvious, which, during the recent tense minutes, had escaped his mind. He stared at Tyron, who immediately noted his serious demeanor.

"What is wrong, my friend? You appear . . ." Tyron's voice trailed off, and he turned toward Lanira, who still looked upon him as one would a god. Now he too understood, and he shook his head, his eyes wide. "It could not be helped! I heard her scream! What could I do? *What could I—? No-ooo*!"

Though still slightly dazed, he rose to his feet and staggered away, his head buried in his hands. The puzzled Lanira stared at Dehril, who hurried after his friend.

"Tyron, please! I understand—!"

The tormented Kalkh whirled about and glared at Dehril. "*You* understand!" he shrieked. "But what of *her*? Why did I listen to that old fool of a magician? This was inescapable! No matter how hard we tried to avoid it, *this was inescapable*! May Zeth forgive me!"

Lanira gazed from face to face as she cried, "Please, will you tell me what is happening? Your words are confusing."

Dehril looked at Tyron, who snapped, "Tell her! Tell her everything! Surely she has the right to know!"

The Berboran nodded resignedly and took Lanira aside, while Tyron turned and stared absently at the Miskanthians. For long minutes the beauty from Shaaf listened intently to Dehril's words, her intelligent face never once betraying the tidal wave of emotions that undoubtedly swept through her as she absorbed the revelations. Then, after all had been said, she strode toward the Kalkh and grasped his hand firmly. So soft had her tread been that Tyron whirled in surprise as she appeared beside him. He noted the gentle smile on her face, though he found it nigh impossible to gaze into the hypnotic eyes. She kissed him, long and hard, then took a step back.

"As far back as our elders can remember, the miskanths have carried off the women of Shaaf," she said. "In my lifetime I knew of one such woman. She was a kind, gentle soul, well liked by all. One evening, she journeyed to the foothills to recover a lamb that had wandered off, and they took her. She returned to the village three days later, though for each day that had passed, she had aged at least ten years. She spoke to no one, but instead was led back to her home by her husband and two small children. Within the first hour she took a dagger to all three, leaving little intact for the villagers to bury. Only then did she thrust the blade into her own heart, her insane laughter being the last sound that anyone, myself included, was to hear her utter."

"It is a tragic tale," Tyron stated. "But—"

"It is no tale, but a fact. What must the mountain devils have done to her, what unspeakable perversions must they have performed, to change her so? That would have been my fate,

Tyron, had you not acted as you did. Given the alternative of death, I would have gladly chosen it, this I swear. Now I have even more, for there is still a chance that I may live."

"Then you do not loathe me?"

She shook her head. "Loathe you? Nothing could be more distant from the truth. Had I observed you standing helplessly on the hill while the miskanth carried me off, then indeed would I have loathed you. But such is not your nature, Tyron; this I know. Here, let me tell you of the other beast you destroyed, the one called Wossekh. Dehril, you will find this of interest, for I sense that even now you do not as yet fully understand the reason for your unexpected welcome in Shaaf."

"That is true."

"Wossekh and his scum were spawned in the village of Mogrhel, a den of pestilence far in the eastern wilderness. Mogrhel itself was leveled by the aghor's soldiers some three years past, the inhabitants either destroyed or sent to the mines. But Wossekh and the others escaped, and the knowledge of the terrain was such that they could not be hunted down. As a result, they began to raid the sector's villages and prey on travelers, their own avowed vengeance for the destruction of their people. During their three-year reign of terror, at least forty people met untimely deaths at their foul hands, and nothing could be done to stop them.

"Because of its remoteness, Shaaf was somehow spared from this; that is, until four months past, when they stormed boldly into the village. Before anyone could react, they had taken the wife and daughter of the bantir as hostages, and because of this, no one dared challenge them. They swaggered about the village partaking at will of food, wine, and women, some of the latter even giving themselves willingly to the swine. Only after they had more than sated themselves did Wossekh notice me, and the foul words that he spoke as he touched my hair with his greasy fingers assured me that he would remember the next time.

"Despite the vigilance of our men they returned two months later, and this time they held the bantir himself. Wossekh immediately stormed to the hut wherein my father and I dwelled, and he demanded my favors. My father tried to stand up to the brute, but for his efforts he received a blade through his heart. In my grief I scratched Wossekh's face, and his pain was such that I felt certain he would destroy me. But one of his scum intervened with a skin of wine and a village whore, both of which he eagerly accepted. I was left to mourn my father's death in peace.

"Subsequent to this, I devised a thousand plans for the cur's demise, until I decided on one that I believed could not fail. When next he came, this barely a month past, Wossekh found a different Lanira, one who appeared more than eager to share her favors. He stood in the portal, a broad grin on his wicked face, while I removed my garment and swayed enticingly toward the waiting cot. But in spite of his eagerness, Wossekh was not the fool that I thought him to be. I was grabbed from behind by one of the others, who had entered through a side window, and before I could react he had wrested from me the small dagger that was concealed in the palm of my hand, the one that I would have thrust into Wossekh's throat before he could place a filthy hand on me. Another appeared from behind Wossekh, and together they . . . I was hurled to the cot . . . they took turns, the three . . . of them . . . *Zhon*!"

Lanira buried her head on Tyron's chest and began to sob while the Kalkh placed a strong arm around her shoulder. "If someday I make the journey to Sharn I will seek this Wossekh out, if only to crush him once again!" he stated grimly.

The golden-haired beauty shook loose from the terrible memories and, after separating herself from Tyron she dried her tear-stained face. "Such is the nature of the monster you destroyed," she told him. "Can you understand my feelings?"

"Yes, I can. But what will you do now?"

"My choice is already made," she stated. "I will go with you."

"No!" Tyron snapped. "You cannot—"

"Listen to me. Even before the miskanth found me this morning, I had already decided that I would not return to Shaaf. I have always despised the small-minded people there. Now, with my father dead, there is nothing left to hold me. I might have journeyed to Berbora, but . . .

"If I indeed have the Scamban malady, then I would not wish to die slowly, horribly, as Dehril described. I would prefer the quick thrust of a dagger to a death such as that. Alone, I might find myself too weak, or too cowardly to carry this out. Do you not see?

"Lastly, if I am indeed fortunate enough to avoid the disease, I would find much satisfaction in helping you seek out and achieve what you so understandably desire. I will not hinder you in the least, this I swear!"

"The road before us is rugged, our future at best questionable," the Kalkh protested.

"My future lies with *you*, Tyron." Her hypnotic eyes again ensnared the helpless mountain man.

"I-I fear that I cannot refuse you, Lanira," he stammered. "But Dehril—"

The young beauty turned to the Berboran, who smiled and nodded his assent. With a cry of delight she embraced each of them, and with a slender arm she gestured toward the west.

"Even if you are skilled, as well as tireless, it will take many days to cross the range, assuming you do not encounter the miskanths. In that direction, about four miles, is the entrance to a passageway through the mountains. It is far less dangerous, and will save much time."

"But that is impossible!" Dehril exclaimed. "The maps do not—!"

"The maps show nothing, for only I know of it. I discovered it as a small girl, and never did I tell anyone, not even my father. For years it has been my private place, my escape from the tedium of life in Shaaf."

"You speak of a cave, do you not?" Tyron asked. "How can you be certain that it does not end halfway through?"

"Because I have journeyed its entire length."

"You—you have been to the far side of the Miskanthians?" Dehril exclaimed.

Lanira shook her head. "Only once did I venture that far, the distance being considerable. I came to within fifty yards, where I saw the daylight at the end of the tunnel. Inbred fear then overpowered my curiosity, for the other side of the Miskanthians has always been regarded as a place of unspeakable horror. I hurried away as quickly as I could, and never again did I approach as closely."

"And you would not be afraid to venture there now?"

"I would not. Legends are indeed for children!"

Dehril thought of the corths but said nothing regarding them. Instead, he asked, "When did you make this journey?"

"Twelve years past. I was ten years of age at the time."

"Then you were considerably smaller. Can the passage accommodate us now?"

"In a few places it may be tight, but we will make it through."

"So be it!" Tyron announced, forgetting the fact that he had looked forward to the upcoming climb for many days. "Our path leads *through* the Miskanthians. Show us the way, Lanira."

Before departing, they recovered their pikes from the carcasses of the miskanths. Dehril then raced up the knoll to retrieve the items he had acquired in Shaaf. There were lengths of sturdy rope, climbing axes, additional furs, as well as food and water. Two joints of beef and a skin of wine would see them feast well that day, though the remainder of the fare was selected with longevity in mind. Dried meats, nuts, and the like, though hardly appetizing, would not spoil, and they would be afforded a welcome change from the tasteless fare they now possessed. They discarded none of the items, even though some would prove of no value initially. With three to carry the supplies they would not present much of a burden, and Tyron reasoned that they might be useful at some later time.

They angled sharply toward the base of the Miskanthians, though their progress could hardly be considered rapid, for Lanira's ankle was still a bit tender, while Tyron's head throbbed from the blow he had received. The sun stood almost overhead when the young beauty motioned for them to halt, and with much relief they dropped to the dusty ground.

"We—are here," Lanira announced breathlessly.

Tyron peered intently at the nearby rocks before exclaiming, "But I see nothing!"

"Of course not," she replied with a mysterious smile. "It would not then be a secret, would it? Only when we are ready to leave will I reveal it."

"Then do so, woman!" the Kalkh roared in mock anger. "We haven't all day to sit here."

The grinning Lanira would have complied, but Dehril held her wrist firmly before she could regain her feet, and he told them, "Hear me, the two of you. It took us hours to traverse little more than a league, for you both appear as walking dead! Not until wounds have been tended to, not until some proper rest, will we depart this spot!"

"But—" Tyron began.

"Dehril is right," Lanira said, as she placed her fingers gently over the Kalkh's lips. "A respite would suffice us well. You are indeed headstrong, as your friend advised me, though I can well understand your desire for haste. Please, Tyron."

"Of course you are right, Lanira, as are you, my motherly friend." The Kalkh sighed. "I suppose that, even if I were insistent, you would refuse me access to your accursed tunnel anyway."

"You are correct," the beauty replied, now unable to suppress the laugh that she had heretofore contained. Tyron, despite his grave onus, could not look upon that vibrant, joyful face without himself being caught up in its aura. At first he chuckled softly, this soon turning into a hearty roar that Dehril had known so well from the many good times they had shared together in Berbora. Soon the laughter of all three pierced the brooding stillness, nor did it cease for a while.

Lanira's ankle had sustained little more than a slight twist, as she assured the concerned pair after the echoes of laughter faded. Indeed, the swelling was almost negligible, even after the pressure that had been placed upon it during the past few hours.

The Shaafian beauty was instead solicitous regarding Tyron's injury, and she showed much determination as she took charge of his care. Dehril might have protested, for he desired both of them to rest; but the change in his friend, so drastically evident during the brief exposure to this remarkable young woman, silenced him. He would not interfere with what little joy the pair might ever know.

With her back pressed against a narrow, vertical outcropping, Lanira ministered tenderly to the Kalkh's head wound, and so gentle was her touch that he did not even wince. Once done, she massaged his neck with her strong, slim fingers, this further soothing the troubled mountain man. With Tyron's head softly ensconced in her lap she hummed a sweet, simple tune, and not until he had fallen into the folds of undisturbed slumber did she stop. She kissed him on the forehead, and within minutes of closing her eyes she joined him in the embrace of temporary darkness. Dehril noted the nearly identical smiles that creased the faces of both, and he beamed as he settled in to see them safely through the afternoon.

The sound from high in the mountains brought them awake simultaneously, though Dehril was the only one who initially scrambled to his feet. While gazing about the surrounding terrain, his sword drawn, the Berboran cursed himself for allowing sleep to overcome him. The sun was descending slowly toward the western horizon, indicating that he had slept for at least three hours. He turned toward Lanira and Tyron, noting that both, while a bit surprised by his actions, were quite well.

"May Zhon strike me down for my laxity!" he admonished himself.

"You needed rest no less than we did, my friend," Tyron told him. "Do not concern yourself with it. The day passed uneventfully."

"But what of the noise that—listen! There it is again!"

Lanira listened to the distant sound as it was repeated, and she said, "You need not worry about that, at least for now. The miskanths are still high in the mountains." She then glanced toward the sun. "But in two hours, perhaps less . . ."

Though still irate with himself, the mumbling Dehril broke out the fine fare provided him by the Shaafians, and they partook of a feast. Lanira chided all good-naturedly, herself included, about over-stuffing themselves to the point of being unable to fit through the oftentimes narrow passageway. But the meal served to buoy their spirits, while the afternoon's rest did wonders for their various injuries, and soon even the Berboran had forgotten about his harmless lapse.

Near dusk they gathered up their belongings, and Lanira led them to a spot about fifteen yards farther along. There, the lifelong secret of the girl's tunnel was revealed to outsiders for the first time. Amidst a clump of brittle brush there sat a small, seemingly insignificant boulder, one that would have not warranted a second look. But its appearance was unquestionably deceiving, for the stone swiveled outward effortlessly at her touch, and a narrow, semi-circular opening appeared. She indicated the hole proudly.

"Behold, the passageway to the far side of the Miskanthian Mountains!" she announced. "Now the knowledge is no longer mine alone, though I can think of no one else with whom I would rather share it. Stay close behind me, for there are a few branching tunnels that lead to dead ends. The journey will at times seem endless to you; but, barring unforeseen delays, we will reach its end within two days."

The strong-willed Lanira entered the cave feet first, with Dehril, at the urging of Tyron, close behind. It proved a tight squeeze for the Berboran, but he too soon vanished into the blackness. The Kalkh hesitated for a moment before following the others, his eyes turned upward to the distant, snow-capped peaks. Even had anyone stood at his side, they would have been unable to understand the words that he uttered beneath his breath.

"Hear me, Zeth, I beg you. Never have I ceased to believe in you, not even after what happened in Berbora. Now I would ask you but one thing: spare her, great God of the Mountains! See that the accursed Scamban plague does not befall her! She made me smile, she made me laugh. Please, Zeth; *do not take Lanira*!"

###

The passageway was cold and damp farther in, necessitating the use of their comforting furs. Droplets of water, the runoff from overhead streams high in the mountains, clung to the cave walls throughout more than half of the lengthy journey. The tunnel occasionally widened to nearly ten feet, though at no time did its height exceed five feet, oftentimes less, this forcing them to traverse the distance on their hands and knees. There were a few tight spots, as Lanira had said earlier, which caused them to remove their bulky outer garments in order to pass. It was indeed a seemingly endless trek through the dull, granite-walled tunnel. But, if nothing else it passed uneventfully, and for this they were thankful. They slept twice during the passage and saw no forms of life save for some small lizards.

Without the guidance of Lanira they would surely have become lost, for the passageway did branch off into countless lesser tunnels, as she had said. But her instincts were unerring, for never once did she appear to hesitate. Nor did she slow appreciably, despite the grueling nature of the journey, until less than an hour from its end. Dehril, who had previously called forth his reserves of strength to keep up with her, suddenly found himself mere inches from her feet. She paused for only a moment before continuing, her pace now slower. The Berboran, believing fatigue to have begun taking its toll, shrugged this off, for the speed at which they now moved was far more to his liking. He noted that Tyron, a yard to his rear, chose not to question the change either.

The tunnel curved sharply twice, and then it straightened out for about a quarter of a mile, its width just barely enough to allow the three ample room for passage. But this eventually terminated, and for the first time they were able to stand upright, the ceiling of the last hundred yards rising nearly eight feet above the ground. Far ahead, they could discern the dim light of morning through a wide cave mouth, this indicating that their journey had taken them as far as, if not beyond, the earliest traces of dawn. Though wobbly they strode purposefully, three abreast, toward the opening, Tyron and Dehril both pleased at the prospect of being freed from this confinement.

"What manner of terrible land do we enter?" the Kalkh wondered out loud as his eyes remained fixed on the adit.

"Even the benevolent magicians of Berbora would not speak of its nature," Dehril replied, as he too gazed at the entrance into the enigmatic land beyond the Miskanthian Mountains. "Lanira, what about the legends of your people? Did they tell anything of—?"

With their eyes straight ahead, neither noticed that the golden-haired beauty was no longer at their side, but rather a few yards behind. Both whirled about as they realized this, and they saw her down upon one knee, her head resting in one hand. They retraced their steps and knelt down alongside her, their concern evident.

"Lanira, what—what is wrong?" Tyron asked hesitantly.

She lifted her head slowly, with considerable effort, and stared at them. Her face, as well as the rest of her skin, had turned a ghastly pale white. She parted her lips to speak, though her weakness was such that she could scarce utter the words they had prayed not to hear.

"I . . . feel . . . ill . . . !"

CHAPTER NINE: VISIONS

Furs were torn from their backs, a bed hastily constructed on the floor of the cave, upon which they gently placed the trembling form of the dying Lanira. Tyron fought back tears of grief and anger as he gazed into the incomparable face of the tall beauty, now so wan. Her body was aflame with the fires of fever, while the first of the dark spots were in evidence on her left arm. Coherency would soon leave her as the suffering, the unbearable pain grew worse, and then . . .

"Lanira! My—Lanira!" the Kalkh sobbed as he clutched her cold hand tightly against his chest. "Zeth! May you be cast from on high into the fires of Sharn! May you be cursed ten thousand times over by the soulless demons that move through its slime! You have done this to me! *You have seen me destroy the woman I . . . I loved!*"

Her eyelids fluttered as these words resounded through the cavern, and once again the vibrant flecks of jade held him captive. Her tapered fingers gripped his arm, while her pale lips formed the barest trace of a smile. She spoke, though the words came forth with great effort.

"Tyron . . . hear me . . . I do not . . . blame you . . . for this! You must . . . believe me! I too . . . love you, my . . . mountain god. We will be . . . together . . . again. Now go . . .! Dehril will do . . . what must . . ."

"Lanira—!"

"Tyron, please," Dehril said softly as he assisted the grieving Kalkh to his feet. "The worst will soon come, and she must not be allowed to suffer any longer than necessary. Go to the mouth of the cave and await me outside. Do—nothing, I beg of you. I will not be long."

The Kalkh tore his clouded eye from the shivering Lanira, and after freeing himself from Dehril's grasp he staggered blindly toward the adit, his legs acting independently of the impulses reflexively sent forth from his tortured brain. Three times he stumbled as he traversed the remaining fifty yards, though this was not his fault alone. Had his vision not been blurred, had he been able to measure each step before him, he would have noticed the small piles of whitened bones, as well as the layers of dried excrement and other assorted debris that dotted the floor of the cavern. But this was of no interest to him, not any more. His unwanted affliction had brought death to untold thousands, including many he had cared about, an incomprehensible onus, to be sure. Yet none could have brought him more grief, none could have pierced his heart more painfully, than the death of the gentle beauty from Shaaf, whose existence he had not even been aware of days earlier. Dehril would soon plunge the blade into her heart, and she would be wrested from her torment, much like a beast of burden would after suffering a broken leg. It would have been more than anyone could bear; it was indeed more than enough for Tyron.

Befittingly, it rained outside the mouth of the cave: a hard, pelting rain, its force such that it drew Tyron from his own internal suffering, this for the first time since leaving the scene of the tragedy. He glanced about, noting that the terrible, cryptic far side of the Miskanthian Mountains appeared little different than Berbora's northern frontier. The rock-strewn tundra was rugged, seemingly uninhabited for as far as he could see, this not a considerable distance because of the dense, gray mist. Ahead of him, toward what he guessed to be north, visibility was little more than half a mile, but to his right he could see for nearly two miles along the perimeter of the sheer rock facings, where the effects of the storm seemed to be lessening. Only to the left was he unable to see more than a few yards past the hole from which he had emerged, for here were stacked countless boulders of varying shapes and sizes, these likely cast downward over the years by minor upheavals, or other acts of nature. The despondent Kalkh deposited himself a few yards from the base of these rocks, his place of rest a flat, shale-like stone of a coppery hue.

For long, unbearable minutes he continually forced from his mind the thoughts that assailed them; but no matter how hard he tried, no matter where he chose to look, his eye inevitably fell upon the broad adit, and the scene within formed before him, its clarity such as to indicate that he had not yet departed. *No more!* his tortured conscience shrieked from within. *It has gone too far! Do what you must, fool of a Kalkh, lest other innocents be made to suffer at your hands! Be done with it, now!*

Tossing his pike aside he mechanically drew his longsword, and with his hands squeezed tightly around the hilt he pressed the tip against the left side of his chest, now exposed through his tattered garments. Thus did he sit, statue-like, his anguished soul shrieking at him to carry out the necessary deed, though as yet the final, telling stimulus was not in evidence. Then, from within the bowels of the nearby cave, he heard the echoes of a short, gasping scream, and he knew there could be no more delays. His knuckles whitened, and with a final imprecation hurled at Zeth he began to urge the well forged Berboran steel into his flesh.

The loud hissing sound snapped him from the spell, for such was its proximity. Centuries of inbred instincts now dominated his actions, and with the speed of a mountain cat he propelled himself forward on strong legs, at the same time whirling about to face the loosely formed outcropping. Others might have cringed before the horror that now emerged from amid a broad, triangular crevice, but not so Tyron. He felt only disgust, loathing, for this travesty of nature. But even more, an association between this thing and the cave he had recently left immediately registered, for he now recalled the broken bones, the foul droppings, and he knew that the end portion of the lengthy tunnel was its lair. If he cared little for his own worthless life, then it was the responsibility he felt for the unselfish Dehril that momentarily stayed his hand. The Berboran, having completed his incomprehensible task only moments before, would even now be traversing the remainder of the cave, where his own torment, as well as the encompassing gloom of the interior, would doubtless prevent him from putting up an adequate defense against the thing that would regain its putrid dwelling. Tyron swore that this would not happen.

Long seconds passed as the monster slithered through the opening, its elongated trunk propelled by untold thousands of filiform tentacles. The arthropodal creature, when finally emerged, measured fifteen feet lengthwise, while its thickness was that of a fully grown Yushan oak. Its nine brown, fleshy segments were identical in size, save for the rearmost one, which tapered drastically to a flat point. Each of the ovoid, jointed sections acted independently of the others, though, contrary to appearances, the haphazard movements seemed to enhance the speed of the thing. The head comprised the first segment, which was no different from the rest, save for two immense, circular black eyes and a bony, squared plate directly above, this undoubtedly the armor-like protection for its vulnerable brain. Two wicked, closely juxtaposed pincers protruded from atop the foremost of its many appendages, the pair clamped tightly about the bloodied remains of a mountain goat, one that had been freshly killed. Initially, no mouth had been in evidence. But as Tyron stared in muted horror, he realized that the huge insect had been feeding during its journey, that even now it was in the process of consuming another bit of the flesh. One of the pivoted grippers deposited a piece of the gray-furred animal into a gaping, beet-red orifice that suddenly appeared only inches below the eyes. This maw displayed no teeth of any kind, though they were hardly necessary, for the pincers made certain that the offering was well mashed. The food was thrust deep into its throat, where obscene muscle contractions bore it far back into the digestive tract. Once done, the pincer was withdrawn, and the hole snapped shut. Thus did the multi-legged monstrosity feed, though from the large portion of goat still intact, it was clear that the thing had planned on devouring the rest within the confines of its own lair.

Tyron would have preferred to face the thing with his pike, but the weapon had been tossed aside and was now beyond his reach. He did not rue this at length, however, for the two eyes now fell upon him, and the Kalkh knew that the monster was well aware of this obstacle to its desired cave. The goat carcass was discarded, and the insect began to wriggle obscenely, the hue of its slimly flesh altering to varying shades of green. It emitted a loud, piercing whistle as its six foremost segments rose upward to a height of nearly ten feet, where the thousands of thread-like appendages rippled in unison, like a wind-blown field of wheat. For long moments it remained poised, until the high-pitched whistle finally ceased. The pincers snapped together menacingly as it lowered the bulk of its torso, and with a series of sibilant, staccato-like hisses it charged the unwanted intruder.

Because of its position amid the rocks it was at first unable to achieve the momentum that it desired, which afforded Tyron a few extra seconds to devise a strategy. Accordingly, he placed more than fifteen yards between himself and the outcropping in the hope of enabling him to witness exactly what sort of offensive the insect would employ. But the thing was hardly devious, and far less than subtle, for once upon level ground it charged headlong toward its prey, its rigid pincers tearing furrows through the muddy earth. The quick-thinking Kalkh described a wide arc around its right side, thinking that it would be unable to alter its course too rapidly. But the thing's rearmost segments seemed to act of their own volition, for no sooner had Tyron raced past its head when he found himself confronted with the tapered, flagellating tail, which had been swung around at blinding speed to intercept him. In an act of desperation he leaped over the wildly swinging appendage, his sword slashing as it passed below. The tip of it was severed cleanly, this causing brown gore to spurt forth. It was in this foul puddle that the flesh continued to squirm.

Tyron, certain that he was rid of the thing for at least a few seconds, raced toward the rocks, where he gathered up his pike. He then whirled to face the creature, where he noted that its rush had carried it some ten yards past the spot he had first vacated. Its jointed torso was twisted around in an O as it gazed dumbly at the bleeding hind portion, the hurt not yet registering in its miniscule brain. But it was not confused for long, for the pain was finally realized, and it began to thrash about, its whistle again shattering the stillness. The dark eyes fell upon the tormenter once more, and its pincers clattered loudly as the insect curled its body into a semi-circle. Again it charged the intruder, this time resolved not to allow a repetition of its previous escape.

The Kalkh, quickly recognizing the nature of this strategy, raced toward the boulders, for he knew that he would be unable to bypass the creature a second time. He sheathed his now useless sword, while the pike was hurled toward the higher rocks as he made ready to climb. The insect neared as he scrambled upward, and had misfortune not intervened, he would undoubtedly have gotten free of immediate danger. The pike had found no place of rest above, and he was forced to react instinctively as it now hurtled down toward him. He leaped to one side, his nimble fingers seeking the nearest handhold. But the unstable pile was such that he succeeded in doing no more than loosening the cluster of rocks, these carrying him with them as they rolled to the base of the outcropping. He now lay in the path of the onrushing horror, and he knew that a second chance of escape was no longer a possibility.

Despite the numerous scrapes he had sustained, Tyron snatched his pike from amid the rubble and leaped to his feet. The thing, now only a few feet away, had slowed, for it knew that its prey could no longer escape. Slowly, deliberately, it straightened out the heretofore curled torso, while the bony grippers came closer to the man. The beet-red orifice opened wide, and a thin drool trickled forth, as though in anticipation of an additional repast.

It was the sight of the gaping maw that led the Kalkh to attempt one last impossible action. With his hands wrapped tightly around the shaft of the pike, he raced forward between the two pincers. The insect did not initially react to the unexpected charge, and because of this, Tyron managed to thrust the weapon deep into the putrid mouth. He shoved it upward at a slight angle, toward what he assumed to be the brain, and only when the barbed tip struck the bony plate from below did he stop, for he knew that the target had been located. This time there was no delay, for the pain registered immediately, and it hissed loudly as its segmented torso stiffened. Tyron would have freed himself from its blind path, but momentum caused him to stumble for an instant, and before he could recover, one of the pincers had wrapped itself around his waist. He grimaced in pain as the life was slowly crushed from him, and with the strength of desperation he attempted to pry apart the vise-like organ. Whether he succeeded or not was questionable, but he fell from its grasp nonetheless. For long moments he lay there, his breath all but gone from him, while the thing thrashed madly only inches away. He was struck by the flailing tail and hurled against one of the boulders at the base of the nearby outcropping. This was far more than his devastated body could take, and after observing the creature for an instant as it swam through a sea of crimson, he was engulfed by a blackness that seemed all but final.

###

At first it was only a yellow blur; but then, slowly, it began to acquire form, substance. He knew that it was a face; it was *her* face. The red lips parted, and words came forth, but for long moments they remained inaudible. He strained to listen, forcing every bit of his limited awareness to the purpose, until finally he heard them.

". . . to what I say! It is I, Lanira! Tyron, please! Can you not hear me?"

A meager smile crossed his face, though his eyelids were hardly parted. "La—nira! You were . . . correct . . ." he gasped in a strange voice. "We would meet . . . in another life, you . . . said. We have . . . done so. Eternity is ours . . . my Lanira . . ."

"But Tyron, I am not—!"

"No more plague . . . Lanira," he continued to prattle. "Death has made me . . . immune. We can . . . make love. No more . . . plague . . . immune."

"Listen to me, you thick-headed Kalkh!" the unexpected voice roared, its volume driving much of the lethargy from his dulled brain. "It is not yet time to die. Pull yourself free from whatever holds you, as you have done so many times in the past. On this I insist!"

His eyes snapped open, and he saw, beyond the incomparable face of Lanira, the stern visage of Dehril. He shook his head twice, three times, before again speaking.

"What has happened to you, my friend, that you should join us so soon in death?" he asked, his voice stronger but his thoughts still jumbled.

"You brother of a cave bear!" the Berboran laughed, unable to contain himself any longer. "None of us are dead! Can you not see that?"

The uncomprehending Kalkh glanced from one to the other, his sight finally resting upon the smiling, tear-streaked face of the golden-haired beauty. Slowly, hesitantly, he raised a trembling hand upward, until he touched the warm, vibrant skin.

"Lanira—you live!" he cried as he pulled her down toward him. They embraced for an eternity, and not until long after her sobs had ceased did they separate. "But how can this be? No one survives the Scamban malady! With my own eyes, I saw—!"

"Calm yourself, friend, for you are still weak," Dehril advised him. "I will answer all your questions. I was within moments of plunging the blade into Lanira's chest when I chanced to gaze down at her left arm, where the first of the dark blotches had appeared. At first it was difficult to see, but upon closer scrutiny I discovered two tiny holes near her wrist, each emitting a drop of blood. Recalling the pace she had maintained through the night, and then the noticeable change toward the end, I reasoned that she had been pricked by the fangs of some tiny serpent or insect, something she might not have even been aware of herself. With this final straw to grasp at, I placed a tight tourniquet on her arm almost as high as her shoulder, for the spots had already reached this point. I then used the knife to bleed the punctures, draining as much blood as I dared."

"Was it then that she cried out?" Tyron asked.

"Yes. Why—?"

"It is nothing. Please continue."

"Once done with this I concentrated on her fever, which, with most of the poison drawn from her system, broke quickly. She opened her eyes, and after assuring me with a smile that she would be well, she fell into a deep, restful sleep. She was still ashen, yet I felt certain that she would survive.

"I hastened to the cave mouth to advise you of the good news, but less than halfway there I heard the grotesque noises from outside, and I knew that you had met with some difficulty. The thing was in the last stages of dying when I emerged, but not until it had perished could I reach you. Though I now realized what the cave was, I nonetheless carried you back into it, my hope being that the terrible insect had been the sole occupant. This way, I would be able to tend to the both of you. So far, my assumption has proven correct."

"Then we must hurry!" Tyron snapped. "Another might come at any moment. How long since I destroyed the other? An hour? Two?"

"The demons of darkness have held you for five days, my love," Lanira stated.

"Five—*days*?" the Kalkh gasped. "That cannot be!"

"Yet you can see that I am well recovered from my own illness, can you not?" Indeed, her face was radiant, her movements strong and self-assured. "Not for two days would this overbearing watchdog allow me to my feet! And since then, three more days have passed. You were badly injured, Tyron!"

These many revelations were far more than the Kalkh's fogged brain could absorb at a single time. He stared at one of the cave walls for a few moments, his head shaking, before again gazing upon the others.

"Then—then I did not pass the Scamban malady on to you?" he asked.

Lanira shook her head. "The symptoms caused by the serpent's venom were similar, and therefore deceiving."

"Nor is there any chance of her contracting the disease," Dehril added, "not after these many days of exposure. Lanira is immune!"

Tyron gazed at the beauty, who nodded and smiled. She kissed him gently on the forehead, and then, despite his protests, she lowered him softly to the furs, for his most recent efforts had fatigued him. Within minutes the Kalkh was asleep, but not before they heard him mumble, "Zeth, great God of the Mountains, my apologies for the names I so unwittingly hurled your way. You have not deserted me yet."

CHAPTER TEN: THE NEST

The next morning, after nearly a full day's sleep, Tyron assured the others that he felt well enough to travel. Though still weak, his numerous injuries had healed sufficiently, and he was anxious to quit the dank cave. The insect's lair had served them well for the duration, since not a single day had passed without torrents of rain falling. Also, the unknown nocturnal predators that howled and bellowed ceaselessly throughout the long nights chose to shun the cave, likely due to the knowledge of its past occupant. Dehril could recall only one that snuffled about the cave mouth, this on the third night. It did not remain long, however, much to his relief.

Tyron wanted to recover the pike that he had utilized in the dispatching of the segmented creature, a task that, once outside the cave, he saw would be relatively simple. The insect's flesh had been picked clean during the days that passed, leaving only a grotesque string of concentric bones, each connected by narrow pieces of cartilage. In another day or two there would remain little more than a pile of dust, for the bones of the last two sections had already been cracked for their marrow. Though no creatures of any kind appeared to be close by, the Kalkh nonetheless cast many wary glances around him as he yanked the weapon from the foremost skeletal segment.

Despite the many puffy clouds that dotted the sky, the sun was visible just atop the eastern horizon, its location indicating that the cave mouth did indeed face due north, their desired direction. No morning fog blanketed the land, thus affording them unlimited visibility. But they found little to see across the barren plain, for the many prowlers of night chose the daylight hours to rest, or perhaps to feed on their most recent kill. The dens of these creatures were surely beyond their abilities to locate, had they even been foolish enough to seek them out.

They traipsed across the rugged tundra for hours, the Kalkh displaying little sign of fatigue, which greatly relieved the concerned Lanira and Dehril. Only once did it rain, a torrential downpour that lasted just a few minutes. Numerous small craters that pocked the plain were rapidly filled with the cool water, enabling them to replenish the supply in their skins. Not until midday did they pause for a brief respite.

While Lanira and Tyron talked, Dehril gazed northward across the seemingly endless expanse of terrain that stretched before them, his thoughts centered on the immense distance that, as Zarthik had advised them, would be necessary to traverse. He was vaguely aware of the dark shadows that covered the land as the sun was momentarily blotted, for it had vanished behind the sporadic clouds numerous times already that morning. It reappeared almost immediately and was just as quickly covered again, the speed of this causing him to glance skyward. What he saw above brought him to his feet, his mouth opened wide in horror.

"What in the name of all the gods is *that*?" he gasped.

The pair first looked at the Berboran, then at the sight that held his attention. Tyron grunted loudly, while Lanira, her skin ashen, pointed a trembling finger upward.

"Zhon! It is a *barrah*!" she cried.

"A *what*?" the Kalkh roared.

"The barrahs are the couriers of Sharn, their task to carry the physical bodies of those deceased into the foul depths after the dark ones have wrested the souls from the unfortunates. At least, so say the legends of my ancestors."

"How can you be certain?" Dehril asked.

"You will see soon enough, I assure you!"

The corvine bird floated lazily in the cloud-filled sky, many hundreds of yards above their heads. It described broad circles as it dropped lower and lower, though not until a broad puff obscured the fiery sun were they able to gaze at it more closely. To all appearances it was nothing but a common raven. The lustrous black plumage measured nearly seventy feet from tip to tip, while its body was proportionately huge. When less than fifty yards from the ground, they were afforded a clear look at its underbelly, where the disbelieving men immediately understood what the sharp-eyed Lanira had meant. Three sets of thick legs were in evidence at evenly spaced intervals, each lengthy member ending in five vicious, gleaming talons that opened and closed continually, as though anxious to grasp and rend something; or, as the legends foretold, to carry off the dead toward a final place hardly of their own choosing.

"We'd best leave here, quickly!" Dehril exclaimed as he knelt down to gather his possessions.

"Wait," Lanira said. "It may not challenge us. The barrahs are known to seek only the dead—"

"Then this one best be advised of its error," Tyron snapped. "See!"

The creature ceased its aimless drifting and with a harsh, deafening cry it hurtled down toward them, its massive wings tucked tightly against its sides. They fell to the ground as the barrah passed above them, its raking talons only inches from their flesh. As the feathered horror rose high in the air, they quickly regained their feet.

"Hurry," Dehril said. "Perhaps we can outrun it!"

"Even if we could there is nowhere that we may run *to*," Tyron countered. "Quickly, your pike. We must make our stand here!"

They snatched up the weapons and stood ready to meet the barrah, which had already completed its arc and was now commencing another descent. This time, however, its approach was slower, more deliberate, as though it sensed opposition.

Knuckles whitened around shafts as it came to within thirty yards, twenty, ten. Then, unexpectedly, it braked to a sudden halt, the vast wings again beating vigorously. The force created by these flapping appendages was such that it drove them from their feet and pinned them against the muddy earth, the now useless pikes falling from their grasp. They no longer controlled their own movements, for they were as helpless as babes beneath the huge, invisible hand that held them there. Closer, closer came the grasping talons, until, one by one, they encircled the unwilling trio. The foremost pair closed around Dehril and Lanira, while Tyron was taken by the second claw on the right. Their attempts to clutch at deeply rooted shrubs were futile, for the thing lifted them on high with a deafening screech of triumph, and they could do nothing but watch as the earth fell away below them. The barrah then sped off toward the north with its squirming victims, its momentum nearly causing them to black out.

###

It soon became clear that the barrah had no intention of destroying them; at least, not during the breathtaking flight. Its steel-like talons, while encircling them tightly, allowed ample room for breathing, though they could do little else. The dizziness that they had first experienced at the rarefied height, nearly three-quarters of a mile, soon left them, though their fear of observing the ground from this unique position could scarce be measured. But none displayed the least sign of this outwardly, nor did they continue their struggles, for the last thing that any now desired was to be freed from the thing's grasp.

League after countless league fell away beneath them, for the barrah could cover more distance in an hour than they would have been able to traverse in a full day, or more. They passed beyond the perimeter of the lifeless tundra, where the terrain altered drastically, and they soon came to understand why the magicians of Zavrhal had lost more than half their number on the journey to Vorhashekkh so many years past. The land was a seething cauldron of huge and terrible life forms, an impossible, nightmarish tapestry that could only have been conceived of in the deepest recesses of a depraved artisan's drug-addled mind. Bellowing saurians fought titanic battles amid the swirling, bloodied currents of vast inland seas. Grassy veldts were home to scores of furry, lumbering shapes, the identities of which could hardly be imagined. Savage, spotted cats, three times the size of the largest tigher to be found in the Krabharkian Forest, vied with the others for their prey, gentler creatures that seemed quite out of place amid the horrors that made their existence less than tentative. Cacophonies of death and torment rose upward from the bowels of steamy, verdant jungles, the denizens of which, mercifully, were obscured from their view. Other reptilian behemoths, these more adapted to land, roamed along the perimeters of these forests, as well as upon the rock-strewn plains not unlike the one farther south. Many were four-legged, though a few walked upright. Almost all appeared to be carnivorous, for, like their sea-dwelling kin, their gore-spattered encounters were endless.

Such was the nature of the grim land that demanded the rapt attention of Tyron, Dehril, and Lanira for the greater portion of the day. No words passed between them, for there was little to be said. The seemingly tireless barrah maintained its steady pace throughout, undoubtedly leaving many hundreds of miles behind them.

"Could the death that we are headed toward be any worse than what we would unquestionably have met below?" Dehril mused. "Most likely not. But one fact is clear: we are still alive, and while alive, there is always a chance of survival, no matter how slim. We *will* endure!" he shouted with much resolve, though the words were lost in the wind, and fell upon no ears.

Mountains appeared on the horizon before them, a less than imposing range that would have been lost amid the vastness of the Miskanthians. Only one peak stood apart from the rest, a large volcanic cone that slanted upward for more than a mile, twice the height of any nearby pinnacles. As the speeding barrah drew closer, they could easily make out the numerous streaks of solidified lava that had run down the mountain's side many hundreds of years past, or perhaps thousands, when the angry earth last chose to vent its fiery venom skyward. They now had little doubt that the corvine bird's destination was the cuplike crater high atop this dormant, though potentially volatile hill.

This range, though situated not far beyond a green veldt that teemed with all conceivable forms of beasts, appeared in itself as a drab, lifeless mound of mammoth rocks to the knowledgeable Kalkh. From this incomparable vantage point he had a clear view for miles in all directions. But he saw no streams, no snow-capped peaks, none of the beasts, predatory or otherwise, that were so much a part of his beloved Yushans, creatures that, more than likely, also existed in the Miskanthians. The granite canyons of this insignificant range were engulfed by deathly stillness, with only the occasional echoes of the barrah's flapping wings to pierce it. Tyron tore his gaze away in contempt and concentrated on the volcano, now less than two miles before them.

The barrah circled the broad crater three times before landing and, despite their increased headiness, the trio was able to peer within. Much to their amazement they did not gaze into a black, bottomless shaft, but rather a smooth, reddish-brown bowl, this barely a few yards below the crater's rim at its deepest point. Some inexplicable phenomenon had caused the immense lava flow to solidify instantly during its final emergence, thus creating the natural aerie now occupied by the immense bird.

Little more could be discerned, for the barrah dropped rapidly toward the bowl, the unexpected motion causing their stomachs to rise in their throats. It deposited them on the lava floor, and they were pinned tightly for a few seconds while the creature maintained its position. It then flew to the rim of the crater, where it perched upon its foremost set of claws. For more than a minute it eyed the captives with its wicked orbs, until finally it loosed a deafening screech that would have caused even the bravest of men to cringe. It then leaped from the rim and was soon gone from sight, though the terrible echoes lingered long past its departure.

After examining their bodies, which appeared none the worse for wear despite the ordeal, the three rose upon shaky legs and glanced around them. They had been deposited near the center of the bowl, the diameter of which measured over one hundred yards. There was nothing within twenty yards of them, save for a huge, perfectly oval boulder, its color a ghastly mottling of brown and purple. Beyond this stood a stack of haphazardly piled timbers, whole acacias, firs, and the like. Their purpose initially escaped Lanira and Dehril, but not so Tyron.

"As the small birds gather twigs, so does this barrah uproot whole trees," he told them. "This is its nest!"

"A nest!" Dehril exclaimed. "Then this rock—"

"It is an egg!" Lanira interjected.

Dehril nodded. "Then we are to be food for its young. But where are—?"

The query went unfinished, for the trees in front of them began to move as the hatchlings responded tardily to their parent's call. Four beaked heads rose above the timbers, and despite their recent torpor they immediately spotted the potential repast. They screeched as they flapped their underdeveloped wings ecstatically, and as a single unit they surged forth from the nest.

"To the rim, hurry!" Tyron ordered, though the others did not have to be prompted. They raced in the opposite direction, with Dehril the first to reach the edge. The Berboran leaned forward and gazed down, the sight causing him to stumble backward, where he nearly bowled over the Kalkh. Tyron could see that his face had turned a pale white.

"Thur! It-it is straight down!" Dehril gasped.

The Kalkh quickly satisfied his own curiosity regarding the sheer cliffs before turning to the others. "We must explore the entire rim," he told them. "It cannot all be—"

"There is no time!" Lanira screamed. "See! They come!"

The young, screeching barrahs were now in the center of the crater, having freed themselves from their erstwhile sanctuary. They utilized their two rear sets of claws in racing across the lava floor, and their trundling gait could almost have been considered comical, had one not stood in their path. Their feathers were colored a dull gray, the glistening wetness indicative of their recent hatching. All were of equivalent size, their height over nine feet as measured from their rearmost claws, on which they occasionally rocked back. Their clattering beaks left no doubts regarding the endless hunger that each possessed, this reflective of their species. The sight of the trio only whetted their appetites further.

"Lanira, can you handle a sword?" Tryon asked as the quartet of horrors drew nearer.

"Most women of the frontier can easily best the men of the city!" she replied haughtily.

Tyron smiled as he handed her his well-used blade. "Let us then separate. This tactic may confuse them, and enhance our chances of survival."

The Berboran drew his own sword, while Tyron pulled his dagger from its sheath. The latter stood his ground as the others strode warily to equidistant points on either side of him, the distance about ten yards. As Tyron had guessed, the uncomprehending young barrahs halted in their tracks, their minute brains not allowing them to understand why these morsels did not remain in one place for their convenience. Their shrill cries lessened to guttural questioning sounds as they cocked their heads. They still functioned as a singular entity, their life spans as yet too brief for them to act individually. The Kalkh realized this, and he had no intention of permitting them the opportunity to reevaluate the situation.

"At them, quickly," he ordered. "We will be afforded no better chance!"

They hastened toward the hatchlings, now huddled together in their confusion. Again they commenced their terrible screeching, and all but one backed away. This creature charged at Dehril, who was only a few yards away. Though surprised by the action, the agile Berboran managed to leap from the path of the snapping beak. Raking talons sought his flesh, a few causing minimal damage. But Dehril retained his balance, and with a powerful stroke he cleanly severed the barrah's head. Spurting gore flew everywhere as the body continued to scurry about reflexively, not crumpling for many seconds.

Tyron believed that this action would send the remaining barrahs fleeing; but, to his unfeigned shock, the opposite proved to be true. The trio appeared belligerent over the loss of their sibling, and they became determined to take out their ire on anything in their path. One of them broke toward Dehril, while the others, both ignoring the rapidly approaching Tyron, charged at Lanira, who happened to be in their line of vision.

The golden beauty, displaying no fear, selected one of the pair, and with her sword poised for thrusting she held her ground until the last possible moment. Then, as the screaming monstrosities neared to within a yard, she drove the lengthy blade into the thing's neck and leaped aside in a continuous motion. The barrah's screeches altered to sickening gurgles as brownish lifeblood poured from its mouth, and it expired in only seconds.

As Tyron raced toward the scene, he realized that Lanira's well-conceived action may yet prove her downfall. She had been unable to absorb the blow as she fell to the hard lava floor, and she now appeared stunned. The other barrah, after gazing upon its dead brother for a moment, turned its attention toward the fallen girl, and with a violent shriek it trundled toward her. Had the Kalkh not acted instinctively, the steel-like beak would undoubtedly have closed upon her. While barely slowing his stride, Tyron scooped up a fist-sized chunk of rock and hurled it at the thing, his unerring aim guiding the missile to the back of the barrah's head. The neck snapped up as the blow registered, this brief action allowing Tyron to narrow the gap. Before the bird could turn around to seek out its new tormentor the Kalkh leaped upon its back, and with one strong arm wrapped around its throat he plunged the dagger repeatedly into any potentially vulnerable spot. The barrah loosed a chilling scream as it tried desperately to cast off the unwanted rider, but its efforts were to no avail. The blade fell again and again, the foul blood of the creature dousing the sickened Tyron. But still he persisted, until, with a final shriek of anguish, the third of the barrahs fell to the lava surface, where it commenced its short-lived death throes.

The Kalkh raced to Lanira's side. She had regained consciousness in time to roll free from the dying barrah's sphere, where she otherwise would have been brutally slashed. After assuring Tyron that she was well the pair turned their attention to Dehril, and both were quickly able to reconstruct what had transpired during recent moments. The creature that set off after the Berboran had somehow managed to separate him from his sword, which had slid almost to the rim of the crater. Dehril had raced toward the weapon and was now close to retrieving it. But the barrah stayed right on his heels, and before Dehril's hand could close on the hilt, the thing knocked him forward. He stumbled toward the rim, his momentum such that, despite the upward curvature of the crater, he tumbled over the brink, with only his clutching fingers temporarily saving him from the fatal, plummeting journey.

With Lanira's cries ringing in his ears, Tyron raced across the lava floor. The feathered horror was perched on the crater's rim, directly above the helpless Dehril, who was moments away from a terrible death. But before the barrah could react, it was struck from behind by a force that most likely shattered bones in its undeveloped body. With a grotesque, sputtering screech it toppled over the rim, and the echoes were audible long after it had come to rest on a broad stone ledge, more than a quarter of a mile down.

Despite the force of the impact, Tyron's momentum still carried him forward, and for a few tense seconds he teetered precariously on the lip of the crater. But he caught his balance in time, much to the relief of Dehril, who was now pulled to safety by both the Kalkh and Lanira, the latter arriving only a moment earlier. The crater was now deathly still as the fatigued trio sought a brief respite.

"We'd best not tarry here too long," Tyron finally said. "One of the parents, perhaps both, may return at any minute."

This revelation proved more than enough incentive for the others. After regaining their weapons they followed the knowledgeable mountain man around the edge of the crater, where, after gazing thoughtfully for long seconds down the western slope, he motioned for them to halt.

"See," he told them as he pointed downward. "This side is not exceptionally steep, and there are many footholds. We should have no difficulty in making the descent."

The others, far less skilled in such matters, acceded to the wisdom of the Kalkh. But before topping the narrow rim of the crater, their attention was diverted by two wide-spread occurrences. Lanira was the first to notice the small black speck in the cloud-filled sky far to the east, and she pointed it out to the others. None had to be apprised of what it was, for its destination was evident. They peered at it for only seconds, when they heard a sound, this one considerably closer. Across the lava floor, bits of the thick eggshell were pushed out from the inside as the last of the monstrous brood began to hatch.

As one, they scurried over the crater's edge and commenced their reckless descent along the side of the volcano.

CHAPTER ELEVEN: THE FANOLLS

With the mountain-bred Tyron setting the pace the western slope, though far from the gentle declivity he had professed it to be, was negotiated without incident. The stunted peaks soon swallowed the outer shell of the penetrating vent, and they were able to find more than adequate concealment amid the variegated formations. They could easily hear the frenzied screeches of the giant barrah from high above them, as the corvine bird bore witness to the bloody scene in its nest. But whatever terrible vengeance the creature sought to wreak would have to be carried out elsewhere for, even it if chanced to spot them, its great bulk would keep the raking talons far from their flesh. The hills were their sanctuary, one that they almost were sorry to surrender when the time came.

"In a way, we owe the barrah a debt of gratitude," Tyron stated, as they peered upward at the elevated bowl. "How many days of journeying, how many leagues of unspeakable dangers, did it save us from by bearing us as far north as it did?"

"Then tell me, my friend, why I somehow do not feel the desire to offer it a debt of thanks," Dehril said.

Lanira shuddered. "Nor do I. But Tyron is right, for perhaps the gods willed it to be this way. We are closer to our destination than we could have ever dared imagine in so brief a time."

Dehril nodded. "That is true; however, if the rest of the land is like what we so recently passed over, we will indeed be sorely pressed to reach the boundaries of Vorhashekkh."

"We will not know this unless we try," the Kalkh said testily. "Let us go."

The others complied without question, though their bodies proved far less willing than their hearts. By the time the sun reached the far horizon, little more than an hour later, they had descended barely a few hundred yards. They paused to rest for the night on a narrow ledge, where they huddled together to protect themselves from a chilling wind that had begun to lash at the range with surprising force. Their furs, as well as their skins of water and most of the food pouches, had been left unwillingly at their earlier campsite, many hundreds of miles to the south. Only Dehril's tasteless fruit layers remained, for not once since the beginning of the journey had he untied the pouch containing them from around his waist. They chewed absently on the leathery victuals, the small quantity proving less than satisfying. Thirsty, cold, far beyond the point of fatigue, the trio nonetheless managed to find a few restless, scattered hours of slumber through the night, this despite the incessant cries of the mourning barrah.

Because of their position on the western declivity the light of dawn was a bit longer in reaching them, and accordingly they waited until an hour past sunrise to resume their descent. Tyron's unmatched lore enabled them to traverse precipitous trails, find handholds and footholds where none appeared visible. He even discovered water in the form of a tiny rivulet that emerged along the base of a shale facing, a trickle that the others would undoubtedly have passed without noticing. The precious liquid was not easy to extract in any quantity, but before long they were all at least partially satisfied. Despite their anxieties, Lanira and Dehril followed the Kalkh's lead without question, and by the early part of the afternoon they once again walked upon level ground.

"You know," Dehril mused as they rested at the foot of a vertical cliff, "I am beginning to understand the exhilaration you feel while in the mountains. I admit that the heights still scare me, though not nearly as much as I expected them to. That you could revel in such a life is something that I now see more clearly."

"And I," Lanira added. "My people, though they dwell in the shadows of the Miskanthians, have never been enamored of the mountains, most likely because of the terrible creatures that haunt them. But my father and I occasionally braved the lower peaks during the daylight hours to hunt for wild goats, and I can remember the sense of freedom that I felt as I gazed over the seemingly insignificant land that spread out below me. Such is the feeling that I experienced this day."

Tyron nodded thoughtfully as a slight smile creased his face. "I will yet make mountaineers of you two," he told them.

The pair laughed, while Tyron turned his attention to the land that stretched north before them. Less than fifty yards from where they sat was the perimeter of a broad savanna carpeted by tall, yellowish grass that waved gently in the afternoon breeze. About three miles distant it terminated at the edge of a wood. Only Zeth knew what roamed amid these trees to further jeopardize their trek, though, if nothing else, it would provide them shelter from the vengeful barrah, which still voiced its threatening cry as it hovered atop the lofty aerie.

During the initial fifty yards they felt naked, exposed, with no concealment. But fortune saw the corvine bird on the far side of the volcano during the few tense minutes on the open plain, and they reached the tall grass unchallenged only an instant before the creature again appeared. To their surprise it was accompanied by another, undoubtedly its mate. Both perched on the crater's rim for many minutes, their combined shrieks echoing through the many canyons. Then, with their immense wings flapping vigorously, they set off toward the east. Their outlines grew smaller, until finally they vanished from sight, much to the relief of the trio.

Passage through the dense, waist-high grass was not achieved with any speed, though with the threat of the barrahs gone, they hardly minded the inconvenience. They encountered untold thousands of insects, a few varieties of which found their sweaty flesh most agreeable and caused them numerous annoying bites. But other than two small, tusked pigs, both of which scurried away as they neared, they saw no other signs of life, and within two hours they arrived at the boundary of the wood.

Coniferous trees dotted the forest, their height and girth such as to indicate immeasurable age. The sun's rays trickled downward sporadically through the dense boughs, though despite their inability to view the orb with regularity, they never once strayed from their path. They were ever alert, prepared for anything that the cryptic land might issue forth as a challenge. But their vigilance went untested, for the wood proved to be a place of tranquility, with only the occasional song of a bird in the distance to disturb the stillness. Three streams were crossed during the day, one of these deep enough for them to cleanse their much-abused bodies. By the time dusk approached, they had traversed a considerable number of miles and were well satisfied with their progress.

Unlike the comfortable climate of the afternoon, the night air proved frigid, which necessitated the lighting of a fire. The forest floor was covered by thick boughs that had fallen from overhead at one time or another, which provided them with more than enough fuel for the duration of their respite. They took turns on guard, still not allowing the serenity of the wood to lull them into laxity. But nothing else, save for the ceaseless chorus of insects, was in evidence. All had a more than adequate amount of rest, though Tyron was still troubled on occasion by the unrelenting nightmares. Had it not been for Lanira's sweet, soothing voice he would have found slumber impossible.

The subsequent four days were much like the first, and because of this they were able to put a considerable amount of leagues behind them. Their almost leisurely pace allowed cuts and bruises to heal, a fact for which all, especially the Kalkh, were thankful. Water was plentiful, but food was hard to find, forcing them to rely on the leathery fare still carried by Dehril, which now dwindled rapidly. The lack of food proved the only damper in what was otherwise a peaceful interlude in their long and deadly trek. Why this place offered such a glaring contrast to the terrible land south of the volcano, they dared not even guess.

By mid-morning of the sixth day the majestic trees began to dwindle, and within hours they had left the quiet wood behind them. Rolling hillocks now stretched north as far as they could see, this not a considerable distance, due to the height of many. They followed a naturally formed path that snaked through these knolls, one that was dry and crusty, unlike the soft loam of the forest floor. This altering of the terrain, along with the limited visibility, served to heighten their awareness to a point not known for many days, as they once again felt exposed to the unknown land. Tyron, more so than the others, experienced much uneasiness, as though hundreds of unseen eyes were cast upon him. He chose not to share this feeling with Lanira or Dehril.

The first of the figures appeared atop a knobby hillock, about two hundred yards before them. There were at least ten, though from such a distance their features were not discernible. With slow, deliberate steps they descended to the path where, three abreast, they strode toward the trio, who now stood frozen in their tracks. Dehril did not glance at Tyron as he waved his arms at the approaching beings.

"Turn back, quickly!" he cried. "You know not what you are doing. Let us pass in peace."

But still they came, either not understanding his words, or not caring. He glanced at the Kalkh, who snapped, "We must seek a way to bypass the fools! Let us retreat."

They whirled about, where, to their amazement, they faced nearly a score on the trail behind them, these no more than fifty yards distant. In fact, the hills on either side of them were now dotted by hundreds of the beings, leaving them with no outlet.

Tyron sighed. "If their intention be to take us as their prisoners, then let us submit. Our internment will not be of considerable duration."

Like docile lambs they quietly watched the circle tighten, and for the first time they had a clear look at their would-be captors. Each appeared to have been shaped from a similar mold, for it was difficult to distinguish between any two. They were all short of stature, this more pronounced by the stooped manner in which they walked. Human characteristics were clear, though they were definitely of a lower order. Filthy, matted hair covered nearly every bit of flesh, save for a circular, exposed area around the mid-section, and one near the small of the back. Their torsos were as thick as wine casks, the arms and legs proportionately as large. Mouths were not visible through the shaggy beards, flat, black noses only partially so. But their wide, bloodshot eyes were more than evident as they peered wickedly at the intruders. All were similarly armed with knobby clubs, crude weapons at best, though doubtless formidable in their hands. None wore outer garments of any kind save for flimsy, animal-hide loincloths, these doing little to confine their bulging genitalia. They were a menacing lot, to say the least, and Lanira pressed herself more tightly against Tyron as they neared.

Once within ten yards of the trio the brutes halted, their silence adding to the tautness of the scene. A single figure then emerged from the group on the road before them, the girth of this one nearly half again that of his fellows. He swaggered boldly toward the three, his leering eyes affixed on the beauty from Shaaf. Even when he addressed them, he did not tear his gaze away from her. They found much difficulty in understanding the words, for the language spoken, while like their own, was of the most primitive, rudimentary form.

"I be Gharf," he grunted, "and I rule the land of the Fanolls for this many miles around." He displayed ten fingers, and for long, tedious seconds he opened and closed his hands continuously, while none of the trio bothered to count. Once satisfied, he continued: "Throw your weapons on the ground. You are prisoners of the Fanolls. The she belongs to Gharf."

Lanira felt Tyron's body stiffen, and she shook her head admonishingly at him, likely fearing that he would attempt a rash action. While casting their steel to the road she whispered, "Do not concern yourself, my love. The swine will not touch me, this I swear. It will be over soon."

The golden-haired beauty, her head held high, strode haughtily past the obese fellow, while a score of Fanolls converged on Dehril and Tyron, their foul odor causing the pair to turn their noses up in disgust. Their hands were tied tightly behind them with thin strips of supple rawhide, and they were urged none-too-gently along the northward path. Because of the crush of countless bodies their attention was confined to the road before them, and they were unable to catch a glimpse of either Lanira or her captor. Beneath his breath, Tyron prayed that he had not made the wrong decision in allowing this to come to pass, for he knew that they could easily have sent scores of these Fanolls to Sharn before falling. Now, only time would tell.

About three hundred yards farther north they traversed a slight incline that split two knobby hillocks on the left of the road, which placed them on an almost identical path leading westward. Throughout the remainder of the long day they followed the twisting path, while the Fanolls, with the need for silence negated, taunted their captives mercilessly. But Dehril and Tyron endured all of this stoically, until finally, near dusk, they arrived at the perimeter of a broad savanna. There, half a mile across the brownish grass, sat the Fanoll village, a fact more than obvious by the bold way in which the large band approached it. For that day, the journey had ended.

The village, which reeked as badly as its inhabitants, consisted of countless shabby hovels, each haphazardly constructed of mud and straw. Scrawny curs nipped at the heels of the pair as they were paraded through the center of the foul place, while unattractive, ill-tempered children hurled stones at them. But worst of all were the Fanoll women, grotesque females who might easily have been mistaken for their mates, had it not been for their ponderous breasts. They shrieked foul insults at the strangers, and they would have torn their eyes from their sockets with long, unclean fingernails had the men not driven them away with their cudgels. *I will feel little remorse upon seeing this vile place expunged,* Tyron thought.

At the far end of the village, the two were cast into one of the larger hovels they had yet observed, this likely a prison hut. There were at least ten other figures within the darkened confines, all bound in a like manner, though some, undoubtedly the more recalcitrant ones, wore thongs around their ankles as well. The latter crouched pathetically on straw mats that were infested with all manner of wriggling vermin. Some of the prisoners came forth to investigate the new arrivals, who saw that they were no different than the creatures that brought them here. Tyron and Dehril kicked them away disgustedly, though the ones able to walk continued to come forth for long minutes. But finally, the furor caused by their arrival died down, and they sought out one of the least filthy corners. There they slumped to the ground, their bodies overwhelmed by fatigue.

"What now?" Dehril asked.

"We wait," the Kalkh replied. "But we'd best not sleep at the same time, for I fear that some of these devils have been pent up far too long."

With nighttime upon them, they were afforded only a meager amount of light through the narrow door from a few of the cooking fires in the village. During the first few hours the most depraved of the occupants sought to reach them, but each time they were repelled by the heel of a sandal. Neither as yet had attempted to find slumber for, despite their exhaustion, they could not bring themselves to close their eyes in such a pestilent hole. But Tyron finally chanced to gaze at the Berboran and saw that his friend could withstand little more.

"Dehril, please! Try and get some rest. I will keep—"

"See! Here comes another one," Dehril interrupted. "Let me have at him, and then perhaps I will sleep."

Tyron nodded, and the Berboran made ready to thrust the approaching form away. Both immediately noticed that this fellow was not one of the three or four that had troubled them since their arrival; in fact, this was the first time they had a clear look at him, for he had remained in a far corner throughout. Both his hands and feet were bound, but, rather than crawl through the filth, he utilized his knees to traverse the hovel. He paused less than two yards from them, where he eyed the pair curiously. He was considerably taller than the Fanolls, and his shoulders, even in light of the obvious deprivation he had suffered, were not stooped. His eyes, as observed in the dim light, denoted intelligence. When he spoke, his tone was strong, well-modulated, this in spite of the fact that the words were meant for none but themselves to hear.

"I would talk to you," he said.

"You may approach," Dehril replied.

The middle-aged fellow shuffled forward, until he was within a foot of them. He was a large man indeed, his height three or four inches above their own, his muscles steel-like in appearance. Only by trickery, or by overwhelming force of numbers, could the Fanolls have captured the like of him. If the latter, then surely he had taken the lives of many before succumbing.

"Who are you, and where are you from?" he asked.

"I am called Dehril, and this is Tyron. We have journeyed here from Berbora."

The fellow thought for a moment, before saying, "I am not familiar with the village. No matter; you are not like these Fanoll devils, that is clear. Perhaps we can be of help to one another. I am Vohon of Dosheel."

"What do you have in mind, Vohon?" Tyron asked.

"One's strength ebbs further with each day spent at the labors that these Fanolls assign. I have been here only two days, after they took me in my sleep, and already I sense the early signs of weakness, as you will. If we can somehow free one another, then we may yet fight our way out of this reeking pit, or at least die in the attempt."

Tyron shrugged. "You will be freed soon enough, Vohon, and you will not even have to raise a finger. Your timing was ill chosen, I assure you."

"My presence here is not by choice, this I assure *you*," Vohon snapped. "But what are you talking about? Your words, they—"

Dehril, with a nod from the Kalkh, detailed all to the disbelieving Vohon, who absorbed it in muted horror. For long moments after the narrative he stared absently at one wall of the hovel, his inner torment not visible to those who observed him. Then, with a shrug of resignation, he again faced the pair, and they were surprised to note the grim smile that he wore.

"If this is to be my fate, then so be it!" he announced. "But I pray that I live long enough to see these devils fall. Promise me one thing, this I beg of you."

"Yes?"

"Do not leave my body to rot upon this foul ground, but return it instead to Dosheel, there to be buried in the rich soil of my homeland."

"It will be done," Tyron stated, "this I swear!"

"Good. Then I suppose that there is nothing left to be done, save to rest. I will share turns with you through the night, so that these ghouls might be kept away from us. They have had little to eat, you know."

Vohon, informed of his possible death only minutes earlier, placed his back against the wall of the hovel, where he fell asleep almost instantly. With a shrug, Tyron motioned for the Berboran to do the same, and he complied. Only when his eyes could no longer remain open, this nearly three hours later, did he awaken Dehril. Thus passed their first, their only night in the verminous prison hovel of the Fanolls.

###

The malady struck more rapidly than any of them would have thought possible. Shortly before dawn a terrible scream of agony arose from the heart of the village, this silencing the nocturnal sounds of the savanna. Vohon, who had been standing guard, woke the others, who were immediately aware of what transpired. Once again they were forced to relive the nightmarish days of Berbora's end, as shriek after pathetic shriek poured forth from various parts of the village. In their own hut, three of the weakest prisoners had already succumbed, quite inexplicably in silence, while all but one of the others were gripped by the fires of unquenchable fever. Vohon, himself not yet affected, was as shocked by the seeming indifference on the faces of his two cellmates as he was by the ugly blotches that spread rapidly upon the visible flesh of the unfortunate ones. Though he had steeled himself as best he could, he was hardly prepared for the reality of it, and at times he was forced to turn away.

As the Fanolls perished all around them, Tyron loosened Dehril's bonds by gnawing through them. This proved a relatively simple matter, for the Kalkh's teeth had long since been strengthened by years of chewing on the tough, delectable rasha nut of the Yushans. Once free, the Berboran untied the others and, after restoring circulation to numbed members, they made their way slowly to the door of the hovel. No guards remained outside . . . none, at least, that could cause them any delay.

"Vohon. Do you know which of the huts belongs to Gharf?" Tyron asked.

The Dosheelian nodded. "I was taken there on the day they captured me. It is the one adorned by countless feathers, on the far side of the village."

"You will lead us there!" the Kalkh ordered.

They raced headlong through the village, though try as they might they could scarce remain oblivious to the atrocities that surrounded them at every turn. The symptoms of the Scamban plague were identical, but the reactions of these primitive people were quite different than those of the Berborans. Like crazed, cornered beasts they lashed out at one another in the throes of their torment. The claw-like nails of the females rent the flesh of any that strayed within their sphere, children not excepted, while the clubs of the snarling, depraved males caved in skull after skull. Tyron, Dehril and Vohon curled their way around spilled entrails, spattered brains, bloodless faces twisted in horror. The Dosheelian, who had seen much in his forty-five years of life, had heretofore doubted whether anything could exist to affect him so. His mind was sufficiently changed that morning.

Two dozen or more of the wretched beings were felled by the trio on their way to Gharf's hovel, with little consideration given to gender. Vohon was the only casualty, having received a deep scratch on his left shoulder. But the burly fellow ignored this as they continued, and within moments they arrived at the gaudy hut.

"Remain here," Tyron told the others. "This will not take long."

The Kalkh parted the flap and peered in carefully. Despite the dimness, he immediately absorbed the scene and was forced to stifle a gasp, lest his presence become known too soon. Lanira, *his* Lanira, lay naked on a straw mat in one corner of the filthy room, her perfectly formed body now bruised and bleeding in places too numerous to count. The grotesque Gharf stood in the center of the hovel, a knobby cudgel raised high above his left ear. His back was turned toward Tyron, who could clearly see the dark blotches on the exposed flesh. The Fanoll ruler had also contracted the Scamban plague.

"You *she-witch*!" he shrieked. "You bring this upon my people! You will die for this—!"

Too weakened to defend herself any longer, the Shaafian beauty lay helpless as the brute neared. Tyron scanned the room quickly, noting that their appropriated weapons were strewn haphazardly near the door, only inches from his feet. In a swift, silent motion he scooped up a longsword and raced across the small room. The steel was guided by more than his muscles as it sliced cleanly through the thick neck, his momentum nearly causing the Kalkh to lose his balance. Gharf's head rolled to another corner of the hut, the expression of disbelief still frozen upon it, while the spurting torso crumpled to the floor, the club grasped in its nerveless fingers.

"Tyron!" Lanira screamed, and with an effort that even she had thought herself incapable of, she staggered to her feet to meet him. The Kalkh held her tightly for a moment, though he knew that there was little time to spare.

"Lanira, we have to go! But—I must know; did he . . .?"

"He did not!" she sobbed.

"May Zeth be thanked! Come."

After retrieving the weapons, as well as Lanira's tattered garment, they exited the hut, where Dehril and Vohon awaited them. The sounds of the Fanoll atrocities assailed their ears as they crossed the savanna, the relatively short distance of which seemed interminable because of the girl's injuries. Less than halfway across, Tyron gathered her up in his arms, despite her protests, and within minutes they were again surrounded by the hills. The unbearable cries soon faded behind them, much to their relief.

CHAPTER TWELVE: THE MOUNTAIN OF THE GODS

Vohon, unquestionably familiar with the surrounding terrain, guided them confidently between the loftier of the knolls, while a few of the least imposing ones were topped with ease. Initially they journeyed toward the east, a direction hardly to the liking of Tyron, though for the time being he chose not to say anything. His greatest concern at the moment was for the battered Lanira, who, perhaps mercifully, had succumbed to the folds of darkness shortly after leaving the veldt. Despite offers of assistance by his companions, the Kalkh refused to relinquish his hold on the young beauty. Not until an hour had passed, when they arrived at the edge of a small brook, did they pause for a respite. Tyron placed the girl gently on the soft earth.

After hastily restoring circulation to his numbed arms, the worried mountain man began ministering tenderly to Lanira's many wounds, few of which proved to be as severe as he had first feared. Once these had been cared for, he dabbed at her face with the icy brook water, a few drops of which managed to trickle down her throat. Within a minute her eyelids parted. The Shaafian beauty gazed upward into the anxious face, and she proffered a meager smile as she caressed Tyron's cheek with her slim fingers.

"I-I am well," she stammered. "Thank you, my love."

With these words Lanira again fell asleep, though this time her breathing was steady, and she appeared to be resting peacefully. Tyron observed her for a few minutes before he was convinced, and only then did he look to his own needs, which, aside from a burning thirst, were few. Vohon was stunned to see the Kalkh display few signs of fatigue, despite carrying the girl for nearly two miles; but Dehril, who knew him well, showed no surprise at the efforts of his strong-willed friend.

While resting comfortably upon the loam alongside the tributary, Dehril asked Vohon, "How far to the east does the land of your people lie?"

The massive fellow shook his head. "Dosheel sits to the north of us, about a two-day trek. We might have headed toward it from the Fanoll village, save for one thing: an immense fissure, caused by some ancient upheaval, separates the land for miles in all directions, making passage impossible. By journeying east we have avoided the worst of it, and our path to Dosheel lies true from here. From what you told me in the prison hovel regarding your destination, it appears that we will be traveling together for a bit longer. If . . . if I should perish from that which devastated the Fanolls, then you will not even be inconvenienced in carrying out the favor I requested."

Tyron, upon hearing the Dosheelian's words, averted his eyes, while Dehril shook his head sadly. Vohon, now cognizant of the Kalkh's torment, would have spoken to him, but the quick-thinking Berboran chose to alter the subject.

"What of the land we seek? Have you any idea of the distance to Vorhashekkh?"

"I can tell you that precisely," Vohon replied, a slight shudder perceptible. "The border of the dark kingdom lies little more than fifteen leagues beyond Dosheel."

"Zeth!" Tyron exclaimed. "Then we have indeed come a long way!"

Dehril nodded. "To be sure. Tell us, Vohon, what do you know of Vorhashekkh?"

"Dosheelians know much of the dark kingdom, though it is knowledge we would just as soon be freed of, I assure you. The core of the evil lies about twenty-five leagues past the southern boundary. There, within a few leagues of one another, stand the citadels of the Three, your destination. But know this: even if you are fortunate enough to bypass the many barbaric tribes as you traverse the land, this questionable at best, you will find each of the strongholds more than formidable. I cannot say for certain exactly what they are like, not having ever seen them; yet I know that forces beyond our understanding see to the security of the Three. They are nigh unapproachable."

"And just how do you come by this knowledge?" Tyron asked.

"We of Dosheel have established an uneasy truce with some of the Vorhashekkh tribes, who journey to our land so that we might barter. They take the crops of our rich fields, food that they are incapable of growing themselves, and in exchange they bring us crude ores, from which we fabricate our tools and weapons. Though coarse beings at best, they nevertheless seem to know much of what is transpiring across the dark kingdom, and they are seldom hesitant to share their knowledge."

"If these tribes are as you described them," Dehril said, "then why do they not utilize force in taking what they desire from your people?"

Vohon shook his head. "You are unfamiliar with Dosheel, and therefore could not understand. My village is nestled amidst a fertile canyon, this located high in the Tengavirego Mountains. Only a few tenuous paths are negotiable to those of limited skills, and these are always well guarded. Those of Vorhashekkh despise the mountains, and seldom do they ascend more than a few hundred yards, though even if they were able to, we would not allow it. All confrontations are made on our terms, without exception."

"Then Dosheel is—a mountain kingdom!" the Kalkh exclaimed.

"Why, yes." Vohon appeared puzzled by Tyron's reaction. "Does this matter?"

Tyron's wistful gaze turned northward, but Dehril faced the Dosheelian and said, "Not yet, my friend. But who knows?"

Though now totally confused, Vohon chose not to pursue the strange behavior of the pair. Instead, he stated, "If . . . when we reach Dosheel, I will see to it that you are well provisioned for the remainder of your trek. I admire your courage, and would see you given every possible chance to succeed."

"Your kindness is appreciated, Vohon," Dehril said. "But what of your people? Would they not be hostile toward strangers?"

Vohon shrugged. "It matters little what they may think, for I am their bantir."

Subsequent to this revelation, few words passed between the tired men, all of whom were preoccupied by their individual thoughts. But after half an hour of idleness they knew that departure was a necessity, lest they be set upon by any of the crazed Fanolls that might have fled the devastated village. Tyron hated to awaken Lanira, who slumbered deeply, and accordingly he gathered her up in his arms as gently as possible. Yet in spite of his efforts the young beauty's eyes snapped open, and the Kalkh cursed his clumsiness.

"You need not scold yourself, my love." Lanira smiled as she rubbed the last vestiges of sleep from her eyes. "I was near awakening on my own, this I swear. Please, put me down, for I am quite capable of traveling now."

Despite his doubts, Tyron complied. Lanira's initial steps were uncertain, but with each succeeding one her confidence grew, for the movements caused her little pain. Within minutes they were beyond another hillock. The Kalkh's sole eye at first remained glued to the strong-willed girl, though as much with love and respect as in concern. But he need not have worried, for at no time during the lengthy day did she display the least sign of faltering. She maintained any pace that the sturdy Vohon chose to set, and on more than one occasion they found her four or five paces ahead of them, to their amusement.

The fissure that Vohon had earlier alluded to appeared before them within the first hour. It was little more than a couple of feet wide where they crossed; but to the west of them, as far as the hilly terrain would allow them to see, it spread out into a gaping chasm, in some places more than a hundred feet across. The black, inhospitable pit seemed bottomless, and all were glad to leave it behind them.

Save for an occasional hare or bird, they observed no other signs of life during the long day, and their progress was not slowed in the least. They paused for the night atop a flat-topped hill, one that afforded them a clear view for many yards in all directions, where each, save Lanira, took a turn at sentry. Though she protested, Tyron was adamant in his desire to see her rest go unbroken, which it did. The night passed uneventfully, and all were refreshed when they resumed the journey shortly after dawn.

By mid-morning the rolling landscape had fallen away behind the travelers, depositing them on a semi-fertile veldt of saffron-tinged grass, the blades of which were scarcely more than two inches high. Herds of chevrotains, as well as other oddly colored ruminants, dotted the yellow plain, some barely raising their heads in acknowledgement of the passing foursome, others thundering away in terror. But the presence of these creatures did not hold their attention for long, for during their first hour on the veldt they bore witness to a sight that was, at the least, awe-inspiring. A dull gray haze, which had limited visibility to little more than a couple of miles since the previous morning, now dissipated, affording them an unhindered view northward. The sun's rays glinted off the white-crowned peaks of the Tengavirego Mountains, these rising to towering heights and blotting the horizon before them. So exquisite was the scene that it appeared almost unnatural, as though a visionary artist had searched his soul to create a watercolor monument worthy of the gods, utilizing the azure sky as his canvas, and the earth itself as his easel. Vohon beamed proudly as he gazed upon his home, while the others paused in disbelief, their tongues lost to them for long minutes.

"I-I never thought that I would say this," Tyron finally stammered. "Next to this range, my own Yushans would be as hills."

Dehril nodded. "It is indeed a splendid sight."

"Some of the peaks rise nearly four miles above the level of the ground," Vohon told them. "At no time during the year are the snows gone from their summits. See there!" He indicated one particular titan, a towering sentinel some miles to the northeast, the top of which was obliterated by dense clouds. "We call it the Mountain of the Gods, for surely its crown reaches upward into the abode of the Masters themselves. Among the Dosheelians, it is a mark of great skill and courage to ascend it. A few succeed, though most are turned back. Some are even killed. I stood atop it in my fifteenth year, alongside my father, and have since scaled it three times on my own."

Tyron, his arm around Lanira's waist, stared longingly at the Mountain of the Gods, and none but the golden beauty heard the words that he uttered softly: "I will climb you someday, this I swear!"

The trek resumed, and with each mile the mountains loomed larger before them. By the early part of the afternoon the land had begun to slope upward gently, but this hardly slowed them, despite the rapid pace that the eager Vohon set. The bantir of Dosheel, if anything, appeared more vigorous since their departure from the Fanoll village, and all, including himself, knew that he had avoided the Scamban malady. Tyron had already offered more than a score of silent thanks to Zeth for this.

Two hours before dusk they stood at the base of a sharp incline after having crossed a narrow mesa. Here, Vohon motioned for the others to stop, and he addressed them: "Atop this slope is the start of a trail leading up to Dosheel. I . . . this is difficult to say. My people are not far from here. . . ." He paused.

"Save your words, Vohon," Tyron stated, placing a firm hand on the bantir's shoulder. "I will go no farther. Dehril will accompany you and receive your kind offering."

The relieved Dosheelian glanced at Dehril, who asked him, "Will I be able to rejoin the others before sunset?"

After peering at the arcing sun, Vohon replied, "We will be fortunate to reach my village by dusk. Even those born to the mountains are loath to risk the traverse during the dark hours. It would be wise for you to remain there overnight."

"Then Lanira will accompany you to Dosheel," Tyron said. "She—"

"I will remain here with you!" the Shaafian beauty stated emphatically, her arms crossed.

The Kalkh shrugged, though he could not have been more pleased. Dehril and Vohon, after a few hearty laughs, offered their hands in a parting gesture.

"Your food will suffice for the night," the bantir said, indicating a meager quantity of thick-skinned fruit that he had discovered on the veldt. "As for water, you will find a trickle amidst a knobby outcropping at the far end of the mesa. I need not explain any further, Tyron, for I sense that you are well versed in the ways of the mountains. We'll rendezvous on this spot shortly after dawn, and I will guide you through the Tengaviregos."

Dehril scrambled up the hill at the heels of the agile Vohon, and once atop the ledge they glanced downward at Lanira and Tyron, who were waving. After returning the gesture they retreated a few steps, the pair below now gone from their sight. The rock-strewn shelf, no more than five yards in width, terminated at the base of a broad escarpment, the practically sheer sides of which rose high overhead. Dehril immediately spotted the narrow traverse, a tenuous path little wider than a foot. He gazed questioningly at the Dosheelian, who smiled.

"If it is any consolation, this is the worst that it will be. Just remember one thing: haste is of no value here."

Vohon mounted the traverse, his back pressed tightly against the escarpment, and with deliberate movements he began the ascent. The Berboran immediately followed, his eyes intent on everything done by his guide. They circled the cliffs at a gentle angle, the ledge soon disappearing behind them. Only once did Dehril chance to gaze downward, where he saw that only a few inches of stone beneath his sandals separated him from numerous jagged outcroppings on the floor of a canyon, more than a quarter-mile below. He quickly averted his eyes, all the while doing his best to force the thought of such a terrible death from his mind.

For more than half an hour the traverse spiraled upward, and on two occasions it appeared to narrow even more, if such were possible. Dehril sweated profusely, despite the coolness of the mountain air, though at no time did he voice his anxiety to Vohon, who continued to sidle deliberately along the thin shelf. But finally the path widened, until they were able to stride forward with quicker, more purposeful steps, much to the Berboran's relief. Though still a hazardous trail, it seemed like one of his former city's broad avenues by comparison. His confidence grew, though at no time did this new self-assurance approach cockiness, for he had heard far too many stories of the mountains from Tyron, and he knew that they must always be respected.

They encountered the first Dosheelian near dusk, a swarthy, well-muscled youth of about eighteen. He stood in their path, his fingers tightened around the oak shaft of a finely made javelin. Only when he recognized the foremost of the pair did his tension ease. He averted the gleaming tip of the weapon and nodded curtly at Vohon, a gesture that was returned. Then, with the formalities over, the two grinning figures embraced, the sounds of their backslapping echoing through the stone sentinels.

"How good to see you, Uncle!" the youth roared. "We feared that your hunting expedition had ended in tragedy."

"It is good to be back, Rajhok," the bantir replied. "Dehril, come and meet Rajhok, the son of my sister."

The two clasped hands, and after a few more words to his nephew, Vohon motioned Dehril on. Three more sentries were encountered along the incline, all kin to the bantir. Then, with the red sun inches below the western horizon, they left the traverse for the floor of a broad canyon, one ringed entirely by sheer precipices and lofty crags of indescribable shapes and hues. Vohon had returned to Dosheel.

Finely built wooden cabins, at least six or seven hundred of them, sat amid well cultivated, bountiful fields and meadows of tall grass, the latter dotted with herds of goats and other domesticated creatures. Comely Dosheelians, men and women alike, tended the crops, while children and elders watched over the beasts. A well-beaten dirt path split one of the pastures on its way to the heart of the village, and it was along this road that Vohon led his guest. But their progress was slow, for the bantir was quickly recognized by his people, and they hastened forth joyously to greet him. Soon the pair was engulfed by a sea of humanity, all seeking to place a hand of welcome upon their beloved chieftain.

The throng suddenly parted in deference to two women, the faces of both streaked with tears of joy as they hurried toward Vohon, arms outstretched. They were both beautiful, and Dehril at first thought them to be sisters, so much alike did they appear. Only upon closer scrutiny did he realize that one was undoubtedly of a like age to the bantir, while the other was younger than him. Their complexions, unlike most of the Dosheelians, were creamy white, their lengthy, cascading hair a tawny hue. Both were possessed of great natural beauty, their faces unadorned in any manner. The former covered Vohon's grinning face with passionate kisses, while the other waited impatiently for a chance to embrace the massive fellow, which she soon did. Once done, the Dosheelian chieftain wrapped his arms around the pair and guided them toward Dehril.

"This is Thiana, my wife, and Veleann, our daughter," he told the Berboran, his pride more than evident. "My women, I would have you meet Dehril, who I am proud to call friend."

The two greeted Dehril cheerfully, and he responded in a like manner. But while he addressed both of them, he found that he could not tear his eyes away from Veleann. The lissome beauty wore thick furs to ward off the chilled mountain air, though this scarcely sufficed to conceal her perfectly sculpted figure. Her radiant face was highlighted by a pair of soft brown eyes, these denoting compassion, while her crimson lips, formed in a pleasing smile, silently begged to be kissed. The Berboran shook his head to be freed of the spell, an action that was noted by most. Vohon laughed uproariously as Dehril's face reddened, while Thiana nodded knowingly. None of them, Veleann included, appeared to be angered by his interest in the mountain beauty.

After seemingly endless introductions to other Dosheelians, Dehril was led to the utilitarian cabin of Vohon, where the earliest hints of a pending feast were already in evidence. His escort was Veleann, who had slipped her hand into his easily, without hesitation. He was only vaguely aware of other people issuing words of welcome as he passed, for her proximity alone was more than enough to make his head swim. Neither spoke, though emotions long dormant in the Berboran were already beginning to surface, and he could sense that she felt the same. For a moment, just a moment, Dehril forgot all else, including his avowed responsibility to Tyron. Save for Veleann, nothing else mattered.

The banquet commenced in earnest, and the two were separated, for many were the eager ears that desired knowledge of this traveler, and the strange land that he had come from. Between mouthfuls of sumptuous food and heady wine he did his best to satisfy them all, though his eyes continually scanned the throng for a hint of the one who had captivated him. But the crush of Dosheelians was great, and on only two occasions was he even afforded a glimpse of the girl. Though overwhelmed by the warmth and acceptance of these people, he silently wished that all, save for her, would disappear from the village, at least for a short while.

Interminable hours passed, until Vohon finally sought him out and led him away from the doting crowd. The bantir had consumed more than a few skins of Dosheelian wine, though he maintained control of his senses. He indicated the far end of the village, and with his arm draped over Dehril's shoulder, he guided him along the narrow dirt path.

"Undoubtedly you weary of answering all of the questions," he stated. "Also, you must be fatigued from our journey, for I know that I am. A cabin has been prepared for you, where you may rest undisturbed until morning. But first, I have news that will be of interest to you and the others. From one of my people

I learned that the Hemghels, a nomadic tribe of Vorhashekkh, approached the base of the northern peaks only days earlier, in order to barter. They told of a new alliance being formed by the Three, something that has not been attempted since the prime of their fathers. With this union, they would seek to crush the unspeakable Cuhthic of Lamnagha."

Dehril's eyes widened in horror. "And if they prove successful, then Tyron's final hope will also be destroyed!"

Vohon's brows knitted as he thought for a moment. Then, with a smile, he told Dehril, "I had not even considered this; but do not concern yourself, my friend, for even if the Three could unite without tearing one another apart, a questionable occurrence at best, they would be sorely pressed to defeat the ruler of Lamnagha. No, that is not what I had in mind, but rather this: the Hemghels were within the spheres of the citadels half a month past, where they learned of the proposed alliance. The word was that Dukkor and Shadil planned on journeying to the citadel of Yathir, the northernmost stronghold, there to attempt consummation of the unholy union. Do you not see, my friend? If your desperate plan is to succeed at all, what better chance would there be than to have the Three together in one place, at one time?"

"Of course!" Dehril exclaimed. "But what assurance have we that all will still be there when we arrive?"

"There can be no guarantees, to be sure. But by the reckoning of the Hemghels, the parley would have commenced only days earlier. Unless they vex one another immediately and disband, they will continue to go forth with their planning. This, I am certain, will take many days, perhaps weeks. Even on foot you should arrive there in time."

"Have you no steeds that we may utilize?"

Vohon shook his head. "There is little need for mounts in the Tengaviregos. The tribes of Vorhashekkh ride fiery stallions, the likes of which would serve you well. Unfortunately, none of the nomads are close by at the moment, or I surely would barter for three of the animals."

"Perhaps we may acquire some along the way."

"Remember what I told you earlier: the people of Vorhashekkh must not be confronted, for they would carve out your hearts as soon as gaze upon you. Your only chance would be to commandeer mounts by stealth; but even this I would advise against."

"Thank you, Vohon; we will be certain to heed your warning."

They paused before the outermost dwelling on the western perimeter of the village, and with a sweeping gesture of the hand Vohon presented the temporary residence to his guest. After promising to awaken him before dawn, the bantir spun on his heel and strode back to the vicinity of his own cabin, where the number of celebrants had already thinned. Dehril stared wistfully at the remaining folk, but he could catch no further glimpse of Veleann. Not until long minutes later, when the village was all but deserted, did the dejected Berboran part the heavy drapes over the portal and enter.

Though sparsely furnished, the interior was spotlessly clean. A thick pile of sleeping furs lay on the floor, as well as a pitcher of wine and a tray of food. The sole remaining item was a basin of water, in which Dehril rinsed away the grime of his journey. He then thrust his fatigued body beneath the mound of furs, though not before chancing one final look out the portal at the now silent avenues of Dosheel.

Despite his weariness, Dehril found slumber difficult to attain. For nearly an hour he twisted and turned, but he could not free his mind from the vision of the tawny mountain beauty. It was because of this awareness that he could hear the gentle tapping on the cabin wall outside. He bade the visitor enter, and the drapes quickly parted. By the dim light of a single lamp he could easily discern the exquisite form of Veleann. He wondered if she noticed the slight smile that he could scarce suppress.

"I have been expecting you," he said.

"I know," she replied in a husky voice. Her loose garment fell to the floor, and she thrust it aside with an unshod foot. The small flame was extinguished, but he was able to observe her silhouette as she swayed sensually toward him. He lifted the furs, and within moments she lay in his arms.

###

"Dehril, I must leave now."

"No. Please, do not go."

"But I must! Dawn is not far off, and Father will come for you soon. Dehril?"

"Yes?"

"You do not really have to go, do you? Please stay here in Dosheel with me. Say that you will!"

"I-I cannot, Veleann; not now, at least."

"But Dehril, I—*I love you*!"

"As I do you, my mountain goddess."

"Then why must you go? Can you not take me with you?"

They had spoken much during their night of ecstasy, and now Dehril told her what little there was left to know. She listened in stunned silence, and when he was done, she realized that her love and respect for this warrior, who only yesterday was unknown to her, had grown even more. Her fiery lips were pressed firmly against his, and the unbounded passions of the night were extended for long minutes. Finally, reluctantly, Veleann donned her garment and made ready to leave.

"Never have I known one like you, my Dehril. Should your love for me be but a small part of your loyalty to Tyron, then I will be pleased."

"It will surely be as much, this I swear. Goodbye, my love; I will return to you soon."

"I know that you will; nevertheless, I will pray to the gods on the mountain for your safe journey."

They embraced for the last time, the lithe girl then gliding silently through the drapes. Dehril observed her as she hastened through the village, and not until she had disappeared into her own dwelling did he return to his furs. Here, with her vision still swimming in his brain, he found another brief period of slumber, this lasting little more than an hour. Vohon then came for him, and his sojourn in Dosheel ended.

The earliest vestiges of dawn were evident as they strode through the village, where only a few were awake to see them depart. Among them was Veleann, who waved mechanically to the pair as they passed, unable to display her true emotions. Dehril smiled sadly as he returned the gesture, and with a final shrug he turned his attention to the traverse. By the time the sun sat atop the horizon they had negotiated much of it; even the deadly lower portion evoked no terror, for the Berboran knew that, when next he sidled along it, he would again be close to his beloved mountain beauty.

They now stood upon the rock-strewn ledge at the base of the escarpment, scant yards above the point of rendezvous. But before they could descend, Vohon grabbed Dehril by the arm and faced him, the bantir's demeanor stern. He had been silent throughout the morning, but now he spoke.

"There is something that I must say to you before we join the others," he stated. He then paused for a few moments, while Dehril fidgeted nervously. But Vohon could withhold his feelings no longer. A broad grin appeared on his face, and he roared, "When you return to Dosheel, I will be proud to have you as kin!"

Dehril smiled sheepishly as the massive chieftain pounded him on the back. The relieved Berboran was speechless, though Vohon expected nothing from him. Instead, he indicated the rim of the shelf, and the two scampered down the sharp declivity. Tyron and Lanira were still asleep at the base, the girl nestled tightly in the Kalkh's arms. Both rose slowly to their feet as the others neared, Lanira stretching sinuously, the mountain man shaking off the last vestiges of sleep, much as a predatory cat would. Once greetings were exchanged, Dehril and Vohon distributed the items that the bantir had so thoughtfully provided. Finely made fur garments and boots replaced their own tattered clothes; a long-bladed knife, only inches shorter than the steel of Tyron and Dehril, was given to Lanira, while each of the trio received one of the sturdy javelins. There were skins of water and wine, as well as pouches of food, though not a great quantity of the latter.

"The victuals will more than suffice the three of you as far as the citadel of Yathir," Vohon explained. "If you are successful, then you will find much there for the taking. If not . . ."

With no further words necessary, the Dosheelian bantir led the trio along the perimeter of the slope. Five hundred yards farther along, the angle of the hill had altered drastically, until they found themselves paralleling the base of a sheer stone facing. Though seemingly impenetrable, Vohon nonetheless guided them into a narrow defile, one hardly visible to the untrained eye. This rock-bound passage twisted and turned through the mountains, and at no time could more than fifty yards be covered without it branching off. Even the skilled Tyron would have been hopelessly lost in the unfamiliar maze; but Vohon strode through it casually, never once displaying any signs of hesitancy in selecting the proper path.

Save for a brief rest and a bit of refreshment, the purposeful trio maintained the mountain chief's brisk pace throughout the day, and by the middle of the afternoon they had left the worst behind them. The pass widened, and they were able to gaze northward for miles. Here, Vohon motioned them to a halt.

"I must leave you now, if I am to reach my village by dusk," he told them. "You will need my assistance no longer. Late in the day tomorrow the Tengaviregos will fall behind you. Continue your journey due north, and, if the gods walk in your path, you will find that which you seek. I pray that we shall see one another again."

Lanira hugged the bantir, while the others clasped his hand warmly. Vohon then departed, and the craggy maze immediately swallowed him. The trio then turned and continued along the pass, which proved of little challenge, save for the many bits of rubble under their feet. They stopped for the night shortly before sunset, where all gratefully partook of the tasty fare provided them by their erstwhile host. Tyron made certain that their encampment was at least a few hundred yards from the closest of many adits they had passed, these undoubtedly the lairs of various predators. But while a secure vigil was maintained during the night, their rest, save for an occasional throaty roar that echoed through a distant canyon, went undisturbed.

Their journey was resumed before dawn, and a few hours past noon they emerged from the range. Here they paused, and Tyron gazed wistfully behind him at the towering Mountain of the Gods. Then, with a shrug, he turned and continued north, Lanira's arm entwined around his own. Neither noticed Dehril, whose own eyes remained affixed on the mountains for a few more moments. His purposeful stare would have led one to believe that he was observing something obscure to all but himself; indeed, the vision of his Dosheelian goddess remained indelibly etched on the side of the gleaming peaks, as well as in his heart.

With a sigh he spun about to join the others, but not before uttering the words that none, save perhaps the mountains themselves, could overhear: "We *will* be back!"

CHAPTER THIRTEEN: THE DARK KINGDOM

For the remainder of that day, and half of the following one, they traipsed across a barren, dusty tundra, this devoid of even the most rudimentary life forms. Not even the scrawny scavenger birds associated with such terrain were in evidence, though they gazed skyward nearly as often as they scanned the surrounding landscape. To all appearances, this ground had not been walked upon by any foot, human or otherwise, for centuries. Yet they knew that the tribes of Vorhashekkh had made the journey to the Tengaviregos many times, and because of this their vigilance did not lessen for a minute throughout the tedious march.

As old Zarthik had told them countless days past, and as Vohon had recently said, they could not help but know when they arrived at the border of the dark kingdom. Since early in the morning the sun had been blotted repeatedly by thick, fleecy clouds, these darkening ominously with each hour that passed. By the middle of the afternoon the sun, as well as the blue sky in which it floated, was gone from their sight and, had they not known better, they would have sworn that dusk had fallen upon them far too rapidly. All prayed that they would again see the light of day in the future, for they could expect nothing more than this while within the confines of the bleak land called Vorhashekkh.

The sameness of the charred, lifeless plain went unchanged for two days, save for an occasional boulder, a jagged tor, or a narrow, bottomless fissure, all the result of past upheavals in the bowels of the unsettled earth. For Tyron, the terrible dreams during the nights spent here differed little from any that had plagued him since the devastation of Berbora; but for Dehril and Lanira, the foul land that now held them brought nightmares on par with those of the Kalkh. Scarce an hour could pass without at least one of the trio being jarred awake violently by the terrible images. Sleep became more feared than welcomed, and their fatigue grew increasingly worse.

Mid-afternoon of their third day in Vorhashekkh found them striding wearily, mechanically, across the rubble-strewn ground. Tyron suddenly motioned them to a halt, for his keen ears had detected something in the distance. The others listened, and soon they too were aware of it. They could see nothing, despite the fact that visibility went unhindered for nearly two miles. With much caution they continued forward, their senses now heightened by the unknown disturbance. But not until three hundred yards had been crossed, where they again paused, could they identify the sound, which now became clearer: a mingling of many voices.

Tyron instinctively dropped to the earth, despite the absence of visible foes, the others following suit immediately. The voices sounded close by, a fact reinforced by the absence of any breeze, which might have borne them from afar. They still saw no one, but a cursory scan on the part of the Kalkh revealed that the ground sloped upward gradually about fifty yards before them, the voices appearing to emanate from just beyond the rim of this incline. Slowly, stealthily, they crawled forward, until they were within inches of the gentle hill's summit. They peered over the edge and saw a less-than-fertile vale. From the appearance of those who strode across the floor, the trio knew that they were seeing the first of those who dwelled in the dark kingdom of Vorhashekkh.

The encampment was hardly permanent, for only a few crude lean-tos were scattered about it, this insufficient to accommodate a tribe of more than two hundred people. They were primitive beings, little farther along the scale of evolution than the Fanolls. The males were equally as hairy as their southern counterparts, though taller, and more trim; but their mates hardly resembled the grotesque Fanoll women. They were tall, of Amazonian stature, with lengthy black hair and dusky countenances that were not unattractive, save for the hard, unsmiling look on each face. Their limited garb, little more than a scant fur skirt, revealed alluring curves in all places save the hips, which were a bit fleshy. Most were proportionately buxom, some even a bit more so. None of the females were shod in any manner, nor were their mates. The few children evident appeared as perfect miniatures of the adults.

These inhabitants of Vorhashekkh aroused little curiosity in the trio, for they had encountered things beyond the grasp of most during the preceding days. But there was something else in the crude village that warranted their interest: horses. Scores of them wandered about the perimeter of the camp, all munching idly on brittle, yellowish shrubs that dotted the floor of the valley. Though they longed to possess three of them, they were all well aware of Vohon's words, which had been passed along by Dehril. They had come farther than anyone could have imagined, too far to risk all for whatever number of days that possession of the steeds would save them in completing the journey to the citadel of Yathir.

Tyron, who knew that his proximity could destroy these people within a day or two, shrugged disgustedly, and with a curt gesture he motioned for the others to follow him, his plan to give the tribe a wide berth before continuing the northward trek. But before the trio could depart they heard a distant thunder from the east, where a puff of dust hovered atop the valley floor at least a mile away. The roar resounded through the once silent vale, and five frothing steeds were soon revealed amid the cloud. Not until they reached the core of the encampment did the whooping riders rein in their mounts. Four of the horsemen leaped to the ground, while the fifth sat stiffly atop his own barebacked animal. However, the action of the latter proved to be short-lived, for one of the others dragged the fellow, whose hands were bound, from the beast, where he fell face down in the dirt. The tribe began to converge on him, but the four that had brought him there fended them off.

A towering figure emerged from one of the lean-tos, and with swaggering strides he approached the scene in the hub of the village. Many stepped aside to allow him passage, and soon he stood before the prisoner. After examining him for long seconds the immense fellow spoke, while the concealed trio strained to catch some of the words.

"By the black heart of Dukkor, it is a Tunhi!" he roared. "What brings you this far west, Tunhi dog? You would spy on the Uruskhs, no doubt!" He struck the bound fellow in the face with the back of his hand, a cowardly action that incensed the helpless Tunhi.

"Uruskh swine!" he snapped. "This is what I have journeyed here to do!"

He spat in his tormentor's face, which caused many to gasp. The massive Uruskh snarled like a savage beast as he withdrew a crude but deadly knife from the thong that held his loincloth. He drove the point, once, twice into the prisoner's stomach, this bringing the fellow to his knees, though the imprecations he chose to hurl at the Uruskhs poured forth nonstop, despite his agony.

Frenzied by the spilling of blood, the tribe now engulfed the Tunhi, and no one attempted to stop them. All the Uruskhs, including women and children, sought to inflict some punishment on the prisoner. His defiant words were soon silenced with one final shriek, and from below the crush of bodies a dark stain began to spread as they proceeded to tear him apart. Lanira buried her face in her hands, while Dehril shook his head in disbelief. Even the hardened Kalkh could no longer stand the sight.

"Let us leave this place," he told them, his disgust evident.

They retraced their steps a few yards before turning west, where they paralleled the rim of the vale for a considerable distance, until they were far from the encampment of the bloodthirsty Uruskhs. The narrow valley was traversed with rapid, anxious steps, and once on the far side they continued north. None had doubted the words of Vohon before; but now, subsequent to their unwanted firsthand observation, they knew that any confrontation with the tribes of Vorhashekkh must be avoided at all cost.

They made camp far from the sight of the Uruskh atrocity along the perimeter of an unexpected grove, one comprised of stately oaks with massive boles and heavily foliated boughs. Such foliage, though hardly abundant, seemed out of place in the shadows of Vorhashekkh. Here the trio endured another night of tormented slumber, one made even worse by the not-too-distant shrieks of unknown nocturnal predators. The morning found them no less fatigued than previously as they made ready to resume their seemingly endless journey.

Dehril, who had stood the final watch of the dark hours, was the first to notice the riders as they began to emerge from the trees, and he quickly made the others aware. They might have been Uruskhs, or Tunhis, or one of any number of nomadic Vorhashekkh tribes, though this mattered little to the three. Each of the eleven riders sat atop a towering stallion, a few the color of pitch, the majority of a chestnut hue. The chilled morning air was visible as it emanated from their flaring nostrils. Most of the animals appeared a bit agitated, though not so their masters, who guided them calmly, silently, to within yards of the unexpected travelers, where they were reined to a halt. For long, uneasy seconds they studied the trio, until one of them, a burly, scowling fellow, stepped forth.

"You are now slaves of the Memnels," he grunted. "Place your weapons on the ground and come with us. I will take the female."

Tyron bent over slowly, as though to relinquish his hold on the Dosheelian javelin, and he motioned for the others to follow suit. But as they did so he addressed them, his voice barely audible.

"I doubt whether we can rely on the Scamban malady to again free us from an intolerable situation," he whispered. "If the

Uruskhs were representative of Vorhashekkh natives, then we will be long dead before the plague consumes these dogs. We must make our stand here and now!"

The skillful Kalkh flicked his wrist, the motion barely perceptible, and before anyone could comprehend what had occurred, the Memnel leader clutched at the shaft of a javelin that protruded from his throat. Lanira and Dehril cast theirs simultaneously, each of the well-aimed missiles felling a startled rider. The trio then stepped back quickly as the huge stallions reared high in terror, their riders cast headlong to the hard earth. Two more of the Memnels were crushed beneath the flailing hooves as the beasts fled eastward along the edge of the grove, not stopping until they had covered more than twenty yards. The remaining six nomads, though stunned, utilized animal-like instincts in scrambling to their feet.

"At them!" Tyron snapped as he drew his well-honed blade and raced toward their enemies. Lanira and Dehril duplicated his action, and within moments their slashing steel had dispatched another pair of Memnels, the spurting neck of one, whose head had rolled more than five yards distant, showering all with blood. But the surviving four, while unnerved, quickly recovered from the shock, and with their own crudely forged blades they were able to offer a capable defense.

Steel rang upon steel for long, tense minutes as the stalemate continued; but Dehril finally managed to penetrate the guard of one, who accidently slipped in a puddle of gore. The fellow died quickly from a gaping wound in his heart, which evened the combatants. Tyron, though forced to parry one powerful blow after another from his skillful opponent, could not help but feel pride as he observed Lanira. The beauty from Shaaf more than held her own against a heavily muscled, scowling Memnel, whose thrusts found nothing but air as she deftly sidestepped each one. She was even able to inflict a few minor cuts on the brute's arm, though, like his brethren, his capabilities with the blade were considerable. The fatigued trio knew that they would be sorely pressed to resume their desperate journey.

A loud, piercing roar suddenly filled the air, rising even above the clangor of the battle, for such was its proximity. Tyron immediately recognized it as one of the cries that had plagued them through the long night. The three Memnels stepped back, their eyes widened in unfeigned terror as they gazed furtively about them. Though they might have utilized this advantage to dispatch their foes, Tyron and the others did not move, for they too were paralyzed by the frightening sound. Within seconds it was duplicated by the throats of many, this being more than the nomads could stand. They cast their blades to the ground and began racing frantically toward the equally terrified stallions, while their former opponents gazed after them, unsure of what to do.

From out of the dawn's gray haze they emerged, sleek, black felines with fiery red eyes and slavering jaws. Usually dormant during the day, they had been drawn to the spot by the scent of blood, much of which had been spilled there. The frenzy of these killers, who usually hunted alone, was such that they came forth in a vast pack, at least a score or more strong. Tyron, familiar with their like from his days in the Yushans, knew that to stand before such an onslaught would be asking for death.

"Quickly, the trees!" he snapped, indicating the nearest of the oaks, less than ten yards away. They traversed the distance in seconds, and without pause they scrambled up the broad bole simultaneously. Only when they sat atop the thickest of the low boughs, more than twenty feet above the ground, did they dare glance down, where an unrivaled scene of carnage was being enacted.

Nearly half of the savage, snarling cats had set off in the wake of the stallions, the latter fleeing in terror into the grove. The three Memnels, despite their haste, were easily surrounded by more of the black devils, their final, pathetic cries drowned beneath a spurting crimson sea. Individual battles then ensued between the panthers for possession of these corpses, as well as the ones that had fallen earlier. Fifteen feral creatures vied for eleven prizes, the victors fanning out across various parts of the meadow, where they began to feed.

While the trio sat frozen in horror atop their precarious perch, the remaining cats snuffled the ground purposefully as they padded their way back to the edge of the grove. After lapping up what little gore was left they cast their attention toward the nearby trees, their wicked, flaming eyes immediately falling upon the potential repast. With a conjoint roar of triumph they hastened to the base of the oak. Raking talons tore off thick layers of bark as they leaped upward, each effort carrying them closer to their goal. Because of their poor leverage on the branch, the three could offer little defense, and it seemed but a matter of moments before they were dragged to certain death below.

"I have an idea!" Tyron shouted as he lashed out with his foot at a thrusting claw, an action that nearly caused him to topple forward. "Open your food pouches and throw them down, quickly!"

Drawstrings were loosed, and the sacks containing the fare provided by Vohon were hurled to the ground. One of the felines immediately scented the partly eaten beef joints that each contained. With a loud roar it pounced on a woven pouch, which it proceeded to rend with razor-sharp talons. With the meat held tightly in its dripping jaws the creature pranced off, not stopping to devour the tidbit until many yards separated it from the others.

Another cat carried off a second beef joint, while the remaining pair, at first slow to act, raced toward the last pouch. Neither could gain an initial advantage, and because of this they lashed out at each other savagely, their blood-chilling screams causing a few of their gorging fellows to glance at them with little more than detached interest. Lanira and Dehril, now aware of the Kalkh's designs, scrambled down the far side of the oak even before he motioned for them to do so. The trio dropped to the ground as quietly as possible, and, while the bestial combatants thrashed wildly some yards away, they hastened into the confines of the grove.

Not forgetting that the first wave of panthers had pursued the Memnel steeds into the trees, Tyron guided the others toward the northwest, this far from the path that the horses had chosen to follow, or so they hoped. During the tense hours that ensued they heard many savage roars. But these came from far off, and as the morning waned they grew more distant, until they were gone. Only then did the exhausted three pause for the first time since fleeing the scene of horror.

Long minutes passed before all finally regained their breath, and only then did they chance to re-examine their situation, which now appeared even more hopeless. They possessed no food, all having been sacrificed in order to escape the cats. Even Dehril's supply of leathery fruit had dwindled to nothing, though for some inexplicable reason he still retained the pouch. Their hopes of finding anything to eat were slim, for the dark land appeared unyielding. But worse: the skins of wine and water provided by Vohon had either been lost or punctured during their combat with the Memnels, and not even the narrowest tributary had been crossed since their emergence from the Tengaviregos, leaving them with little hope of finding more. They knew that, without food, they might still reach the citadel of Yathir; but with no water . . . The skins were squeezed tightly for their few remaining drops, and the dejected trio continued their interminable trek.

Soon the sparse wood that had held them terminated at the edge of an alkaline dust plain, the choking silt of which swirled about in the currents of a less than gentle breeze. Not a word was spoken as the three, after gazing out across its bleak expanse for a moment, began treading mechanically upon the ever shifting top layer. They slogged on until nightfall, when they finally stopped to rest in the midst of this gray desert. But in spite of their exhaustion they found rest barely attainable, due largely to the overwhelming thirst that they were unable to quench.

They rose at dawn, or what they guessed to be dawn, and once again set off toward their enigmatic northern goal. Only the lack of intense heat allowed them to travel as far as they did that day, a distance of more than four leagues, before they paused for a respite. They had been loath to partake of one, for they had no idea if they would rise again. Now, they realized that their fears had been well founded, for their shaky legs refused to obey the impulses of their brains. Tyron managed to remain upright longer, but his futile attempts to assist the others proved the Kalkh's undoing. He fell to the ground alongside Lanira, and for a few tense moments he straddled the thin line of consciousness. But the gentle beauty's sweet voice, though barely audible, pulled him from the depths. They continued along upon their hands and knees, for they knew that to pause now was a concession to the gatekeepers of Sharn.

None of the trio could have even guessed at how long they crawled forward, for their movements were reflexive, and they were scarce aware of them. Tyron was the first to notice the variance in the terrain as his keen nostrils were assaulted by a vile smell, the overwhelming stench of decay that emanated from the rotted vegetation they now traversed. He shook the cloud from before his sole eye and peered downward, where he saw the foul humus clinging to his hands. A backward glance revealed the choking dust plain many yards distant, and he was surprised that he had not been aware of the change sooner. In a rasping voice he sought the attention of the others, and once snapped from their lethargy they paused. They quickly studied the surrounding scene, and all were mildly stunned at what they observed.

The putrid loam stretched unbroken as far as they could see to either side of them—a short distance due to the murky haze. To the north, vague outlines of gnarled trees and jagged tors could be discerned, foreboding sentinels that stood silent guard before only the gods knew what. But what held their attention was no less than fifty feet farther along; there, the humus was split by what looked like a road, a well-beaten dirt ribbon nearly ten feet in width. It emerged from the southeast, its many curves belying the levelness of the ground. Not until one hundred yards past them did it straighten, where it soon disappeared between the outcroppings on its northward journey. Countless hoof prints and wheel ruts attested to its extensive use, though at the moment all was still.

"We must . . . bypass this path," Dehril gasped. "If we are found by—"

"No! We *must* be found!" Tyron replied, his rasping voice barely audible. "Without water we will die soon anyway. But there is always a chance that the Vorhashekkh nomads, should they find us, may choose to keep us alive initially, for we would be oddities to them."

"I-I agree with Tyron," Lanira stammered.

"Your point is well taken, my friend," the Berboran said. "Let us go."

After negotiating a nearly imperceptible incline they crept to the center of the road, where they followed its few remaining twists for what seemed forever. Night had fallen by the time they passed between the first of the tors, and it was here that Dehril went beyond the limits of his endurance. Lanira was the first to notice that he no longer kept pace, and she tried to advise Tyron of this, but the words held in her tortured throat. Calling forth untapped reserves of strength, the young beauty narrowed the few yards that separated her from the Kalkh, until she was able to grab his arm. At first startled, Tyron quickly glanced back in the direction that she indicated, where he saw his loyal friend sprawled on the solidly packed ground. His own torment forgotten, the concerned mountain man scrambled to Dehril's side, and with trembling hands he gently rolled the Berboran to his back. The face of the limp warrior was bloodless, and Tyron first feared that he was dead. But a cursory examination revealed that Dehril still breathed, though barely.

"Lanira, help me," Tyron gasped. "We must—!" His words caught as he glanced up the road at the golden beauty, noting that she too had succumbed. He would have raised himself to his feet and hastened toward her, but his own incomprehensible fatigue, coupled with the heart-rending sight of the two who meant so much to him, was more than he could withstand. In silence he toppled forward, and only his proximity to the edge of the road, where his head struck the foul loam with a soft liquid sound, saved him from immediate injury. A scarlet haze soon clouded his vision, this rapidly turning to unfathomable blackness.

CHAPTER FOURTEEN: YATHIR

Dehril saw the hand as it floated ethereally before him, its proximity such that he could have reached out and touched it, if he so desired. The appendage was immense, of a ghastly olive hue, a bloated, clutching monstrosity with dagger-like fingernails. It drifted closer, closer, the gnarled digits opening and closing obscenely as they sought his throat. The terrified Berboran would have swatted it away, but his arms were pinioned tightly, and he was unable to move them. He opened his mouth to scream, but not even a whimper came forth. The spectral fingers surrounded his neck as he continued to struggle futilely.

###

"Young man, please don't fight me! I would only help you. Please!"

Dehril's eyes snapped open, and he gazed upward into an ancient, wrinkled countenance, one that showed much concern. The old fellow might have seen sixty years, or twice that number, though Dehril could not even begin to guess at his age. Two sparkling gray eyes peered out from atop a long, aquiline nose. A wispy mustache grew above thin, taut lips, while a small, white goatee depended from the narrow chin. The curled hair upon his surprisingly large skull was equally as white, and abundant. He stood quite tall, though incredibly thin, almost skeletal. This was especially true of his bony fingers, which were tightly wrapped around the Berboran's wrists. He was not possessed of great strength, this further attesting to Dehril's own weakness, for he was helpless in the elder's grasp.

"Ah, that is better," the old man said as Dehril ceased his efforts, his leaden arms, once released, falling to his side. "Here; I only wish to offer you more water. I could manage only a few drops down your throat while you lay unconscious."

He raised a splashing gourd to the Berboran's lips and guided small quantities into the parched throat. This life-giving liquid proved a sufficient remedy to Dehril, and with a meager smile he nodded his appreciation to the elder.

"M-my friends!" he suddenly rasped. "Where—?"

"The others are well," the old man replied. "See!" He gestured across the road, where Tyron and Lanira lay alongside each other, their breathing steady as they slumbered peacefully. "They recovered long before you, for your own condition was considerably graver. Both are resting comfortably now, and I suggest you do the same."

"But who—?"

"There will be time for that later," the elder stated firmly. "Now rest."

Dehril needed little prompting, for the efforts of the past few minutes had already caused him to waver. The old man saw to it that he lowered his head gently to the road, and within seconds he had once again succumbed to sleep. This time, however, there were no more visions.

###

The Berboran might have slept for hours, or even days, though in no way could he be certain, for in Vorhashekkh it remained dusk. His awakening was greeted by a most inviting smell, that of meat being broiled over a crackling fire nearby. He sat up slowly, stiffly, and after wiping the fog from his eyes he surveyed the scene around him. The old man sat by the blaze, carefully rotating a huge joint of beef that had been skewered on a longsword. Lanira, her back turned toward him, was already devouring a share of the feast, while Tyron tore off a portion for himself. The Kalkh, seeing that his friend had awakened, broke off an additional helping for him. Dehril immediately noted Tyron's strong steps as he approached. With a grateful smile the Berboran took the meat, which he eagerly attacked. Not until most of it had been consumed, not until he had quenched the ensuing thirst with copious swallows of water, did he speak.

"It appears as though the gods did not desert us after all," he said, his voice as strong as it had been prior to the ordeal. "I have always wondered what Thur might look like, assuming that he had substance. Now, I believe that I have discovered the answer." He smiled gratefully at the old man, who chuckled softly.

"I would not be of a mind to dispute your words, my friend," Tyron stated. "Surely—"

"Please, my children." The elder blushed. "You cause me no slight embarrassment. Ah, see! The meat is done throughout. Now indeed shall you feast!" He deposited the joint atop a wooden tray, deftly removing the blade as he did so.

Lanira, now joining Tyron and Dehril, protested, "But we have already eaten so much!"

"Nonsense," the pleasant fellow retorted. "I would not see my guests waste away before me. Indulge yourselves, so that the flesh might not fall from your bones!" Again he chortled beneath his breath, as though sharing some private joke. "Dine well, my children, please."

None could refuse him, so famished were they all. The elder beamed with satisfaction as they attacked the meat voraciously, with even the city-bred Dehril exhibiting little decorum in devouring the repast. Tyron, in the midst of an immense mouthful, gazed curiously at their benefactor; but before he could voice a query, the fellow shuffled off toward his steed, which was loosely tethered some yards farther up the road. From a large pouch draped across the horse's back he withdrew three shiny goblets and a corked skin, which he carried back to the others. After distributing the silver vessels, he filled each one to the brim with a reddish liquid. Dehril sniffed the strange brew, the pleasing scent of which was not unlike wild Berboran plums. Yet in spite of the aroma, he hesitated in drinking it.

"The wine is brewed from the fruit of my own fields," the elder stated. "Its gentle appearance belies its headiness, I assure you." He winked slyly at the trio. "Go ahead, taste it. I daresay you will not be disappointed."

While Lanira and Tyron observed him, Dehril chanced a hesitant sip, this quickly followed by a generous swallow that drained more than half of the goblet. Not since he had last partaken of the fabled Kharkian wine in Berbora's finer inns, this seemingly ages ago, had he tasted the like of this exquisite, potent drink. After catching his breath he grinned broadly at his friends, and the three drained their cups simultaneously. The old man, beside himself with glee, refilled them almost immediately. Amid roars of laughter, which shattered the silence of the bleak landscape, they continued their unexpected banquet. The elder joined in their revelry, though at no time did he share in any of the victuals.

Long minutes later naught but a whitened bone remained before them, all having far surpassed the limits of their appetites. After long weeks of careful rationing, and recent days of deprivation that brought them near death, none questioned their right to indulge in such a manner. The elder had continued to pour his fiery brew throughout, until Lanira, her belly full and her head swimming from the potency of the liquid, finally succumbed to a dreamy half-sleep, her head nestled snugly against Tyron's chest. Dehril was also a bit light-headed, though, like the Kalkh, his drinking had only just commenced. Both thrust forth empty goblets at the old man, who shrugged.

"The skin is also empty, I fear," he admitted, squeezing the few remaining drops into Tyron's cup. "I apologize, for—wait! Yes, I do have another skin, I'm almost certain of it! Let me go and see."

He returned to the side of his mount and began rummaging through the oversized sack, while the others observed him with interest. Tyron, who had once consumed a full cask of Kharkian wine without ill effects, was well in control of his senses, and it occurred to him that the identity of their benefactor was still unknown.

"I would ask something of you, old man," he stated.

"Yes?" the other replied, his back still turned.

"Your presence in this foul place, though welcome, is a mystery to us. Who are you?"

The elder turned slowly, a slight smile evident on his lined face as he replied, "In Vorhashekkh, as well as other lands, I am referred to in many ways; but you need only call me by my name, which is—Yathir."

Dehril, upon absorbing this revelation, unwittingly dropped his goblet to the road, where it struck an embedded stone, the ensuing clangor wrenching Lanira from her stupor. Yathir resumed his search for the skin of wine as the girl, smiling dully, reached for her own cup, still half full. Tyron, momentarily frozen by the old man's revelation, pulled himself free before the rim could touch her lips, and with a sweep of his arm he knocked the goblet many yards distant. Their host's countenance altered to a mask of bewilderment as he watched the Kalkh hurl his own vessel in the wake of the other.

"Is this how you thank one for his kindness?" Yathir snapped. "Why . . . ah, suddenly I understand! So you too have heard of me; then I forgive your hasty actions, for doubtless I would have reacted no differently in your place. But what have you to fear from me? You think that I poisoned the wine, or the meat that you ate? You were near death when I found you and, had I wished it so, I needed to have only sat back and awaited the inevitable, which would not have been long in coming. No, my young friends, you have not been poisoned, this I swear."

None could find their tongues at first, and for long moments they stared at the smiling Yathir. This benign elder, by his own admission, was one of the Three, a dreaded dark magician of Vorhashekkh! Could Zarthik have been so in error regarding the nature of these supposed fiends? Was this concerned old man, who had displayed nothing but kindness, one who they had traveled countless leagues to—destroy? *If not for him, we would have perished long before this!* Tyron thought. He saved our lives! The tithe of Cuhthic would not, *could not* be met, not this way, at least. But—what of the plague? Must I carry it to my grave, and beyond? Perhaps Yathir would know . . .

The Kalkh, who had strode forward reflexively a few paces while listening to the magician's words, now glanced behind him to observe the reactions of the others. To his dismay he saw Lanira, who had been sitting upright only moments before, lying prone on the hard earth, her arms folded across her chest, as if in final repose. Dehril knelt upon one knee at her side, gazing down at the still beauty in muted silence.

"Dehril, what is wrong with her?" Tyron cried as he hastened to join them. "Why did you not advise me . . .?"

The latter query went unfinished, for the uncomprehending Berboran toppled forward as Tyron grasped his arm, and had the Kalkh not guided him gently to the ground he would doubtless have injured himself, or Lanira. A cursory examination revealed the flesh of both to be of a sickly yellow hue, while their eyes, which remained open, bulged obscenely. The horrified Tyron glared at Yathir, who had remained alongside his steed throughout, the same vague smile frozen upon his face.

"What has happened to them, magician?" the Kalkh snapped. "Tell me!"

Yathir shook his head. "It was the wine, unquestionably. I should not have allowed you as much as I did, in light of your deprivation. Your friends exceeded their limits—"

"You lying cur!" Tyron shrieked. "I have seen Dehril consume ten times the amount without ill effects! The truth, quickly, before I carve out your heart with . . .!" He reached instinctively for the hilt of his blade, but found it no longer sheathed in his belt. "So you have taken our weapons also, have you?" he growled. "No matter; I'll need only my hands to—*oh*!"

The Kalkh had taken no more than five steps toward the grinning magician when his legs buckled, the rubber-like appendages no longer able to obey his will. Waves of nausea coursed through him, and a scarlet haze clouded his vision; but still he moved forward, every inch achieved at the price of unbearable agony. He could hear Yathir speak, though the voice was hollow, detached.

"If it be any consolation, young fool, I never once lied to you. My desire to see the three of you live was strong, though for reasons of my own concern. The wine was not poisoned, merely drugged; the effects that you suffer will be of short duration, though you may yet pray to your accursed gods that they were far longer." He laughed wickedly for a few moments, before continuing: "Your resistance is commendable, for most would have succumbed long before this. I even feared that I had drawn forth the wrong skin. How fallible that would have been of me."

Tyron tried to focus on the wizened figure, but the vague outline of Yathir appeared as an ethereal vision, one that floated languidly in a hazy sea of ever-changing hues. The Kalkh began to sink in this swirling rainbow tide, and only one thought echoed in the recesses of his tortured mind before the colors altered to unyielding black: *Zarthik had not been wrong!*

CHAPTER FIFTEEN:
THE THREE

The circular room was large, its diameter between thirty and thirty-five yards. Its walls, as well as its lofty ceiling, were built of mortared stone. Despite the absence of windows the vast chamber was well lit by scores of torches, these set in brackets at evenly spaced intervals along the walls. There were at least twenty doors of varying shapes and sizes, all apparently forged from heavy cast iron. The floor was solid, though a layer of coarse, grayish sand was strewn atop it. A thick-beamed balcony protruded from one portion of the wall; it sat twenty feet above the gritty floor and was at least twice that in length. Two doors of average height and width provided entry from another level onto the overhang, which at the moment was unoccupied.

Tyron, Dehril and Lanira eyed the chamber with little interest from their position on the wall opposite the balcony, where all had regained consciousness only recently. Tight manacles surrounded their wrists, while heavy chains, each four feet or more in length, ran from these cuffs to broad, rusty rings set solidly in the wall. Save for throbbing heads, all were none the worse for wear from their recent ordeal on the road. None had any recollection of being brought here, though it was not difficult to guess that their place of internment was the citadel of Yathir.

One of the larger doors on the wall below the balcony suddenly opened, and a figure silently emerged into the chamber. Lanira gasped, while the others watched its approach in muted horror. The visitor was a black man, his features not unlike those of the ones that Tyron had observed along Berbora's docks. But this fellow stood a head over seven feet, the rest of his body proportionately as huge. He wore only a narrow loincloth around his middle. The beads of perspiration gathered on his flesh caused it to gleam like obsidian. Hair was absent from his bony skull, nor was there a single strand to be found anywhere on him. His face, though not unhandsome, was a mask of cruelty, of primitive savagery. They could hardly guess his reason for being there, though all feared that their survival beyond the next few minutes was at best questionable.

The black first approached Dehril, who struggled futilely against his shackles. Soon the Berboran ceased his efforts, and with a shrug of resignation he awaited his fate. But the giant chose not to harm him; instead, he paused less than a yard before the captive, his brow knitted as he studied the fair-skinned fellow from head to foot. A minute later, when satisfied, he moved on to Tyron, where the ritual was repeated. But the short-tempered Kalkh was of no mind to withstand an examination.

"I would not be gaped at like some beast in the zoo of Sargonna," he snapped. "Get away from me!"

At first startled, the black leaped to his feet and retreated a few paces. Then, his face twisted in rage, he smashed the back of his hand against both sides of Tyron's face, the blows nearly snapping the Kalkh's neck. Lanira screamed, while Tyron, the blood trickling from his mouth, pulled helplessly against his chains, for he was certain that the black would now destroy him. But the huge fellow, despite his anger, somehow regained control, and with a snarl he turned his attention to Lanira. His demeanor altered for the first time as he eyed the golden beauty, and his lips parted in a broad grin, which revealed rows of broken, rotted teeth. Lanira's body stiffened as he caressed her arms and legs with his meaty hands, while Tyron again resumed his desperate efforts.

"Don't touch her, you scum!" he shrieked, the words resounding through the chamber. But the black paid him little heed as he continued his groping, the thick fingers now fondling her golden tresses. He then touched her softly on the cheek, an action that he was quick to regret. Lanira twisted her head around, and in a continuous motion she sank her teeth into the brute's thumb. The black's mouth formed in what would have been a scream of pain, had he not been devoid of speech. He pulled the digit loose, and for long moments he stared in horror at the blood that poured forth. Then, glaring at Lanira, he raised his huge hands to her throat.

"Bordu, back!"

The piercing voice shattered the tension of the chamber, even rising above the terrible clangor of the rattling chains. Lanira's would-be killer, heeding the command, relinquished his hold only seconds before life would have been wrested from the helpless beauty. With a last wicked scowl at the shackled trio, the mute black retraced his steps across the floor of the chamber toward the door beneath the balcony, where he knelt subserviently before three robed figures that had entered only moments before. Not until Lanira had shaken off the effects of the vicious attack, not until she had assured Tyron and Dehril that she was well, did they turn their attention to the new arrivals.

Foremost of the trio, more than a head taller than the other two, was Yathir, resplendent in a shimmering emerald robe. Even from across the broad room they could clearly discern the fires of malevolence that burned in his eyes, fires that he had somehow been able to shield from them during their encounter on the road. The remaining pair, also ageless, appeared to have been poured from a like mold. Only upon closer scrutiny could it be noted that one, who wore a caftan of red, was a bit stockier than his counterpart, whose own magnificent garment had been fabricated from yellow satin and studded with blinding jewels of incomparable wealth. The faces of both were masks of intense evil, even the countenance of Yathir paling by comparison. None doubted for a moment that they looked upon the Three, the dreaded dark magicians of Vorhashekkh.

"Your fool of a servant would have spoiled Yathir's fun, Shadil," the bejeweled fellow hissed.

"I will see to it that Bordu is punished," the stocky one replied. "Perhaps an ear this time. What say you, Yathir; will this suffice?"

"Leave the dolt be, both of you!" Yathir snapped. "Even had he carried out his designs, the flesh would have still been warm, and quite acceptable. Only the joy of watching their torment would have been wrested from us. No, he shall be spared this time—though I would desire him out of my sight."

Shadil indicated the door with a brusque motion of the hand, and the groveling Bordu crept silently from the chamber. Then, turning toward the others, he said, "Let us be done with this spectacle, Yathir. I grow weary of your desire for games."

"I do not object to the diversion," Dukkor interjected, "but I daresay you could have chosen another sport. The chamber of the Crawling Death would have sufficed, or perhaps—"

"Listen, the both of you!" Yathir shrieked. "I did not select these three to be used in any *games*! Come, gaze upon their flesh, and tell me if you have seen their like in Vorhashekkh before."

The magicians approached the helpless trio and, like herders seeking out breeding stock at auction, they poked at their bodies mercilessly. Tyron would have appealed to Yathir, in hope that some of the past kindnesses shown were not entirely feigned; but a glance at the old man's fiery eyes assured him that such an action would be futile, and accordingly he withstood the abasement in silence. In addition to their reputed powers, these men appeared to be quite mad.

"I concede the quality, Yathir," Shadil said, once the examination had come to an end. "But—"

"But nothing!" Yathir snapped. "Do you not realize what this means? The Dungeon Spawn have not feasted upon the likes of this since the days of our sires, and they grow more surly with each passing year. They are dissatisfied with the flesh of the vermin that dwell within the borders of our land, and more often than not the barely gnawed corpses are left here to molder in the chains, while they return unsatisfied to the depths. However, they will be more than pleased by this unexpected offering, I assure you!"

"My own Dungeon Spawn are not as hard to please," Dukkor boasted, "and are quite amenable to disposing of any malcontents that I may chance to cast their way. Why the bother with these? It was no different with your father, and will likely not change in the future!"

"Nonetheless," Yathir said, "before this day is over, before any discussions of an alliance recommence, we will observe their dance of ecstasy! You will talk about this for a long time afterward, the both of you. Now come!"

The bickering of the incomprehensible Three continued across the floor of the chamber, this lending further credence to Vohon's assurance that any union between them, if ever consummated, would be long in coming. Once through the portal beneath the balcony the heavy door clanged shut, and the chamber again fell still. Tyron, Dehril and Lanira, all of whom had gazed after them in disbelief, now stared at one another, the Kalkh being the first to break the silence.

"In the name of Zeth, of your own Thur and Zhon, and of any other gods that chance to populate the world beyond the clouds, *what manner of horrid death have I led you to*!"

"First, my love," Lanira said, "you have not *led* us to anything, for we have come of our own accord." Dehril nodded his agreement, and she continued: "As far as what these fiends have planned for us, I submit that any speculation on our parts would avail us little. We will learn the answer soon enough, I fear."

The steel-jawed Kalkh gazed at the pair as he said, "I am a man of few words, as you know, and can scarce express what the two of you mean to me. But know this: the Three will not have your lives so easily! Somehow, some way, I will see you from this foul place safely, I swear it!"

Both smiled at Tyron, and for the time being they chose to believe him, despite the apparent hopelessness of the situation, for such was his determination. No further words passed between them during the hour that ensued, preoccupied as they were in seeking some way to rid themselves of the confining shackles. But the heavy metal remained unyielding throughout, and when one of the upper level doors finally opened, this disgorging the terrible Three onto the oaken balcony, they ceased their futile efforts. Lanira and Dehril now realized that, had it not been for Tyron's resolve, the time spent in awaiting the inevitable would have passed with agonizing slowness; they were quite thankful for what he had done, though they said nothing to him.

But the Kalkh had not spoken his promise in vain, and now, as the magicians appeared, he swore at his inability to free himself from the fetters. Quite aware that the next move belonged to Yathir, he glared silently at the gaudily dressed elder and his foul brethren, all of whom still argued amongst themselves like customers at a street market. He watched as the lean Yathir, dismissing the complaints of the others with a curt wave of the hand, strode to the far end of the balcony, where he opened the second door. Tyron could see little of what was within, his angle affording him a less than advantageous view. The only certainty was that the door led into a dimly lit cubicle, in which numerous strands of thick hemp depended from above. However, Yathir's subsequent words and actions left no doubt regarding the purpose of the room.

"Cease your bickering, fools," he shouted at Dukkor and Shadil. "Observe the floor of the chamber, for I would open the first of the doors!"

The pair, now silent, fanned out along the overhang and leered down expectantly, while Yathir began to pull on a few of the ropes, which Tyron now realized were part of a complex system of pulleys. He then joined his brethren on the platform, while four of the doors below began to open inward, the metallic clanking that each made resounding through the chamber. Soon the noise terminated and for long, tense minutes the captives were engulfed by a deathly stillness, as though they had been dropped into an airless void.

Tyron, his senses heightened above most others from his years in the deadly Yushans, heard the sound first. It emanated from the blackness of a large portal far to their left, though at first it could not be identified. But moments later, when Lanira and Dehril became aware of it, the Kalkh was already well attuned to what most closely resembled a bulky object being dragged slowly across a hard floor. The sound was not steady, but rather sporadic, stopping occasionally for long seconds before again resuming. It grew louder, louder, while beads of sweat formed on the flesh of the tense captives, despite the chill of the cavernous room. They became vaguely aware of a second, similar sound, this from a smaller door on the far wall; but their eyes remained glued on the first portal, from which, minutes later, the thing emerged.

A gelid gust of air permeated the chamber as the horror, after pausing for a moment in the doorway, resumed its shuffling journey across the gritty floor. It appeared as a translucent, gelatinous mass, and only in the midst of its obscene undulations could one discern the misshapen appendages, the mockery of a head by which it might have been compared to a human being, however remotely. Despite being stooped it stood more than six feet, while its girth was half again the height. Some semblance of a face was in evidence near the center of the uppermost ovoid blob, and it was the sight of this, above anything else, that sent waves of revulsion coursing through the trio. No proboscis was visible, the two black, lidless eyes instead sitting directly atop a broad, circular maw. Rows of gleaming, filed teeth gnashed together in the beet red orifice, while a brown, mucous substance oozed forth from its jaws and fell in large globules to the floor, this trail of slime spreading out in the thing's wake. Though it moved slowly, unsteadily, there could be no doubt as to the destination of the silent monstrosity: its shambling gait would lead it to the three frenzied, struggling captives, whose flesh it craved.

###

The chamber, the dungeon horror—all were gone, and Tyron drifted spectrally in the midst of a milky haze, not knowing up or down. He seemed only mildly surprised at the presence of the fog, and only a bit more so as his sole functioning eye fell upon the enigmatic red sphere that glowed dully in the distance. But as the thundering, monotonic voice shattered the stillness of the white vacuum the sphere flared brilliantly, until he could not look upon it directly. Instead he absorbed the words, which emanated from the fiery core.

"Tyron, my son, the currents of time have chosen to play the most wicked of games with you. Even I was forbidden to intervene, or you might have been spared a destiny of such incomprehensible torment."

"Great Father of the Mountains," the Kalkh uttered. "You have not forgotten me."

"Forgotten you, my son? Through all your suffering subsequent to the devastation you never once abandoned me, though your reasons were justifiable. I have not been far from your side, Tyron, although you could hardly have been aware of my presence. Your unwavering loyalty must be acknowledged."

"Then you can help me now, and those that I love, my Father?"

"I can, Tyron."

###

In spite of her terror, the wide-eyed Lanira glanced at Tyron and was stunned to see that he no longer fought against his chains, that he stood limply, his eyelids shut. But ere she could call out to him, he became instantly alert. An enigmatic transformation seemed to take place as he absorbed the surrounding scene; fires appeared to radiate from the depths of both sockets, even within the false eye of glass that had been fabricated for him so long ago in Berbora. His teeth were bared in a savage grimace as he coiled one of the chains around his right arm. Blood rushed to his head as he strained mightily, while veins protruded from his glistening sinews. Though similar efforts of the hour past had proven futile, Lanira somehow sensed that the powerful Kalkh had called forth previously untapped reserves of strength, these unknown even to him, until now. Long moments later, when the endmost link separated from the deeply set ring with a metallic groan, she knew that she had been right.

With Lanira and Dehril spurring him on, with the Three hurling vile threats from above, Tyron duplicated his incredible feat with the second chain. The fires quickly left him, though his muscles remained taut. After casting a grim smile at the others he faced the apparition from the bowels of the citadel, noting that, despite its slowness, it had neared to within a few yards.

Denying the waves of revulsion that swept over him, the Kalkh voiced a chilling cry as he raced toward the translucent horror, his chains describing broad arcs as he swung them around his head. The thing, never before challenged in its eternity of life, ceased its progress in the face of this unexpected assault, its brown drool, stimulated by the proximity of warm flesh, forming a puddle at its feet within seconds. Ten times Tyron swung the well-forged links at the monster, each pass tearing loose large chunks of its vile substance, these pieces continuing to squirm obscenely where they fell. Not until the bulk of the pulsating mass had spread out across the gritty floor did Tyron cease his efforts, for he knew that it could do no one any harm.

"Young fool!" Yathir shrieked from the overhang. "You dare to destroy one of the Dungeon Spawn? Soon you will regret your action, this I swear!"

The gaunt magician raced toward the cubicle, where rope after rope was drawn downward. Heavy doors throughout the chamber began to open simultaneously, but the Kalkh chose to ignore this as he raced across the floor, not pausing until he stood below the balcony. Dukkor and Shadil, the former withdrawing a shiny blue globe from the folds of his garment, continued to revile him as he wrapped the chains around one of the heavy wood beams that braced the overhang; but not until Yathir had rejoined his brethren and peered below did any of the dark ones realize his designs, though far too late.

"He would drag us down with him!" the sorcerer screamed. "Quickly, the—*ayiieee*!"

Despite its thickness the oaken balcony gave way like balsa to the one whose strength, at that moment, was more than human. The blue globe flew from Dukkor's hands and burst into a thousand shards on the floor, as the sorcerer screamed. Tyron, neither knowing nor caring what powers Dukkor might have summoned from the enigmatic object, stepped aside as the heavy overhang shattered against the floor, the impact temporarily stunning the magicians. But somehow, inexplicably, the trio regained their feet within moments, and they glared at the sinewy mountain man, now unraveling his chains from the beam. Yathir was the first to speak.

"Know what you have done, fool!" he hissed. "Every door is now open, and soon *all* the Dungeon Spawn will rise! The portal above is beyond our reach, while the sole one here leading to the primary corridor can only be opened from outside. We are trapped!"

Tyron smiled grimly. "Then we will soon find out if the horrors from below also relish the flesh of their sires," he told them.

The raging Yathir reached into the folds of his robe and drew forth a slim, gleaming dagger. With lengthy strides he narrowed the distance between himself and the Kalkh, whose resolute smile remained frozen on his face. Three times the magician thrust the blade forward, but Tyron deftly sidestepped each one. Silently, with a single swipe of his chains he caved in the chest of the shrieking Yathir, his momentum nearly severing the sorcerer in two. Yathir crumpled to the floor, his evil soul now consigned to Sharn for all time.

Upon seeing their comrade fall, the wide-eyed Dukkor and Shadil fled across the floor of the chamber in opposite directions. A quick glance behind him revealed to Tyron that no more of the Dungeon Spawn had as yet come forth to menace Lanira or Dehril. The Kalkh searched through Yathir's robe hastily, discovering the ring of keys that he sought within seconds. Once rid of his own shackles he hurled the keys in the direction of the others. He then turned his attention to Shadil, where he saw that the rotund magician, quite unused to running, had stumbled over his own caftan only a few yards away, near one of the open portals.

"My ankle!" he whined. "Please, help me!"

Certain that the pathetic Shadil would not be going anywhere, Tyron set off after Dukkor, who stumbled aimlessly about in the middle of the chamber. But before he could draw close to the magician, he heard Dehril cry, "Tyron, the other one, quickly! He must not be carried below!"

The Kalkh whirled and saw another of the gelatinous travesties emerging from the portal near the gibbering Shadil who, blinded by terror, crawled directly in its path, scant yards away. It reached the magician's side in seconds, and with its vicious cuspids the horror proceeded to rend the stocky body, the scarlet caftan now stained an even deeper hue.

Preoccupied as it was, the Dungeon Spawn remained unaware of Tyron's approach until too late. The Kalkh had scooped up the previously discarded chains, and with these formidable weapons he duplicated the destruction of the first. A cursory scan of the chamber revealed that Lanira and Dehril, now freed, had cornered the desperate Dukkor, who menaced the pair with his own dagger. Though his friends were unarmed, Tyron had no doubt that they would prevail, and he quickly turned his attention to another matter of necessity. In the bloodied folds of Shadil's robe he found a large knife with a jewel-encrusted hilt, the edge of which could easily have split hairs. The Kalkh's stomach churned as he cleanly severed the head, an action that left him with little remorse. Once the majority of the blood had been drained he tucked the grisly prize under his arm, and with a last glance at the still wriggling bits of the dungeon horror nearby he strode purposefully to the side of Yathir. The unspeakable chore was repeated in haste, and the heads were wrapped in the lean sorcerer's robe, which Tyron had torn away.

Seven, eight of the dungeon travesties now emerged into the vast room of death as Lanira and Dehril, the latter bearing the head of Dukkor, hastened to rendezvous with Tyron. The reunion was brief, for they guessed that more of the horrors were even now crawling upward from the slime-drenched depths. But how would they find a way out, if what Yathir had said was true? Frantically they sought an answer, an attempt even being made to level the immense door that led to the corridors of the stronghold, an exercise that proved futile. Dehril finally pointed at the door high above.

"Up there! If we utilize the remnants of the balcony, then perhaps we could reach it."

"But the creatures!" Lanira cried. "They will be upon us soon!"

"Our last alternative is to pass through one of the portals into the depths of the citadel," Tyron replied, "an idea that I would quickly reject. Dehril is right, for this is the only way. We'd best proceed, now!"

They had barely begun dragging the fallen overhang away from the wall when the main door suddenly opened, and the giant Bōrdu, a huge scimitar in one of his meaty hands, entered the chamber. His proximity was such that the black's wicked eyes first fell upon the trio, and from the way that he fondled the curved blade there could be no doubt as to his intentions. But the stench of death that permeated the room caused him to glance about, and his eyes nearly bulged from their sockets as he absorbed the grim scene. During these moments of uncertainty, Dehril drew forth Dukkor's dagger and hurled it into the black's midsection. Bordu flinched slightly as the steel entered his flesh, though little more than one would after being stung by an insect. He extracted the blade almost casually, and with his teeth bared he hastened toward the three.

Tyron, after a quick glance to the rear, shouted, "Let me have at him. The Dungeon Spawn are nearly upon us!"

The sinewy Kalkh raced forth, and in a blinding motion he kicked the scimitar from Bordu's hand. Reacting quickly, the black placed an arm lock on his foe, one that would have snapped the limbs of most. But Tyron's leverage enabled him to counteract it, and for long, tense moments they remained at a stalemate, while the shambling Dungeon Spawn drew closer. Tyron finally broke the hold, and with a loud grunt he hoisted the massive black high above his head. With the strength of desperation he hurled Bordu more than twenty feet across the chamber, the black falling in the path of the two foremost horrors. The shrieks that now poured forth from the throat of one so long silenced were beyond comprehension, and only the clanging of the metal door behind them as the trio passed into the corridors of Yathir's citadel freed them from its chilling sphere.

CHAPTER SIXTEEN: CUHTHIC

The bleak, granite-walled corridor of the citadel twisted and turned, though not once did it branch off, and the three were able to follow it unerringly until it terminated at the base of an angular stairway. They mounted the steps without hesitation, the portal at the top depositing them into a large, ornamented hall. Tapestries lined the walls, while thick rugs covered nearly every inch of the floor, the colors of all a ghastly mottling of the darkest hues. There were statues carved of obsidian interspersed throughout the hall, all representative of unspeakable demons, grotesque horrors both formed and formless.

Yathir's retainers wandered through what Tyron now realized was a dining hall, men and women on an evolutionary par with the Vorhashekkh nomads previously encountered. The trio was at first wary, but they soon realized that the mindless servants, without the guidance of their master, were harmless. They deposited their grisly trophies on a long banquet table, one laden with all manner of tempting food, though their appetites, in light of recent events, were something less than ravenous. Dehril then removed the pouch that had been tied around his waist since their departure from Berbora, and for the first time he explained his designs to the others.

"Never once did I doubt that Tyron would bring us this far," he stated, winking at Lanira. "Accordingly, I reasoned that some preservation of the heads was necessary, lest the flesh rot from the skulls during the last portion of the journey and allow Cuhthic to accuse us of duplicity. These waxed layers will more than suffice."

After nodding their admiration of the Berboran's foresight, Lanira and Tyron began gathering food and water for the remainder of the journey to Lamnagha, while Dehril undertook the grim task of encasing the foul prizes in the treated paper. All were done within minutes, a fact that relieved them, for the ominous hall of Yathir was beginning to tell on their already taut nerves. They glanced around for a way out, finally noting a large set of double doors at the far end of the room, the only others aside from the one through which they had entered. Tyron cast the twin portals outward, and the trio emerged, quite unexpectedly, into the light of day. With the death of the Three, the pall that had engulfed Vorhashekkh for hundreds of years had been lifted, leaving the dismal landscape bathed in the rays of the long-denied sun.

At least a dozen people wandered through the courtyard of the sturdy, walled stronghold, but they were even more bewildered than their brethren inside, and they offered no resistance. Dehril discovered their discarded longswords at the base of the wall some yards past the doorway, and they felt relief as they hefted the familiar steel. But even more satisfying was the sight of horses, seven in all, loosely tethered along the perimeter of the north wall. Three of the best were selected, and, after a few uneasy moments the stallions responded well to the kindness of their new riders. They thundered through the open gate, and not once did the trio glance behind them as the citadel of Yathir fell away in the distance.

No longer fearful of any chance encounters, they followed the well-defined dirt road as it continued northward, finally pausing when darkness, true darkness, fell upon them. A half full moon, as well as a myriad of flickering stars, appeared before a black canvas, and not once through the long night did even a single cloud obscure their view of the tranquil scene. They feasted well before retiring, and when they awakened at dawn they felt refreshed, invigorated, for the first time in recent memory. The journey resumed on a note of optimism, and many leagues were consumed that day by the tireless steeds.

During the latter part of the afternoon, the trio approached the border of Lamnagha. Its proximity was not difficult to determine, the keen senses of their mounts providing them with the initial clues. The animals had grown increasingly skittish during the preceding hour, culminating with Dehril being hurled headlong from his own horse, which now appeared terrified. Though uninjured, the shaken Berboran could not recover in time to grab the beast's reins, the frothing stallion setting off at a brisk trot toward the south. The others followed in its wake, Tyron's attempt at reining his to a halt resulting in a fate similar to Dehril's. Lanira, skilled as she was, dismounted gingerly before her horse had attained its top speed, and together the trio gazed helplessly at the fading puff of dust. Then, with a conjoint shrug, they gathered up their strewn belongings and resumed the journey on foot.

As they had guessed, the border of Lamnagha was little more than two miles beyond, a fact evident from the top of a slight incline they had reached only minutes after the flight of the stallions. Unlike the gradual variance from the land north of the Tengaviregos to the southern perimeter of Vorhashekkh, this line of demarcation left little to the imagination. It was as though a black mantle, one that stretched as far as the eye could see, had been dropped from the heavens to obliterate all before them, which indeed it did. They approached it with much trepidation, and for long moments they paused at the edge of the foreboding pall. Then, their arms unconsciously linked together, they passed into the blackness, which, like some immense, living entity, swallowed them.

It was midnight in Lamnagha; not early twilight, or dusk, but the darkest of the dark hours—moonless, starless. Minutes passed before their eyes became accustomed to the gloom, and even then they were afforded a view of little more than a few yards before them. Their fur garments, more than sufficient in Vorhashekkh even prior to the demise of the Three, availed them little here, and they shivered uncontrollably against the gripping chill. That they would know only eternal darkness while within the confines of this wretched land was an unquestioned truth, and it sufficed little in warming them.

Tyron finally motioned them forward, and they resumed the trek at a brisk pace, if for no other reason than to maintain the circulation in their veins. The defoliated earth beneath their feet was solid and, despite their preoccupation with potentially hazardous footing, they made more than adequate progress. Only when fatigue finally overwhelmed them did they pause, countless hours after entering the sinister land. It might have been dusk, or true midnight, or even morning of the following day, though they could not say for sure, having lost all track of time. They sought slumber upon the bleak tundra, but the visions that assaulted them were by far the worst of all, and they suffered greatly.

The chill lessened a bit within hours of their departure, while the earth upon which they strode altered considerably. Soon they left deep footprints in the spongy humus, and with each succeeding step they sank deeper, until the reeking bog clutched at their ankles. This swamp, though befitting of such a place as Lamnagha, now slowed their progress to the pace of a land tortoise, and they rued the delay. Intertwining creepers of surprising thickness were hacked away, at the cost of much time and effort; undetectable pools of quicksand pulled each of the trio downward on at least one occasion, the subsequent extrications, made exceedingly difficult by the lack of leverage, further draining the strength of all. Little more than a scant few miles, if that much, were traversed through the mire before the trio, exhausted almost beyond caring, finally collapsed upon a small area of firmer loam.

Soon aware that continued torpidity might see this swamp as their final place of rest, Tyron shook loose from the fog that permeated his brain, and his persistent badgering eventually saw the others sitting upright, however unwillingly. The Kalkh distributed food and water, which all partook of absently. Many long minutes passed before Lanira broke the stillness.

"In the name of Zhon, when will this all end?" she uttered in a husky monotone.

"Soon, my love, soon," Tyron assured her, his arm encircling her numbed shoulder. "The gods have brought us this far, and they will not desert us now."

Despite their fatigue none initially sought the folds of slumber, so fearful were they of the visions borne by sleep in this unspeakable place. Instead, they gazed blankly at the marsh gas that surrounded their sanctuary, foul-smelling, purplish vapors that curled upward sinuously and formed bizarre patterns against the dark backdrop. It was in the midst of these swirling wisps that Tyron first saw the face, though initially he did not react, for he feared that his overtaxed mind was again seeking to torment him. But the others saw it too, leaving little doubt that it did indeed exist. The Kalkh sought to study it more closely, but it rose skyward, carried by the snaking gas, and in moments it was gone.

It appeared once again to the left of them, this time twice the size of the former apparition, and they were afforded a more than ample view of the leering countenance. Like the Three of Vorhashekkh it was an ageless face, one that had known a hundred years, or perhaps twice that number. The large head was hairless, save for a few thin wisps of white, the protruding blue veins quite evident. Two steel-gray eyes sat atop a bulbous nose, while the thin lips that surrounded two rows of uneven teeth were parted, revealing the most wicked of grins. The pointed ears were disproportionately small, as was the angular chin. It was a gaunt face, its white flesh pulled tightly throughout, not even the least wrinkle apparent.

This larger specter also vanished, only to be replaced by two more, and then four, all mirror images of one another. Moments later they wafted upward amid the marsh gas endlessly, until it became impossible to look away from the evil face. But worse, a distant, mocking laugh soon began, one that seemed to emanate from no particular direction. It drifted closer with each passing second, until it became necessary to cup trembling hands over ears that were assailed mercilessly by the deafening cackle. As it grew louder, the numerous heads rose about them in an endless procession. None of the trio was even vaguely aware of the screams that poured forth from their own throats in the midst of this onslaught.

Silence, deathly, stifling silence suddenly prevailed, though none were at first willing to accept this. But one by one they lowered their hands and glanced upward, where they saw nothing but a few thin wisps of vapor floating upward from the still marsh. Tyron and Dehril rose simultaneously upon shaky legs, both immediately assisting the wide-eyed Lanira up. They peered out into the blackness, words escaping them for the moment.

"By the black heart of Sharn, what brings the likes of you to Lamnagha?"

The overwhelming voice shattered the stillness, its force again bringing Lanira to her knees. But the others, despite their terror, continued to gaze into the unyielding darkness, with Tyron being the first to speak.

"We cannot see you!" he shouted. "Why do you not show yourself?"

"You have seen enough of me for the time being," the voice replied. *"Now, you have left a question unanswered."*

"We seek the one called Cuhthic," Dehril stated. "Do you know of him?"

The laughter resumed, and not until many seconds had passed did it cease. Then, the voice again spoke: *"And what do you desire of this Cuhthic?"*

"You are the one we seek, are you not?" Tyron asked.

"How perceptive," the voice mocked. *"Now, another query has been posed."*

"We desire a boon," Dehril said.

"A boon? You desire a boon of me?" Again the laughter resounded through the swamp, and this time it seemed to last an eternity. Cuhthic then said, *"Know you who I am, what I am?"*

"We do."

"Though fools, I cannot help but admire your audacity. But if you know what I am, then what makes you think I would grant whatever it is that you desire?"

"Nothing would be asked of you without something given in return," Dehril said. "We have come well prepared to meet your price."

Again the laughter, though briefly. *"What could the likes of you have that I would desire? Show me, quickly!"*

Dehril shook his head at Tyron, and the Kalkh replied, "Not until we stand before you, Cuhthic, will we reveal the nature of our offering. If acceptable, then you must agree to grant our request, which we know is within your power."

"And if not?"

Tyron shrugged. "Then we are at your mercy."

"You are at my mercy now, *young fools*!" Cuhthic snapped. *"But I am intrigued nonetheless. Very well; I agree to your terms."*

"How will we find you?" Dehril asked.

"To the north you will see a light. You need but follow it to my citadel. I will say no more until you stand before me."

Laughter ensued, but this quickly faded, leaving the swamp in silence. Lanira, now upon her feet, assisted the others in scanning the darkness, and her keen eyes were the first to fall upon the dim glow. Without a word they began walking toward the distant light, the Shaafian beauty in the lead. Inexplicably, they were able to traverse the mire with little effort, the firm loam that had marked their temporary sanctuary remaining constant throughout. Tyron guessed that the hand of Cuhthic was somehow involved here, for he believed that they had whetted the magician's curiosity, that the dark one desired an audience as quickly as possible. They paused for only a minute, while Dehril fumbled about within the folds of his pouch, the one that bore the grisly prizes. As they observed the malleable wads being cast away, both Tyron and Lanira were well aware of what the Berboran was doing.

The light grew brighter with each subsequent step, and in less than an hour, by their estimate, the three stood before the portals of a gloomy, rock-walled building. Their beacon, a blazing torch, was held by a small, hooded figure, who awaited them in the doorway. A hand emerged from the folds, and they were beckoned forward, into the citadel of Cuhthic. They complied and, though none uttered the words, all were well aware of the ominous clang with which the door closed behind them.

Their silent guide led them along a bleak corridor, one devoid of life. The light from the single torch allowed them to see the outlines of figures painted on the gray walls, most of these similar to the sculpted horrors in the hall of Yathir. But they shrugged these off as they continued in the wake of the purposeful figure, who soon turned into a dimly lit room on the left. It was not a large chamber, and had little appeal, decorated as it was in the manner of the dark magicians. The singularly predominant object was an immense chair, one carved from gleaming obsidian. It sat atop a stone dais in the center of the chamber, the additional height provided by the platform making it all the more imposing. It was toward this chair that the robed figure glided, and once at the base of the dais their guide, whom they had assumed to be a retainer, whirled about to face them. The cowl was drawn back over the head, and the three stifled gasps as they gazed upon the leering countenance that had tormented them earlier, the face of Cuhthic, ruler of Lamnagha.

Cuhthic ascended the platform, and not until he had hoisted himself atop the oversized throne did he address the three. His voice was sibilant, almost meek, quite unlike the amplified thunder that had overwhelmed them in the swamp.

"Not since the prime of my father's father has anyone sought out the heart of Lamnagha," he hissed. "Those earlier intruders came seeking the riches that they were certain abounded here—not a false assumption, to be sure. They too were young, and because of their audacity they suffered the excruciating tortures every day for the remainder of their lives, a period of nearly fifty years. Perhaps you also come for the treasure of Lamnagha?"

Though fearful that the evil one would not keep his word, Tyron nonetheless stepped forth boldly. "We spoke the truth earlier, Cuhthic. Our purpose here is to barter with you, nothing more."

"And still you believe that you can offer me something beyond my power to possess?"

"We are staking our lives on it."

"Indeed you are. Hurry then, for I weary of this talk! I would be amused to set eyes upon your offering."

Dehril, pulling the drawstrings on the pouch, stepped forward. "Very well, magician," he snapped. "See if you are amused by this . . . and this! And this too!"

The heads of first Dukkor, then Yathir, and finally Shadil were placed upon the dais near Cuhthic's feet, Dehril's deliberate positioning causing the bloodless countenances, the expressions of horror still frozen on each, to gaze upward at the sorcerer. Cuhthic's eyes widened, and as he rose upon shaky legs they saw that his slight frame trembled. He knelt on the platform and examined each head closely, until he was satisfied.

"It is them!" he murmured. *"It is—them!"*

Cuhthic began to laugh as he leaped from the dais, his ceaseless peals resounding off the walls of the chamber. Like some uncontrollable dervish he whirled about the room for minutes before regaining some semblance of control. The wicked grin was now frozen on his face as he returned to the obsidian chair, where he gazed down once again at the grisly trophies.

"The heads of the Three!" he crowed. "Never would I have believed it possible!"

"Then you concede that we have earned your favor?" Dehril asked.

"Anything that you desire is yours, my young friends," he told them. "Whatever I may be, I would not go back on my word, especially in light of this! Oh, if I could have been there to see them destroyed . . .!"

"Hear me then, sorcerer, for our journey has been hard and long," Dehril said. "This is what we would ask of you."

Cuhthic listened in silence while the Berboran, still wary, related all that he believed was necessary for the magician to know. Once done, Cuhthic pondered thoughtfully for long moments before gazing at Tyron.

"The removal of the Scamban plague is within my realm, though a degree of agony must be endured before it is done."

"It is the least of my concerns," Tyron assured him.

"The erasure of past thoughts is a simple process," Cuhthic continued. "But know this: singular memories cannot be wrested from your mind. If we go forth, then you will awaken almost as a new babe."

Tyron glanced at Lanira and Dehril before replying, "I have decided against this. Never, *never* must I be allowed to forget what these two, whom I love more than life itself, have done for me. The memories, the nightmares will stay with me, though perhaps someday they will be tempered. For now, I choose to retain my thoughts."

The three fatigued travelers, so near the climax of their incomprehensible journey, embraced warmly, while Cuhthic, with a shrug, retreated to a nearby cubicle, where he sequestered himself. Their strength all but gone, the trio crumpled to the dais, where they awaited the magician's return. More than an hour passed, and, despite their need for the long-denied rest now afforded them, they chafed at the delay. When Cuhthic finally emerged he carried a tall beaker of amber fluid, which he handed to the anxious Kalkh. He then guided him to the door of another cubicle, where he ordered Tyron to down the contents of the vessel. The empty beaker was soon handed to Dehril, and Cuhthic motioned the gagging mountain man into the small room.

"Whatever you hear, whatever you think, you must not interfere," the robed sorcerer warned Lanira and Dehril. "Do you understand? You must not interfere!"

The pair nodded, and Cuhthic followed Tyron into the cubicle, the door closing tightly behind him. In only minutes, the first muffled scream sounded from within. Dehril stepped forward instinctively, but Lanira placed an admonishing hand on his wrist. In the nearly two hours that ensued they suffered as much anguish, if not more, than at any time during their long and terrible trek. Tyron's endless shrieks pierced the thick walls, as well as their hearts, and Lanira could not withhold her tears.

The room shook, the heavy door often appearing close to snapping from its hinges. Dehril wondered how Cuhthic, despite being what he was, could withstand the unleashed force of the powerful, tormented mountain man in such a confined place. But they continued to heed his words, no matter how greatly it pained them.

All within was suddenly still, the stifling quiet, which lasted for endless minutes, proving as difficult to withstand as the previous cries of agony. The door then opened slowly, and the slight form of Cuhthic emerged unscathed, his wicked grin replaced by a smile that might even have been considered gentle.

"It is over," he told them. "Your friend is no longer a carrier of the disease."

The sinewy mountain man, though pale, wore a smile as he followed the sorcerer from the cubicle. Lanira fell into his arms, while Dehril pounded him on the back. None noticed Cuhthic as he glided back to his obsidian throne, into which he crumpled from exhaustion. Not until the mist that clouded the vision of all had passed did they see him, and they immediately hastened to the dais.

"Cuhthic, are you—?" Tyron began.

"Please, my young friends, do not concern yourself with me," he stated, one palm extended. "I require no more than a bit of rest. And do not offer me thanks, I beg of you! The boon has been more than accounted for by this offering." He indicated the pasty white heads. "Now go from here, quickly! This is no place for you. Though you have asked no more of me, you will find, once outside the citadel, that my gratitude is unbounded."

Cuhthic's attention returned to the grisly prizes, and the trio knew that no more need be said. They exited the chamber in silence, and once within the corridor they hastened toward the main portal, anxious to be free of the dismal place. But Tyron was far weaker than he at first appeared, and the others had to assist him, which slowed their progress. Despite their concern, the Kalkh assured them that he was well, that an adequate amount of rest far from this land would prove a sufficient balm.

He then changed the subject, lest they worry themselves any further.

"Dehril, what are your plans beyond the borders of Vorhashekkh?" he asked.

The Berboran had previously told them of Dosheel, but never had he spoken of Veleann; now, amid the bleakness of Lamnagha, he advised them of all—or nearly all—that had occurred during his brief sojourn in the mountain kingdom. Tyron and Lanira recognized his great love for this daughter of a bantir, but neither could understand why they had not heard of her sooner.

"Had you known of Veleann and me before we departed the Tengaviregos, what would your reaction have been?" Dehril asked.

"Why, I would have insisted that you remain there with her, rather than subject yourself to what we have endured!" the Kalkh roared. "I . . .!"

No more words were necessary, for Tyron and Lanira now understood. The Shaafian beauty embraced Dehril, while Tyron cuffed him affectionately on the side of his head. In the midst of this byplay they arrived at the door of the citadel, now open, where they observed what Cuhthic had meant by his final words. A gleaming, well-beaten road, one that they were certain stretched to the border of Vorhashekkh, split the blackness of Lamnagha. Awaiting them at its point of origin were three gentle, well-provisioned stallions. The Kalkh, sensing the termination of their once hopeless journey, was afforded a renewed vigor, and he shook himself free from the others, despite their protests.

"Let us depart this dark place quickly, while Cuhthic's cup of gratitude still overflows," he told them, mounting one of the steeds.

Lanira, who had been close on his heels, pulled herself astride a second horse, and the two made ready to ride. But Dehril, only now gathering up the reins of the last stallion, hesitated for a moment as he gazed at the pair.

"But what of you two?" he asked. "You have not spoken of your plans."

"It appears that we will all be putting up with one another for a long time to come," Lanira replied cheerfully. "Now hurry, fellow Dosheelian; my man has a mountain that he must climb!"

10512521R00112

Printed in Great Britain
by Amazon.co.uk, Ltd.,
Marston Gate.